Here, There, GONE

Karen D. Nichols

An Amazing tale of Spirit and Courage in the Face of an Impossible Ordeal

Nichols' Books

In Black & White
Florence, OR

ISBN 13: 978-1985832596
ISBN 10: 1985832593

Cover Design by Karen D. Nichols
Web site, http://karendnichols.com
Email: nicholskaren222@gmail.com

Books by Karen D. Nichols

Each of Nichols' novels includes ties to Oregon, a special dog, a mystery, a love story and an intriguing ending.

Thornton House: Mysterious love transcends time and opens death's door.

The Unexpected Gift: Love finds a Marine and his dog—an inspirational novel with plenty of action. *Very Inspirational*

Second Chance Heart: With Love, two families recover from their loss, celebrate their blessings and experience a miracle. *Very Inspirational*

Triumph Over Fear: In the wild, a young woman survives with her wits and the aid of her dog.

Roots of an Oak . . . A coming of age novel with all the traumas, capers and adventures of a young man entwined in the shroud of mystery.

The Moral of the Story Is . . . Pithy short true tales—from poignant to hilarious.

ACKNOWLEDGEMENTS

I'd like to thank a woman named Betty Edwards for her class, *Drawing on the Right Side of the Brain* that incited a dream outlining a whole book plot. After that, my brain burgeoned with story ideas. I couldn't have proceeded without all my friends and relatives becoming the special characters in my life and my books. They have made it all worthwhile. This story has a bit of reality with genuine characters. A chance friendship culminating in an accident spawned this story. The news story about this incident served as a steppingstone into my imagination resulting in this fictional tale.

I appreciate the Coastal Writers whose edits greatly enhanced my work. A special "thank you" goes to friends for a much-appreciated edits. Thank you Roberta for your edit. To my remarkable husband I wish to offer my undying gratitude for your help, your editing and your support in all that I do. (Like making sure I eat!)

Here, There, GONE

Karen D. Nichols

Chapter 1
Prologue to Natty's Story

After collecting my mail, I shuffled to the bottom of the stack to a slim package. "Hmm . . ." An unexpected package always intrigues me. I usually take my mail to open on the beach while I'm lounging around with my seagull friends and before I edit my book pages.

Standing at the sink in a ray of bright sunshine, I grabbed my kitchen shears then chopped open the brown paper wrapper taped with an overload of Scotch tape. Eventually, I ripped open the final flap. I couldn't help thinking. *This person wants to make sure this information is secure.* A paperclip held a note to a faded blue thesis booklet containing a stack of hand written scraps and full pages of scribbled memos. With raised eyebrows, I read the attached note while I wondered who had sent a package with no return address and a smudged cancellation mark. I didn't recognize the neat printing.

"Dear Karen,

I know it's been a while since our beach days. I've just come to a place where I could let you know that I am okay. I hope you are okay, too. I saw one of your books on sale at a store in town. Congrats.

These notes I am sending to you because if anyone could make this into a story, you could. I think it is an unusual tale that needs to be told. I tried to arrange the ideas and happenings in a logical order.

As you and I sat on the beach, I'd sing little songs that rippled through my brain. You'd read your writings to me.

They were truly amazing stories. We'd share your lunch while we tossed the crusts to our seagull friends, Commander White Head, Peg Leg and all the fun names you gave them— except when my Mutt leapt up and plucked the crusts out of the air.

You have no idea how those days on the beach with you helped me get to where I am now. After so many negative passages in my life, I needed to learn to trust.

When a car mowed me down on Coast Highway, my memory began giving me bits and pieces of my former life slowly revealing my past. My name is Natty Wilson.

By the time you finish your manuscript, I pray there will be a happy ending.

When I get settled somewhere, I'll let you know where I am. Now I know where my fear of trusting anyone originated.

I hope you will find my story worth your time. I'll contact you soon.

Love you, Natty"

When the package arrived, it had been at least a year since my friend had disappeared. Although, I thought of her as a friend, I didn't know her name. That's because she also didn't know her name. Amnesia. It makes sense now. She vanished much the same way she appeared. I never knew what happened to her after I read the article about her accident in the Huntington Beach newspaper. She'd left the hospital when I checked there.

The note answered my prayers for this tender soul who found herself homeless. She can now move on with her young life.

Her scrawled pages immediately caught my interest. With a sigh of relief, I flipped through, giving them a quick scan for more in depth study I planned to do later.

No ideas had come to me for my next novel. The blank page in front of me seemed daunting. Perhaps the reason lay in the pile of notes. The gift of this pack of notes answered my prayers. Practically tripping all over myself, I headed to my office and booted up my computer. I settled the stack on the desk next to my computer.

Where to start? I smiled when I thought back to the first time I met Natty.

I wasted no time. My fingers jumped across the keyboard, starting with an introduction where I fit in the story.

She did finally send me her final notes so this is the complete story.

Chapter 2
Deep dark Hole

For someone like me who loves to swim, nirvana describes my living a block from the ocean in Huntington Beach, California. With palms waving in the breeze, broad white sandy beaches with fabulous waves rolling toward the shore, it is the best stretch of beach on the west coast. No wonder it is known as Surf City.

About 15 years ago, I taught school in Cypress, California. Those summers, I would traipse daily to the beach, swim and body surf off and on for the whole day. While I curled my toes in the warm sand, I'd recheck a hard copy of my novel. As the sun dried me, I maintained my year-around tan. In the morning, I would surge ahead keying in the next chapter, then head for the beach.

Propped against our beach chairs, on weekends until the weather chilled, my husband, Ralph and I fed the seagulls and pigeons with dollar loaves of bread. After a couple of summers we created names for all of 'our' birds. As soon as they saw us making our way down to the water's edge, the seagulls squawked overhead until we set up chairs and spread our towels in the sand. The gulls would peck bread bites gently out of our hands. Like watching an air show, the birds dove as they snatched hunks that we threw in the air. Keeping eyes on our feet became quite necessary as our feathered buddies nibbled at our tasty toes when they finished off our bread supply.

Since I taught school, I could spend my summers on the beach while Ralph worked.

One day, I noticed a lovely bronzed girl as she strolled along Pacific Coast Highway pulling her red wagon. Everyday, just about when I dragged my homemade cart of beach paraphernalia across the highway, there she'd be. With her long, dark hair, matted and dirty and banded in a knot on her head, she wore tattered layers of mix-matched clothes. She hummed as she sauntered along. Wearing a Mona Lisa smile, she stared ahead with her head atilt as though she were thinking the most beautiful thoughts.

Her rusted-out, red wagon brimmed with all of her belongings wrapped in a dingy Army blanket.

Atop her pack sat a mutt that looked like a cross between a wolf dog and a Rottweiler. His ratty fur appeared as though he housed a flea circus. His name, Mutt, suited him perfectly. When anyone came too close they'd be met with bared teeth and a guttural growl.

Pinched between her thumb and forefinger, she always carried three or four dandelions she picked from the grassy knoll, running parallel to Coast Highway along the wide span of white sandy beach.

Then one day, I noticed her coming toward me. I spoke softly to the dog as I reached into my lunch bag and took out my sandwich. "Here," I held it out. "This is an extra sandwich." The dog looked at it, tail scooching back and forth on the sidewalk but still snarling. "I'm just not that hungry today."

She paused for a moment to examine the sandwich. When she reached for it, her hound ceased growling. He licked his lips. She opened the Saran Wrap and pinched off a hunk. The scrufty dog sat for a moment while she fed him his tidbits then she took two huge bites for herself. She rewrapped the remainder and carefully tucked it into her towel. She walked on without a word.

Each day thereafter, I packed an extra sandwich and tidbits for later. Since Ralph and I owned two furry cockers, I also packed some dog treats.

She began to say, "Thank you."

After a couple of weeks, I learned her favorite, cheddar cheese with dill pickles on it, just like me. Once she said, "I think I like ham with cheese, too." So I alternated.

What I didn't learn—her name. Very simply, she called herself Girl and her dog, Mutt.

Perhaps she thought of me as a bag lady too as I dragged a homemade cart behind me, carrying my beach chair, towels, writing paraphernalia, books and newspapers to read along with the lunch I now fixed for two.

I always situated myself by Lifeguard Tower #6. When I sat within shouting distance of a lifeguard, I felt safer while I swam out to ride the waves and dodge the rip tides.

Wherever I plunked down and laid out my extra towel, she dropped down next to me just staring out at the ocean. Her dog lay next to her with his head on her lap almost smiling while she stroked across his black fur and his brown head. I used to wonder why a lot of homeless seemed to have dogs. It didn't seem fair to the animals. Watching her, I realized that when the homeless take a dog, the dog is lucky. The canine gets to stay with its master all the time unlike working people's dogs. For a woman like her, this dog probably also doubled as a bodyguard. Not a long time later, she followed me to my house a half a block from the beach which is in the midst of the new three story homes changing the landscape in old town Huntington Beach.

One day, Girl began to sing. What a beautiful voice. She always sang softly into the wind. Her song whispered in the air as though she breathed in the music of the wind and released a voice from inside her heart.

She did indeed have lovely, ethereal thoughts filling her mind that found their way into her songs.

Mutt joined her with a whine that seemed to be in the same key as her tune. I encouraged her singing when I found an old guitar and helped her fix it up.

I told her how much I loved to swim and how I dreamed of one day having an indoor swimming pool so I could swim all year.   She said she enjoyed watching me swim, catch a wave and ride my Boogie Board. She often applauded when I caught a wave all the way to shore. Sometimes she and Mutt joined me. After she trained him, Mutt loved to ride my Boogie Board, which attracted a group of onlookers. Too bad they didn't have You Tube then. Mutt would have been an instant star, wind in the face, ears back with teeth exposed in a goofy grin.

After inviting her home for cookies and milk, she finally accepted. The first time she came, she sat outside. She would come into our three-story house.

Later she hesitantly inched her way inside. I offered her the opportunity to go up stairs and use our shower, but she refused. She did accept a bar of soap, a towel, toothpaste, and toothbrush as well as a comb and brush to use at our outdoor shower by the side of our house. The dog seemed to love a good scrub. At least he smelled better and his beautiful, black, shiny coat glistened. He seemed almost as lovely as she appeared with her naturally wavy, dark auburn, hair clean and shiny and brushed. Sometimes late at night through the window, I would hear her in the outside shower. I recognized her gentle voice singing to the moon with Mutt harmonizing. She would never consent to sleeping indoors. Once I hung some clothes, underwear, and a coat, across the back gate. On top of the comforter, I left a note saying, "Free, please take." There were other vagrants, so I didn't know if the items would be gone before she found them.

The next day the fence stood bare. I hadn't seen her for a couple of days. I never saw her wear a whole outfit all at once, but the comforter sure dressed up a red wagon filled with a stack of her belongings.

At the end of the summer, I didn't see her anymore. I read a story in the paper about an accident involving a young unidentified woman. When I checked at the hospital, she'd gone. No one knew anything more. I feared what might have happened to her. Besides I missed her company. Who needed a radio with such sweet songs streaming right next to me?

However when I returned to my teaching after summer, I thought little about her other than hoping that her circumstances had changed for the better. When I didn't see her there on the next Easter vacation, I began to worry. After a few prayers for her safety, I realized I would likely never see her again.

I hadn't yet started a new writing project. Now after receiving her notes, I could hardly wait to find out what brought her to Huntington Beach, how she became homeless and her final triumph over homelessness.

Holding her notebook close to my heart, I looked skyward. "Thank you Lord. What a relief to know she emerged from what ever deep dark place she landed."

After reading through Natty's notes, I shuffled through the papers for a moment thinking how I might approach this task of turning them into a book. Since her notes were in first person, I decided to write in first person as well. It helped me get inside her head.

As I found out, dark didn't quite capture her tale of adversity. So here's my version of her story.

Book One

Here, There

Chapter 3
Natty's Story

Still fighting with my brain cells to reveal my life prior to becoming homeless, I find it strange that random memories float back, though much of my early childhood has yet to materialize.

One memory transcended all the rest. I didn't understand its importance, when it first came rushing like a movie scrolling through my brain. But time would show me.

The recollection took me back to my thirteenth year when I spent time on my grandfather's ranch. Several times a year I visited dear Poppy, Mom's dad, up in Oregon. When the memory of Poppy came streaming back to me, I felt an ache in my heart. After all that has happened to me, he could have died. I didn't know. How long my amnesia lasted, I didn't know either, but I knew it would take time to fully recover.

Living in Southern California, in the midst of crowds, those escapes to Oregon became my favorite adventures. Almost like a scene from a pastoral painting, one green rise led to another as the flat lush valley of farms and ranches lay cut by the North Fork of the Siuslaw River.

Poppy's ranch nested between thick dark green spruce forests and open fields where his cattle roamed or huddled under the shade of a large, gnarled, old oak tree. Poppy compared himself to that tree. "I'm knotted and bent yet still standing with plenty more living to do."

The larger field gave his three horses a place to romp and nuzzle each other. The cows and horses visited at the fence between their fields.

Early in the morning, I'd help Poppy saddle the horses so he and I could ride out to catch the sunrise over the forested hills. Sometimes we visited a neighboring ranch or rode to the top of the bluff. We enjoyed the view or we'd sit in a meadow eating while visiting with the resident creatures.

After horseback riding, we rode back to the ranch where I still remember the fragrance of alfalfa mixed with the smell of horses and cattle.

The big red barn set the scene for the rabbits dashing about or stopping for a treat I held out for them. I could never understand why the barn cats only toyed with the other animals, but they were fierce with any rats or mice. I still envision those poor rats, held captive by the cats' sharp teeth, squealing, feet and tail scratching the air never to be seen again. I wanted to rescue them but Poppy said that's why farmers kept cats so the rats wouldn't overrun the farm.

While in the barn to feed the horses carrots and apples, I loved to catch one of barn cats. A moment's cuddle, surprisingly gentle with me before they demanded their freedom. Only Grandpa knew how I loved the barn cats. I begged him to let me take one home.

But alas, the toms were old, set in their ways, and too wild to live indoors.

Poppy stood with his hands on his hips. "Besides, who would keep the rats at bay—unless you want the job?" He raised his eyebrows while he smirked.

"Ew, Poppy, how gross."

After our rides, Poppy and I lounged around the fireplace warming up and harmonizing. He had such a beautiful tenor voice. We even wrote songs together as he strummed on his guitar. That's where I learned to play—on his instrument.

What a surprise Poppy had in store for me on this one Christmas vacation when we rode our horses over to his neighbor's ranch.

Have you ever met a person and, in a moment's time, you felt a connection so strong that the meeting lingers forever in your mind? My interaction with that boy who gave me his kitten, proved to be that special kind of incident—even with so many other memories eclipsed, it's amazing that this recollection remains so vivid in my mind. Being the first memory that broke through the silence of my past, it surprised me.

As it turns out, the return of this memory influenced how my life has turned out.

Chapter 4
Magic Moment

Prior to Christmas, Mom took me to the John Wayne airport. Poppy invited me to stay for one week to celebrate a few days before Mom and Dad would drive up to join us for a family Christmas. Excitement shot through me like an electric shock. I felt all grown up when I kissed Mom goodbye sending me out the jetway to my very first 'solo' flight (without parents) clutching a lunch to eat on board.

Amazing! As the plane lifted off from the end of the runway, my stomach flipped. I stared out the window, watching John Wayne Airport grow smaller and smaller. As the scenery below shrunk to miniature, it became a sculptured, toy train set with Hot Wheel cars moving along the freeway. It didn't take a real long time for a 13 year-old to feel like someone broke the clock, with hands that never moved and no mom to ask, "Are we there yet?" I found an empty seat next to a little girl. She ruffled her curly red hair and invited me to play fish with her deck of cards. Time sped up.

When Poppy met me at the Eugene Airport, his cowboy hat rose above the crowd as the tallest one there. I ran to him. Swept up in his strong arms, he swung me around and round. His hat fell clear off exposing his mass of curly, steel, gray hair. "So good to see my favorite granddaughter."

"Good to see you too, favorite grandfather."

Growing so fast, I'll bet he didn't pick me up to give me his favorite greeting again after that day.

His manly smell and strong arms made me feel so snug.

"Oh Poppy, set me down." Giggling, I planted a smacky kiss on his cheek.

Once on the ground, I let Poppy know the first thing I wanted to do. "Is it too late to ride horses? I missed Candy so much. "

"It will be almost four by the time we get home and get you settled in. Then saddle up and go out? It'll be dark."

I named Candy when I helped Poppy and the vet bring her into this world. On her wobbly newborn legs, her deep reddish brown fur shone while still damp—just like a candy apple. I called her Candy for short.

"You still have her, Candy Apple, I mean. Don't you Poppy?"

"You can say goodnight to Candy, maybe give her a carrot or two. How about a ride about first thing in the morning?"

"Oh, I guess." I put on my exaggerated pouty face as I pointed to my luggage.

"Come on, Sugar. Let's go." With that he dragged my suitcase off the carousel. "What you got in these bags, a bale of hay?"

"Mom says that girls never travel light!" I struck a girly pose with one hand behind my neck.

"Well, I hope you brought some warm clothes. It's been a bit chilly up here."

I rolled my eyes.

On the way home to Poppy's ranch, driving through the farms, by Fern Lake and by the Siuslaw River, we sang funny songs all the way to Florence. It made the time go so fast. I could hardly believe it when we turned on the gravel driveway into his ranch with the white clapboard farmhouse next to the big red barn. The rocking chairs were still sitting on the broad front porch, a perfect stage for Poppy, Mom and I to use as a stage while we sang and danced. Summers were the best! I loved my room up the squeaky oak stairs in the attic. I'd look at the rafters as I lay in the big brass bed under the multicolored quilt Grammy made for me.

Whisking the lace curtains aside, I'd watch the livestock, chickens and cats frolicking about, or watch the sun rising over the forested hill.

That morning, Poppy and I arose at 6 o'clock. After I bundled up, I met him at the barn.

The sun had just dawned. I recall how the glow of the not-yet-risen sun beaming over the mountain backlit the forest treetops. By the time Poppy saddled Storm and helped me throw the saddle on Candy, the sun shot rays that sparkled across the dewy field. It also burned away the fog that nestled between the hills.

I dragged myself up by the horn without a boost, and threw my leg over Candy's saddle. Watching my tall, handsome grandfather don his cowboy hat and mount his horse with flair, I hoped I'd marry someone just like him someday.

We took off in a slow trot, with our breath streaming out like a steam engine. "C'mon, I'll race you to the trail." With me clicking my tongue and controlling the reins, Candy kicked up her hooves as we clopped ahead of Poppy then took off in a canter.

He hollered, "Wait'll you see your Christmas surprise." With anticipation of a surprise, I slowed up. Then he cantered ahead of me. Not to be outdone, I charged up next to him and we set off to—I didn't know where. Soon we came to a dirt road where a yellow farmhouse, a big red barn and outbuildings dotted the landscape.

"Where are we going, Poppy?"

"You'll see."

Moments later, in a cloud of fine powder, we pulled up in front of a sleek modern red barn where we were met by a man who very much reminded me of my dad. He squared his shoulders and strode toward us. "Hey, Grant!"

"Jed, this is my granddaughter, Natty. Natty, this is Mr. Stone."

"Howdy, miss." He tipped his cowboy hat.

Poppy nudged his hat back on his head and slicked some stray, gray hairs off his forehead with the brim of his hat.

We dismounted. Poppy plopped his hands on his hips. "Say, I don't suppose you have that little thing we talked about the other day?"

"Hey, Jimmy," Mr. Stone called out. "Could you come here a minute? Bring that box out, will you?"

A few minutes later, a lanky boy brought a cardboard box out of the barn, leaned over to set it in front of me. When he stood, he brushed a blond sprout of hair back from his face. "Should I open it?"

I found myself lost in the bluest eyes I think I ever saw. We just stood there staring at each other for a moment until I heard the mewing. He lifted the lid. The box contained three little kittens, one black one, a soft gray one and a calico cat. They climbed all over each other trying to escape the box.

"Oh, Grandpa!" I jumped up and down. "Please, tell me I can have a kitten!"

He nodded.

"But what will Mom . . ."

"Spoke to her yesterday."

"We have to . . ." Jimmy's voice broke, "give away all of the kittens." He knelt and picked up the gray one. As he handed it to me, our eyes connected, resting for a long moment. "You can have any one you want." Jimmy stood their grinning, as proud as if he were the mama cat. He stroked the kitten and nuzzled it.

"This one. May I have this one?" I held it close. The kitten nuzzled and licked my cheek with her warm, pink, sandpapery tongue.

"Just promise to take good care of her. She's my very favorite." Suddenly his big sapphire blue eyes filled, spilling tears down his cheek. Abruptly, he turned away. He charged toward the barn.

I returned the kitten to the box and tapped her polka dotted nose. "Wait! I can choose another one!" I gathered up the box and followed Jimmy from the bright sunlight into the shade of the barn. Jimmy stood leaning against a wooden post with his head in the cradle of his elbow.

"Really. They are all so cute. I'd love any one of them."

"I know."

"Really, it doesn't matter which one I have." I set the box down next to him. "Honest."

Chapter 5
A Boxing Match

Jimmy glanced up as he wiped his forearm across his eyes and nose. He squinted into the sun streaming through the open barn doorway. His red nose beamed as he knelt down and lifted the gray kitty holding her close, kissed her tiny head, then handed her to me.

Just then Poppy struck his head in through the barn doors. "Why don't you stay? You can play for a few minutes while Mr. Stone and I palaver." That's what Poppy called conversing about business with his neighbors. I heard them talking and belly laughing while they took care of 'business'.

When he patted the ground next to the box, I eased in close to Jimmy.

"Look, let's get something straight. I have to dispose of all the kittens, one way or another. Pa said so."

"I don't like the sound of that."

He nodded. "Pa says we have too many barn cats already."

We reached our hands over into the box. I teased the tri-colored cat with a chicken feather while Jimmy rubbed the black's tummy. The gray one pawed my arm for attention with her greenish yellow eyes attempting to melt my resolve and doing a very super job.

Jimmy aimed his stare straight into my eyes. "Look, I like your grandfather a lot. After meeting you, I decided that I want you to take this gray one. That's why I picked her up first. I hoped she'd wheedle her way into your heart. You adopting her is better than some other family I don't know. Besides . . . I don't think you'll make her a barn cat."

"Why? Is that bad?"

"Barn cats get pretty independent. She'd have to live out of the house. I'd want her inside with me."

"Well." Looking her over, I held her up as her little paws patted the air. Her pink nose twitched. With her white snout looking like someone spattered her with gray paint, I decided what to name her. "If you are sure, I'll take Polka Dot with me."

"I'm sure."

Nestling her in my arms, we both stroked her back. I closed my hand around her tail. I discovered that her tail had a mind of its own as it wavered and turned.

"Polka Dot, huh. That's a perfect name for her. I didn't name any of them." He looked away. "It hurts more to let them go when they have a name."

We played for a while until the kittens began falling asleep. Jimmy set them back in the box. "Want to take a walk?" He shot up and dusted himself off. He reached out and took my hand for a boost up. "I'll be back in a second." He hurried off.

"Okay." I knelt to give the kitties some more attention.

Carrying a bag, Jimmy returned in an all-out run. "You ready to take that walk?"

As we strolled along, the smell of the farm disappeared into the sound and aroma of the forest. The fragrance of the spruce with the overhang of the woods, wrapped us in a reverie of sounds: chirping birds, swishing feet in the soft dirt path and the whisper of the wind.

Suddenly we started humming at exactly the same time. We laughed as he took my hand. He knew some Irish songs my grammy used to sing.

While we wound through the forest, we sang, chatted and laughed until we came to a shallow outcropping of the river. "Pa dammed this up for swimming. You'll have to come back in the summer. We could go fishing too."

"I'd love to. Next to horseback riding, swimming is my favorite sport. I don't know about fishing. Never done it."

A fallen log gave us the perfect spot to sit. "Then I'll teach you."

"I'm hungry." Jimmy lifted his bag. He broke out two fried chicken drumsticks, with two apples.

It's kind of hard to eat while you're laughing and smiling, but we managed.

Humming along the way back, we watched a set of black-headed junco birds as they puffed out their white chest feathers. They looked as though they'd swallowed Ping-Pong balls.

I pointed. A chipmunk stuck his head out of knothole, scolded us with his chirping.

As we neared the barn, I wished this day would last forever. I hated to return, not with me feeling as happy as I'd ever been.

We stopped for a moment in a beam of sunlight. I looked into Jimmy's eyes. For a moment I felt a chill as the flitting in my stomach started up. He took my face in his hands and kissed me. Did I see stars or were they just flickering in my stomach? My hand in his felt so comfortable as we separated and started back on the path.

My first kiss! I almost leaped in the air.

We sauntered back to where Mr. Stone and Poppy stood chuckling. "Say," Mr. Stone pushed his hat back on his head. "We missed lunch."

"Some of us didn't." Jimmy grinned until his dimples

caved in.

"Well then, I don't suppose you two would like to stay for cookies and milk?"

"Could you, Mr. Dawson?" Jimmy shielded his eyes from the sun as he looked up at Poppy.

"Sorry son. It's late. It gets dark pretty fast this time of the year. I think Natty and I better head back." Having said that, he mounted King.

I tried not to pout. "Bye Jimmy, Mr. Stone. Thank you, Jimmy. I love Polka Dot. I'll take good care of her. I'm calling her Dotty for short."

When I handed the kitty to Poppy, he placed her in a leather pocket attached to his saddle.

"Come back anytime." Jimmy gave me a boost into the saddle. When he winked, I tingled all over. "Hope to see you soon."

Poppy invited their family over for Christmas Eve with my family.

That next summer's swimming with Jimmy turned out to be the best ever. We saw each other every day that week I spent at Poppy's. We rode horses together, fished, sang, laughed, and picnicked in the meadow. Sometimes I can still recall the softness of his kiss and feeling of his arms around me.

But sadly, Jimmy moved away right after that summer. I dragged myself around for the longest time. I wondered if Jimmy ever thought of me. I never forgot those blue eyes and how the nearness of him set my heart pounding.

I prayed it wouldn't be the last time I would see him. But alas . . . never could I have imagined what perils I would endure before or if I'd see him again.

Chapter 6
A Song In the Air

The years in between that trip to Grandpa's and the passage of time until I finished college were still hiding from me with snippets returning now and then. Memories pop into my head when I least expect them. Certain smells, tastes, sights, or sounds suddenly send me a picture. Recently a train blasted its whistle, which conjured up a flash of my parents and me when we boarded an overnight train from California to Oregon, to see Poppy. That proved to be a very exciting trip. Sleeping in a compartment seemed elegant. I think the more stirring the memory the sooner I recall it.

My father had been a Marine. Since he didn't have a son, so guess who became his little 'Marine'. He taught me some wrestling holds but mostly karate for self-defense—real handy for warding off unwanted advances. Using Daddy's techniques didn't really endear me to a few guys I dated, but ever so handy with my adversaries.

The most vivid recollections resulted from interacting with music: singing, playing, dancing or listening. They created a highway into my past.

With all the memories rattling around in my head, I still struggle to pull it all together.

Because of Poppy, I chose The University of Oregon so I could spend more time with Candy and him. Plus I could bring Dotty. Poppy took care of her until I visited on weekends.

My days at the University of Oregon I do remember well.

As a music major, I sang plus played in several ensembles. Roommates, Mindy, Vicki and I formed a group we called the Three Tiers. I sang tenor, Mindy alto and Vicki soprano. All of us in the Three Tiers also played several instruments. Vicki's older brother bartended at *Sam Bond's Garage.* That's a brewery in Eugene. He got us a gig at the club. If I do say so, we brought out a pretty good crowd for our performances.

Being a computer science minor, I became a whiz on the computer, so I fought between which lab to spend my spare hours—the computer lab or the music lab. Music gigs didn't pay enough so I had a part-time job at Silicon Shire where I became adept at a number of computer systems. I didn't spend much time hacking because my parents must've imbued me with a moral bias against dishonesty. Although I did hack sometimes, just to see if I could. I never changed grades, or stole any info or money—that is until I had a chance at retribution. (I'll tell you about that later.)

My senior year I took a couple of psychology classes. Well, if I didn't like where life might lead, I might come back to study psychology. Even though it's a little late for another minor, I found something that really interested me. My fascination with abnormal psychology definitely served me well during my ordeals.

In our dorm room, after graduation festivities, Mindy, Vicki and I stood packing to return home. Time to become adults—a scary little thought. The fact of breaking up our Three Tiers band set a brooding mood that hung like black clouds over us. None of us felt like talking much. The silence unnerved other people in the dorm as several friends rapped on the door to see if we were okay.

Mindy dropped the sweater she held up ready to fold. Her face lit. "Hey, Natty." Her excited voice broke the emotional hush.

"Yeah? Why so cheery?"

"Well, I'm excited for YOU. I just remembered that you'll be going to Southern California."

"So?"

"I had to turn him down but I have a friend in Hollywood who's in a band, a trio that just lost its lead singer."

Mindy grabbed my phone. "I'll put his info on your phone."

"Why aren't you taking . . .?"

"You know I'm an absolutely fab back up singer. I'm not lead material. Besides I don't want to live in California."

She put her finger to my lips as I started to object. "This is your chance. Take it."

Reclaiming my phone, I checked her input into my phone. "So, Willy McGuire . . . All right I'll give it a try."

She fumbled around the chaos of clothes strewn on her bed and found her cell. "I'll call Willy to give him a heads up." She told him I would call back in a few minutes.

Trying not to burst a blood vessel, I grabbed my guitar and raced out the door, "I'll be back shortly." With my guitar slung over my shoulder, I hopped on my bike, racing over to a music room with good acoustics where I could make the call. I hoped Willy would answer and that he'd listen to me sing. I hesitated for a moment then tapped in the numbers.

Willy surprised me with a "Hi, Natty. My buds and I are sitting around having a beer. Let's do face time. I'll call you back."

Before it rang, I clicked down the little stand on the back of my phone and situated myself away far enough to get the guitar with me in the picture.

"All right, Natty. Why don't you wow us with your talent."

For a minute I swallowed. My voice came out as though I

had a mouthful of hot cereal. "Okay."

"Let us hear what you got. I'll turn up the volume."

My throat tightened. "Okay." I croaked out. Something had a strangle hold on my vocal chords.

"Well?"

I clutched the guitar. Slowly my fingers found the strings and I strummed *Hallelujah* while I cleared my throat.

Would I choke up?

When they started playing along with me, I drummed up the courage and wailed out my best version clear and strong.

As they played a few popular songs, I knew the music so I picked along with them and I sang. When I offered one of my own pieces, they were enthusiastic.

We jammed for nearly an hour. At 11 p.m., we finished up.

His buddies left so Willy and I talked another hour or more about the band and their plans. That's when Willy gave me his address. "Google will have directions. How soon can you be here?"

"Um . . . I don't know. How long does it take to drive from Eugene, Oregon to Burbank, California?"

"Depends how fast you drive."

"Well, I can't be getting any tickets. Also, I don't want to drive at night when I get sleepy."

"It's Thursday. Get here by next Thursday and you're in."

"Great. See ya then." I knew it only took two or three days, though I'd never been to Burbank.

Kicking up my heels, I squealed all the way back to the dorm. "I'm in!" I crashed through the door. Vicki and Mindy rolled over as they pulled the covers over their heads. My boxes, bags and suitcases filled up slower than I imagined. I rambled around unearthing my stuff. Fortunately my friends could sleep through anything. After I carried the boxes to my car, I snapped everything into my last duffle bag and zipped it up. I checked around for all my small stuff in the bathroom. I wrapped up my CDs, iPad and CD player. By the time I stacked several boxes with my books and sheet music, lugged them to the car, then bagged up some snacks, I must've been up and down the stairs 100 times! I noticed the early morning sun lighting the sky and sparkling the dew outside on the grass courtyard. What I thought would take minutes, took hours. A glance at the clock read six in the morning. I looked around at my sleeping friends. I shouted, "Yeeha!"

They both shot up in unison like a couple of Jack-in-the-boxes.

Bending over, I kissed them both on the cheek and gave a few lengthy hugs. The thought of not seeing them for a long while had my eyes burning. I spit out my farewell in rapid fire. "I left a couple of sweaters there. If you don't want them, give 'em a toss. The band wants me to come right way. I'm so excited. I'm leaving right now. I love you guys. I'll call you soon and let you know what's happening."

"You better!" Mindy hollered as I dashed out the door, escaping before I fell apart. After a few minutes sitting in the front seat of my old Toyota jalopy, I wiped my red nose. My cheeks drizzled with stinging tears.

Without a look back, I drove away. I couldn't sob and drive.

I never got a chance to call them before my world fell apart.

Chapter 7
Haunted?

Even though I tingled at the thought of my career taking off so suddenly, this had me wondering—right move or not? Knowing I had a week to make a two or three day trip to California, I planned to stop at a few interesting spots, especially art galleries, which might help dissipate the anxiety over my upcoming debut. I had just seen my parents at graduation. I told myself to call home, debated whether I should call Mom and Dad. I finally decided no. *Surprise them!*

I stopped along the way to snap some photos of a couple of covered bridges and horses in fields. I moved up close to shoot a brown and white cow with white eyelashes that captured my heart with a loud, MOO. My side trips took me a little out of my way. *Who's in a hurry, anyway?*

As I drove along, I practiced songs for my opening gig using an overkill of gestures. Funny, I found people staring as they drove by me.

With an empty gas tank and a stomach also rumbling on empty, I pulled off I 5 Freeway at Wolf Creek. Almost immediately, an arched sign, *Wolf Creek Tavern, Tasty Cuisine* caught my eye. I think my stomach said, "Let's stop." I slowed, loving the double decker porch of the quaint building housing a restaurant with a sign, *Bed and Breakfast; the Wolf Creek Inn founded 1883.*

As I parked around back, I admired the garden's burst of

spring flowers still blooming in profusion. I followed the stone trail through the flowerbeds as I headed around front. Aromas of delicious food quickened my pace.

Passing the rockers on the quaint porch, I entered the lobby. The grandfather clock in the corner dinged 3 o'clock. "No wonder my stomach screamed, "Starving!" I perused a small menu tacked on the bulletin board until a waitress welcomed me. I smiled back at her infectious grin as she tucked a gray curl up into her bun.

She patted some crumbs from her costume, an old fashion white bibbed, lacy apron over a long, baby blue, flowered dress. "Sit anywhere you like." She handed me a menu, "We're just switching from the lunch to the dinner menu, if you have time to wait for the cook to slice the turkey."

"Absolutely. So that's what smells so good! I haven't had turkey for a long time."

I took a stroll around the inn then returned.

Antique tables and chairs filled the dining room. I wandered past tables topped with crocheted tablecloths and vases of flowers. One elderly couple put their napkins on the table. When they got up I asked, "Hi, How's the food here?" I smiled.

The man used one hand to swipe his well-trimmed goatee. "Primo!" He gave me the okay sign.

His wife slipped her bag over her shoulder. "Even better than that."

While they exited, I picked a seat by the window where I could watch the birds, bees and butterflies flit around the flowery English garden.

The waitress adjusted her lace cap. "Well, the hot turkey sandwich or a full turkey dinner?"

"Since I didn't eat breakfast, I think the full turkey dinner is a must! Extra butter please." Unable to concentrate on the garden, I nearly drooled all over myself waiting for my food.

"Watch the plate. It's hot."

Her flowered oven mitt validated that instruction. "Enjoy!"

"After I eat, might I see one of the rooms?"

"They are lovely."

After dosing my potatoes and peas with mounds of butter, I scraped my plate clean of mashed potatoes, hunks of turkey, dressing, gravy and peas. I spread butter on my huge fluffy roll then wrapped it for later.

Eating until I should have exploded, I forgot that turkey makes you sleepy. I looked over at a sign that said, '**ROOMS 75 CENTS.**'

My waitress came by to collect my money. "You wanted to see a couple of rooms?"

"Martha," it said on her nametag. "May I, please." I pointed at the sign. I don't suppose the rooms go for 75 cents?"

"Not today," she smiled, "Right this way. " She handed me a brochure on the way by the desk. "Prices are in there."

The well-worn oaken stairs creaked while we climbed to the second floor.

"Clark Gable slept in this room." She swept her arm out, inviting me in. "It has its own bathroom."

"Wow, it smells wonderful in here."

"Maybe that's a forerunner of a spirit presence. No matter what I do in here it always smells this way."

"Good thing the smell is just faint and pleasant. Maybe it's Clark Gable's aftershave!" I glanced around. "Oh, so quaint. I love it. Maybe he haunts this room." The windows were draped with a dark blue pattern that matched the patchwork quilt. I touched the plump, handmade quilt that drew me to sit. When I sat, I knew I wouldn't take another step. "Do you suppose I could stay in this room tonight? Maybe Clark Gable will give me a kiss."

"That's why I showed it to you. I saw you yawning at your table. It's the only open room for tonight." She patted my shoulder. "You do look tired."

I glanced into oval mirror attached to the marbled-topped bureau. My reflection confirmed her suspicions. After all, I had been up all night. "I'll just go and get my things."

"My husband can help you."

"Not necessary. I just have a little overnight bag. I saw a sign downstairs that this inn is on a list of haunted places. Is this inn really haunted? Maybe Clark really will stop by."

"Well . . ."

"It won't change my mind. I'm up for a little excitement."

"My husband and I just reopened the inn a few months ago. The locals say they have seen some spirits, though we haven't been introduced to our ghosts . . .yet." She grinned. "If it is, I hope it could be Clark too, however, our ghosts are apparently local from a long time ago. I've also been told they are mostly very nice."

"Well that's mostly good to know."

"Tomorrow you might have a look at the guestbook down stairs. Some famous people have left notes about their experiences."

After registering downstairs, I climbed the stairs back to the room. I took my make-up bag and toothbrush to the bathroom. When I dumped a small dose of bubble bath from one of the plastic mini bottles, I filled the claw-foot tub to the max. After I submerged myself in a pillow of bubbles, I soaked taking a long luxurious bath then I rinsed off in the shower. I think the shower served as the pièce de résistance.

After, the shower, I thought brushing my teeth with tangy toothpaste would wake me up. It didn't.

When I sprawled out on the bed my eyes couldn't focus on *Cold Mountain* the book I tried to read. When I went to draw the drapes, I noticed no one could see in. The twilight moon cast a beautiful glow into the room—*just perfect. This is the atmosphere that might invite a spirit.* Before I dropped off, I turned out the light without even worrying about ghosts or spirits.

Chapter 8

A visitation

Dreaming of colorful flowers, I could see a man riding toward me on a white horse, mane blowing in the wind. He kept riding though not getting any closer. I waved my arms and smiled. "Yes, come!" *It must be Rhett Butler!* I jumped up and down clapping my hands and swirling my ruffled hoop skirt.

Dust hid him as the cloud engulfed the rider. At last he trotted up near me. "Whoa!" While the dust settled, in deed, Rhett drew up and stepped from the cloud. He swept off his hat, hooked his arm around my slender waist and spun me around. "Oh Rhett, you're here!"

Suddenly music filled the air. We glided around a dance floor to the tune of a full orchestra playing, *What Child is This?* After circling the room, Rhett guided me to the balcony. I felt the breeze in my hair as I gazed up to the star filled sky. He took me in his arms. I felt his warm breath on my shoulders. His mustache tickled as he kissed my cheek. At a closer look, his very blue eyes reminded me of Jimmy, whom I hadn't seen for years. I reared back and stared. "Jimmy? Is it you?"

Suddenly I awoke. Standing on the window ledge, my toes gripped the edge. I screamed a silent scream as I teetered on the edge of the second story window of the inn. Trembling, I let myself down. As I sank into the quilt on the bed, head spinning, I contemplated what happened.

I had never walked in my sleep.

Chilled from the open window as well as my window ledge experience, I sat on the edge of the bed rubbing my arms. I drew the covers over me still shivering.

I lay against my pillow, my eyes wide open, I prayed, "Okay Lord, if there is a specter in my room, let him rest so I can too, please."

In minutes, I did fall asleep. Feeling something odd, I swatted the air and opened my eyes. Though still dark, very clearly a whispy, blonde-haired woman bent over me. She collected the covers and snuggled them around my shoulders, next to my neck. "Sleep tight, my little darling. Tomorrow will bring you danger, but fear not, He is with you. Everything will be all right." I felt a gentle kiss on my cheek. With that she vaporized. I started to sit up. A strong hand held my shoulder down. "Sleep my little one." She made feel so protected. I did exactly as she requested.

When the early morning sunrise lit the room dimly, I woke totally refreshed in spite of the night's strange visitors. I couldn't be sure if I dreamed or whether I actually hosted a ghostly figure in my room.

My phone told me the time: 5:30. I put my phone in my purse. Breakfast wouldn't be served until seven. I felt so energized I didn't feel like waiting. I showered, brushed my teeth, combed my hair and dressed in my jeans, a white blouse and my jean jacket. I packed up in about 30 minutes.

Noise in the kitchen let me know the staff's breakfast crew worked early. I stopped by to tell them about my spirit adventures.

Martha stood in the corner. "Hope you slept well."

"You probably won't believe this, but I did have a couple of spooky visitors last night."

"I've started writing a book about the Wolf Creek visitors.

"Do you mind telling me . . . and could I take notes then add your story to my book?"

"So you do believe that I might have seen a spirit?"

She grinned and nodded. "I am hoping to see my own vision to add to my book."

"Well, good luck and here goes." When I finished my tale, Martha told me about a few antique buildings about 3 miles up the road. "Since they are never open, you could look inside the windows and wander around the Heritage buildings and the old farm equipment, six thirty or not, you could still enjoy them."

"Thanks. I'll recommend your place. With the exception of my near nose dive, I loved it all, including my apparition." I reached for the bookshelf. "Oh, let me buy one of these." I paid for the book of haunted places in California and Oregon. "This will do until you write yours."

"Here, take a sweet roll." She flashed a broad smile. "They're homemade cinnamon rolls." She handed me a paper cup. "Pour yourself a cup of coffee."

I wrapped a cinnamon roll in a napkin. "Thanks Martha." I grinned up at the clear blue sky as I walked back to my car through the flower-laced garden. The sun already peeked over the top of the trees.

When I took off, the turkey dinner stayed in my mind to tease me. Little did I know—that turkey feast would be my last good meal for a very long time!

Chapter 9
On the Road Again

When I left the inn, I took Martha's advice to see the State Heritage Site, which included an old mercantile store, a church, and a barn. I cupped my hands around my face when I pressed my nose against the windows and peeked in. Some old, rusty tools sat in a meadow of daisies. Maybe these old structures played home to some ghosts, too. After shooting a few shots of the old buildings and movies of the resident rabbits, I watched for ghosts but alas, no spirits.

At the car, I checked in the rear view mirror and found my nose almost black from pressing against the windows.

Before I took off, I sipped my coffee while enjoying the delicious, sticky, cinnamon roll. The last of the sugary treat disappeared when I licked my fingers and wiped them on my jeans.

I flipped a U-turn to go south. I had decided to sightsee on the side roads, to avoid the freeways as much as possible.

Taking a few small roads that looked interesting, I found little town stores and antique dealers. I bought Mom a filigree silver pin. Other than graduation, it'd been a while since I had spent much time with my parents. I realized how much I missed them. This road also reminded me of one Poppy, Jimmy and I rode up at Poppy's ranch. While I traveled on, I noticed some smoke ahead graying the azure blue skies. Getting closer, with smoke, embers floating in the air, my eyes watered as I breathed in the fire's vapors.

The State Police woman stood in the center of the highway, slowing me down. She waved her arms, signaling the detour, a small two-lane road. *Oh well, I wanted to have an adventure! Besides, detours are usually marked clearly. Also I have a GPS.* I heard somewhere that the detours in life are often the most remembered parts of a trip. As it turned out, I ran into something I'd like to forget.

I rolled down my window and called out to the Police woman. "Is this fire threatening the redwoods?"

"Just a small brush fire. We have it under control. We will probably mop up in an hour or so."

"So glad to hear that."

The narrow detour road proved to be much more scenic as I passed green farms, strolling cows then patches of dense woods. Stopping often, I photographed some young horses galloping, nickering and chasing each other. When I saw a sign for a local fish hatchery, I headed through scattered trees before the forest thickened with huge redwoods or were they old forest firs? I asked when I toured the fish hatchery, fir trees. Everything fascinated this young city slicker.

Back out on the rural road I reached a fork. With one way heading toward a wall of smoke, I chose the left hand road. I should have known. *GPS.* I didn't listen to myself.

Such beautiful country! The road narrowed as it wound upward through beautiful woods with bits of sunrays splintering through the branches. The flickering made it a little hard to see. It felt like a fairytale forest, the overhead branches almost covering the road in a tunnel. Somewhat mesmerized by the beauty, my mind filled with remembrances of the delicious turkey dinner I'd had yesterday for lunch. When the wheel wells pinged with gravel, I realized that the road had transitioned to a dirt road.

Maybe I should turn around. Were there other options to this road? I'd just barely had that thought while I reached for the GPS. *Oh no!* I hit a boulder about the size of an armadillo. At least it felt like that, big enough as it jostled me around in the car. I whacked my head on the steering wheel.

For just a second, I took my eyes off the road. I looked up at the rearview mirror to see a cut oozing a little blood. I must've hit the gas pedal, or hit a curve when I suddenly smashed into another rock or tree. The windshield filled like a movie screen. Trees and rocks, dirt and brush all flying in the air mixed together, battering the windshield, heading right at me.

I covered my face. A fleeting thought about a balloon popping out of the dashboard to save me didn't happen in my old Toyota. *It felt like the car raced 100 miles an hour.* My body rattled around, as though I rode inside a cement mixer. *I should have fastened my seat belt.*

Everything went black.

Chapter 10
Who, What, Where

Not knowing what happened sent spasms down my aching spine. I woke up in my crumpled car. Lying on its side, the wreck left me squished against the passenger door. The car must have rolled. Blood dripped from somewhere down onto my face. I moved my legs and my arms. Sore but nothing broken, nothing trapped. I wiped my face with my sweater then I picked up a shard of what remained of the rearview mirror and focused on my forehead. A new cut slit my brow, stopping just short of my eye and parallel to the first one. *Pretty lucky, I guess.* Applying pressure, I assessed my situation. I dabbed and pressed until the bleeding stopped.

I glanced around. *I need to get out. But how?* When I tried to figure out my location, I had no idea. Nothing looked familiar. Where had I been I going? I had no clue, when I suddenly remembered the fire and the detour. After I opened the glove compartment, I withdrew two crumpled maps, one of California and one of Oregon. I must be in one or the other. Behind the maps there I found nothing of any use. I didn't know what info to feed my GPS. Taking a 360-degree view, my wreck landed in the middle of small, fenced, weed field. The hole battered through the pieced-together, split-rail fence, my doing. I could be sure of that if nothing else. Behind the car, my gaze followed the tire tracks to a fairly steep hill. *If I had to go that way out of here, I wouldn't make it.*

The way my body felt, I'd not be climbing for a while.

Facing the side window, I could barely make out the peak of a roof with a chimney trailing out a thin curl of smoke.

"Thank you, Lord." At least if my body could hold up, I had a destination. Help waited for me in that house in the distance.

Tugging myself forward, I reached the driver's side of the car. The GPS didn't work. Over the top of the steering wheel, I pushed the automatic window button. Nothing. The crink in the doorframe stopped the door from opening. *What was I thinking? Nothing is working.*

Just to make sure I had company, a couple of deer, a big-eyed doe and a fawn, looked over the fence. With an agile leap, the mother came close enough for our glances to connect. She studied me for a moment then she sauntered back. With a graceful bound over the fence, she returned to her fawn. The deer weren't going to help me, but they did make me smile with hope as their white tails disappeared into the forest.

Returning to my immediate problem, *Okay, now what?* I arched my legs across the steering wheel. Drawing my knees back and grunting, I let loose with a monster kick. A lot of power went into tilting the wheel but not into cracking the window. *Yeah! Shatterproof glass—saving me and now imprisoning me.*

Surveying the interior for something sharper than my soft-soled running shoes, I saw nothing.

My canvas suitcase sat jammed between the backseat and the passenger seat with me in it, way too flimsy to break the window. *I have a pair of heeled tap shoes!*

"I could use a little help here, God." I scooched, twisted, pushed and pulled myself, getting my body out of my own way then struggled to tilt the seat forward. The case still wedged, I managed to pull and shove it back and forth until it wiggled free. The bags frame bent at an odd angle. I let out the breath I held, as I remembered the warning in my haunting dream of last night. *"Tomorrow will bring you danger, but fear not, He is with you."* That thought is what sustained me through what I endured later.

"Okay, Jesus, forgive my rudeness . . . please." After I clicked the latch, applied force then created a gap, I pushed in my arm like a lever into the case. At last it popped open. *Ah, my tap shoes.*

Now the problem would have been much easier if the space hadn't been crushed small and my height hadn't been at five foot nine. *How did my feet get so far away from my hands?* Finally I unlaced my shoe and exchanged it for my tap shoe. I smiled at the steel toe. Some inner music danced through mind as I tapped a hard kick smashing right through the crumbling glass— only one foot needed. After I pushed out the rest of the window, it collapsed leaving my right foot hanging out. Thank goodness for Levis; no cuts resulted. I took my bloody sweater, covered my hands and pulled out the large, left over sharp glass sections from the window frame. With a lot of grunting and groaning, I wormed my way outside.

After dragging myself past the glass shards, I collapsed in a heap. "Ah." I laid out flat on my back, with my hands under my head. "So this is what it's like to feel old." I remembered my other tennis shoe and struggled to reach inside for it. That shoe proved much easier to change in the free space of the grass field.

Resting for a few minutes, my furrowing my brow just hurt as I rubbed my arms and legs checking for more injuries. Luckily I found none. Still, getting up I tried to figure out what hurt worse—my body or my head.

Checking to see if I could walk, I limped forward. The deer watched from afar as if to say, "Good, you're okay." The deer's watchful eyes filled me with hope. *Did you come back to check on me?* As if I expected an answer, I glanced at them. "So what should I do now?" They stood still for a moment, a wildlife painting, before they disappeared.

The beautiful, darkening, blue, evening sky began to twinkle with stars between the clouds. My choice of actions reduced down to one—try to reach the house in the distance before the darkness stole my light.

Forward march!

After slogging through the tall weeds, the cabin, in the distance of about a block, became clearer.

Realizing I forgot to take a few things, I looked over my shoulder. I couldn't go back to the car right now. I couldn't even see it. The sky became darker by the minute. I faced the house, and plodded on. *Later.*

Who owns own this place? Maybe it's haunted. A resident curmudgeon might slam the door in my face—or a lecherous beast could be waiting to attack, No! I pushed that thought aside. I didn't have another option. *Besides it could be just a sweet old lady who would be glad to help me out.*

I sniffed the air. As I drew closer still, the smell of the fireplace mixed with the aroma of food drew me to the log cabin. Without the dog barking, without the lighted windows or the smoke drifting skyward, I would have thought it an abandoned building. If there had ever been any paint on its gray-brown window trim, it'd been long since eroded away. A rusty washing machine sat on its side at the end of the porch. A faded old rug looked like it'd been flung across a bench next to a three-legged chair. Weeds poked through the porch planks. Flowerpots lay in profusion dumping out dead plants. Inside, rags comprised the curtains stretched across the windows. I couldn't get a peek at what or who might be inside.

The sound of the growling dog and its paws scratching at the door made a bigger impression.

I paused. *What would the resident think when he or she opened the door and saw me in ripped clothes drizzled with blood? Would the dog attack as he smelled the blood all over me?*

A chill crawled up my neck. Shivering made me remember. *I should have grabbed a sweater or coat. I guess I had been in a sweat as I maneuvered around trying to free myself. Why didn't I look around for a flashlight, for my purse, my driver's license, credit cards, and money? What about my phone? I must've lost some brain cells in the accident.*

I stepped up to the door and knocked.

Chapter 11
Finding Help

While I stood in front of the cabin, I stared at the gray floor of wide, worn boards with weeds growing between the slits. It hadn't been swept for quite some time. Minutes dragged. Finally solid footsteps inside the cabin told me a man slowly approached. A dim overhead light flicked on, startling me. A woman might have asked, "Who is it?" The steps would have been lighter.

The latch clicked. I stared at a rusty hinge as the door creaked open. A slim wedge of light settled on the dusty porch. Looking through the crack revealed a bloodshot, brown eye beneath a bushy brow. "What d'ya want?"

The dog's snout poked through growling with its teeth bared. "Please little sweetie. I won't hurt you, I promise."

"Shut up, Mutt!" The dog closed his mouth. He backed down his growl to a mini grumble while he sat.

I trembled. "Uh . . . sir." I pushed a stiff strand of hair from my face. "I had an accident. My car went over the hill." I pointed, "There, in the field. It rolled over. Uh . . .I."

"You alone?"

"Yes, I need help."

The door squeaked wide open. "Stay put, Mutt."

"You're a Rottweiler, huh? Good boy."

The huge black dog sat.

The man looked me up and down before he spoke.

I wondered his intent when he curled his lip.

"Yes, you do need help. You're injured. Come in." As he swung his arm out, a crooked smile inched across his unshaven face. After he rubbed his chin with one hand, he stared at my forehead.

Even though the dog still rolled a low guttural sound in his throat, I stepped in. "Thank you."

"Good boy," I changed to my doggie voice, the dog let me pat him on his broad brown head. " Thank you to you, too."

I raised my eyes up at the man, which let me know me he stood well over six feet tall. His rumpled plaid, flannel shirt and jeans, faded and dirty, made him fit perfectly in this cabin. He ran his hand across his short-cropped buzz cut then his unshaven chin. He could be as young as 30 or as old as 45. "Let me get a towel. You need to wash up so we can see that wound." As he walked to fetch a towel, he favored one leg.

"Sit there." He pointed to a kitchen chair by the table. I dusted some crumbs off the chair onto the floor to join the others and sat. The dog must have thought the man intended that command for him as he sat next to me with his head in my lap turning his sniffer on high—because of the bloodstains decorating my clothes, I assumed.

A quick scan around the dark, wood-paneled interior didn't give me a lot of confidence of a sterile environment. Filthy dishes, fringed in green growing stuff, stacked in the sink and old clothes laying about told me he most likely lived alone. A couple of taxidermied deer heads stared down at me.

How foolish, as if MY clothes were clean, I should have brushed me off. I picked off some weeds stuck to my jeans.

Limping over to a cupboard he reached in for a towel. I relaxed, taking his concern and the help all I needed as proof of goodwill. With a tremor, he washed his hands and wet the towel. "Here. Wipe your face. Leave your forehead alone. That seems to be the source of the blood."

Mom. Where are you when I need you? This is the kind of moment when you know you're not as mature as you thought you were. After I washed my face, I felt better. Taking the towel, he dabbed my brow. "Hurt?"

I scrinched my eyes closed. "Not much."

"Two cuts on your forehead. Not too deep. Don't think it'll scar that pretty face." He touched my chin.

"Good." My cheeks burned.

After he retrieved a broad Band-Aid from a drawer, he taped it across my wounds. "This has antiseptic on it already. By the way, I'm Bud."

I know he expected me to introduce myself. Rubbing my hands on my pants, I took a minute to think of what I should say. *Should I make up a name or stick to the truth?*

"Your name?"

"Uh . . . Natty."

He rolled his eyes then squinted while his face registered annoyance, "I need to know your last name, too, if you want me to help you."

I stared at my hands while my eyes blurred. "Natty Wilson." I sucked in a breath.

"What happened?"

"The only memory I have is waking up crumpled in that wreck out there in your field." I pointed. "The tire tracks lead up that hill. I think I hit something and lost control."

He handed me a Kleenex.

The dog sat at my feet and let out a tiny whine. "When I left school yesterday, I headed south to California. My parents live down there."

I wiped my nose. "I obviously hit my head. Maybe . . . I don't know . . . I'm sore everywhere." I rubbed my ribcage.

"Is there a hospital around here?"

"About an hour away."

"Police?"

"Our local sheriff is with the firefighters."

Wondering what to do, I shrugged. "Seems like I remember something about a fire."

"Looks like you'll have to stay here." A crooked smile crossed his face. "I live on a private gravel road about five miles from the main road that's closed."

"May I use your phone? I should call my parents." I ran my hands through my tangled, matted hair.

He stepped to the stove. "I have beans and franks—if I haven't burned them. Are you hungry?" That crooked smile reappeared.

I didn't know how to read his expression, but one thing I did know—the smell made me concentrate on food. When I breathed in the aroma of the bubbling pot cooking on the stove, my stomach growled like it. How long since I fed it? The dog also let us know he'd like some too.

Bud hadn't answered me about a phone. I surveyed the pine-paneled room. Without shades, two over-head, single light bulbs hung from the ceiling leaving much of the room in darkness except a small glow from the dwindling fire. An elaborate computer system filled the desk under the small window, clouded over with a layer of dirt. No clock. No phone.

He must have a cell. "Your phone? I have to tell my parents where I am and what's happened. They might have to come and get me."

After setting silverware on the table, he filled a bowl and set it before me. "Don't have one." He sat across from me, shoveling in his gourmet beans and franks.

I looked up at him, wide-eyed. "How did you find out about the fire?"

He pointed. "Ham radio."

"Oh."

The beans and franks captured my attention. The steam swirled from the pan as the aroma fill the air, a contender for the best food I'd ever smelled. When he dished it into my bowl, I took a giant bite. "Okay. Maybe we can use the radio later."

I eyed the dog. He connected his big brown eyes to my green ones. I cut off a piece of the wiener about to let him have a bite.

"Don't feed the dog from the table."

"Sure." I tried to retrieve the frank. His massive snout engulfed it.

"No! It's okay. He'd probably rip your arm off it you took it back now.

"Tastes good." I popped a bite into my mouth.

Silence sat at the table with us as we ate. When we'd finished, he got up and cleared the table.

"I feel so grubby."

"Maybe you want to take a shower. There are towels in the bathroom."

He walked to hall. "In here." He opened the bathroom door.

That sounded so good. I stood looking blank. *What if* . . .

"I'll turn the heater on."

"Okay." I followed him. "Thanks." *There's nothing to worry about.*

Chapter 12
Clean Up

Inside the bathroom, I noticed the door had a lock. It made me feel more secure when I pushed the button. As the door clicked I sighed. Although the bathroom looked like it needed a good scrub, there were clean towels in the cabinet and a bottle of Suave shampoo on the shower shelf.

"He's been very nice to me. There's no need to fear him. Is there?" I mumbled aloud.

Having made a quick decision, I grabbed some towels, turned on the shower and undressed. I put one towel down on the tub floor. It covered a month's worth of dirt. "That's better," I told myself. With the barrette and pins removed from my hair, I shook my wavy mop. After I stepped into the nice warmth, drew the curtain closed, a flash of "Psycho" chilled my whole body. I turned the spray of water down so I could hear if the doorknob turned. It didn't. *How silly.*

An empty soap dish? Being careful of my injuries, I squeezed out a handful of shampoo, scrubbed down my body and my hair then rinsed. Shampooing the dried blood out of my hair—Wow! The dark pink water flowed down the drain. After I dried myself, I twisted my hair into a towel turban. I opened the door a crack and peeked out. "Do you happen to have a hair dryer?"

He rubbed the top of his head. "Don't need one."

"Okay."

"There are some clean clothes there for you so I can wash yours."

"Thanks." I picked them up from the floor. Back into the bathroom, I unfolded them. I expected they'd be some of his men's clothing, but they weren't. I touched the soft pink cashmere sweater. The lacy pink set of bra and panties surprised me. The jeans fit but the sweater clung a bit too tight. The pink furry socks felt great against my cold feet.

I grabbed another towel, rubbed thoroughly to dry my hair as much as I could.

As I rolled up my bloody clothes, I found a comb and a finger nail file and a pen in the pockets. Because I didn't have a brush, I finger combed through the snarls first then used the comb. I rolled a knot on top of my head and pinned it with three pins then stuck the barrette in back. "There. That should hold it." When I let my hair down it would be wavy, not so curly. Looking in the mirror, I patted my dark russet hair and a thrust of my chin in the air. *What luck to land here! Everything will be okay now.*

After I came out, I decided to help. I headed for the sink to wash the mound of dishes. "Maybe after I finish the dishes, we could use your ham radio."

"Sorry, for my mess. I ran out of dish soap."

That's okay. I headed for the bathroom. "Suave will do nicely." After I rinsed the dishes off, I held the bottle up and squirted the liquid shampoo.

A hot water and soap applied to the dishes in the sink began to remove of the stuck-on residue.

"Hey, you don't have to do that."

"Of course I do. You've been very nice to me. The clothes belong to your wife?"

"Not married."

"Oh." That gave me something to think about. *Did she die*

in an accident; he does drag his leg. Maybe they belong to a girl friend. I didn't ask anything else.

He didn't add any more information. Though, even when I asked about a wife, the cabin interior gave every indication that a woman hadn't been anywhere near it for a long while.

"I already used the radio to contact the fire chief. He said the crew is mostly mopping up, but it'll probably be late tonight or early tomorrow before any of his crew goes home or the roads will be open. One of his men will come by for you in the morning."

"OH. I guess that's okay if you don't mind me staying."

He pushed the lever on his recliner and leaned back. "Sometimes it gets a little lonely out here for an old geezer like me. It's been nice having you." He picked up a book and started reading as I returned to the sink.

"What's your dog's name?"

"Mutt. Mr. Mutt, this is Natty."

"Hey Mr. Mutt, are you hungry?" I bent to set his already full dish on the floor. He bounded over.

"Don't usually feed him until I hit the sack. He howls all night if he's hungry."

I reached to pick it up.

"No!" He signaled with his hand. "He'd probably snap your arm off it you picked it up now. It's okay this time."

It didn't take too long to get the dishes draining on the sideboard.

"Maybe you could stay and do all my dishes for me. Thanks."

"Nice idea, but I think I'll go in the morning." I glanced at his bookshelf. May I read one of these?"

"Sure."

Dust flew when I picked one out entitled, *"Fiend"* with a skull and crossbones on the cover. I slipped another out with the title *"Kaiju: Age of Monsters"*, and eyeballed a few other titles which were quite grim. That gave me a flavor for his taste. I am surprised that I didn't think more of it at the time, but I didn't. An old encyclopedia Volume 19, R-T, seemed a better selection for me. I turned to the page with Teddy Roosevelt's smiling picture. I plunked on the couch and began reading.

Eleanor caught my attention next, a *little better than Bud's macabre taste.*

Mutt jumped up on the ottoman where Bud's sock feet were crossed. "Get, you stupid mutt!" He pointed, pushed then kicked him off. "Get!"

Mutt crept over with his tail between his legs. I patted the sofa next to me where I curled. I drew up my knees to give him room. With a graceful leap he landed, circled and settled in. When Mutt joined me, I ran both my hands under his chin cuddling his big head. I scratched his ears. "You're a good boy, aren't you? So you like your ears scratched. I've never seen a dog smiling." *They usually bare their teeth so it's like a scary grimace.*

I screwed up my face into my version of a grimace. He just licked my cheek and pawed my leg for more attention.

"I'd watch it. Out here I need Mutt for detection and protection."

"This cabin is fairly isolated."

"He's trained to attack so I'd be careful of any swift moves. He's unpredictable."

"Hey," Bud got up and walked to the kitchen counter. "I just made some tea. Would you like some?"

"Okay, sounds good."

"Milk? Sugar?"

"A little sugar."

Mutt watched Bud hand me a steaming coffee mug of tea.

"Thanks." I took a taste. "Just perfect."

After I drew my legs up tight I sprawled out, resting my head on the pillow propped against the arm of the couch.

I went back to reading and sipping while Mutt rested his head on my hip. The tea plus the dog curled close, took the chill away and made my eyes blink trying hard to stay open.

In minutes, Mutt snorted and carried on with a pleasant little snore, the sound of which began to make me feel like joining him in a snooze. Bud and I hadn't discussed sleeping arrangements, so I continued reading. I pulled the blanket around my shoulders.

After shaking my head a few times, my eyelids became as heavy as elephant ears. Feeling safe and cocooned here in the little cabin in the woods, I nodded off.

Chapter 13
In the Darkness

At the sudden jarring of my body, I jerked my head up. With only a small lamp lit in the small, dark, log cabin, I couldn't make out objects. Everything blended together. The room blurred. I couldn't focus. The strong odor of smoke made me sit up. Mutt barked as Bud swept me up in his arms. The smell of his sweat blending with the smoke made my stomach turn. Like a bad dream, I couldn't move my arm or legs.

"What's happening?" I looked up into Bud's indistinct face that swam in front of me.

His curled his lips to the side in half a smile. "Take it easy. The fire is out of control. Headed this way. I wet the house down with the hose. We'll go to the basement where we can wait it out." The glow from the front windows verified a close fire.Things seemed to be swirling around. My eyes strained as I craned around trying to make out where he headed. "I can walk now that I'm awake."

"Okay."

"Will a basement really keep us safe from fire?"

Out the window, flames leaped in the open field. Smoke filled the air and filtered into the cabin silently through the cracks.

"You're okay. I'll take care of you." He set me down.

My feet almost felt detached from reality. I stumbled.

"Please." I struggled against his arm around my waist.

"Hold still. You might fall." He leaned me against the wall as he reached for a rusty metal door. "The basement will be safe."

Feeling a bit dizzy, I braced against the door jam. "I can walk."

Bud shouldered into the door and yanked. "Sometimes this door really sticks. Finally, after a few hefty jerks the door, like a witch's scream, squealed open.

The stairs appeared indistinct. *Have I been drinking?*

"Let me help you. The stairs are kind of steep. Everything is fine."

But everything was not fine. Something shrill in his voice, in his sinister expression had turned menacing.

"I know it's fine, so just . . . Ahh. . ." My vision hazy, about half way down the stairs, I don't recall whether I tripped or collapsed.

Thudding, I rolled over the remaining steps, feeling every bump on my already aching body. When I stopped at the bottom, still blurry, he loomed over me. "Help me!" Trembling, I floundered.

"Are you okay? I'm so sorry. Are you hurt?"

"No, I don't think so."

"Wait a minute. I'll turn on the light." He dashed up the stairs. "Don't worry. You'll be all right. I'm just going to hose around the yard some more."

Before I could even think, the door closed. Like a slow motion, horror movie, the darkness engulfed me to the squealing cacophony of the rusty hinges. The door slammed with loud metallic clang. My eyes scrinched shut. When I opened them, I strained to see my surroundings. When I breathed, the mustiness made the blackness seem far worse than being in any old dark room. I waited a minute absolutely sure Bud would open the door and help me up.

"NO! Damn it!" I banged my fist down on the floor. Damp! I wiped the floor's wetness off on my jeans.

Only dim illumination escaped from the crack around the door. I sniffed. From the moist, damp floor and the distinct odor of mildew, verified the location of the room—definitely the basement.

"Hey Mutt. Are you here?" Slowly my eyes adjusted to the minimal light. I could make out a few things. The dog wasn't one of them. I viewed the stairs I'd just rumbled down.

It all likelihood, there would be a light switch at the top of the stairs. I waited.

He'll be back shortly.

I hope the dog's okay. I waited. *In a fire, a dog might run off trying to escape. Why didn't he leave Mutt down here? If there really were a fire, wouldn't the dog be barking? Sitting in the dark is stupid.*

Reaching for a handrail, I pulled myself upright. My legs wobbled. Teetering, I hauled myself up the stairs, expecting that he'd open and say, "The fire is out now. We're safe."

Surely when the fireman came . . .

The click I heard—I hoped against all–that the door hadn't locked when the door slammed. I jiggled the door. *Maybe if I jiggled the door really hard . . .* I yanked, but no. Had it locked or just stuck? I took two deep breaths, gathered my Herculean strength, gritted my teeth and seized the handle. I tugged as hard as I could. Locked! I screamed silently in my core. I sank to floor bracing to catch myself from another roll down the stairs.

I listened. In the kitchen, Bud clanged something around in the sink. *He'll be back soon.*

At the top of the stairs, I felt around for the light switch. When cobwebs stuck to my hand, I let out a squeal. But I did find the switch. *Would it light?* Crossing my fingers behind my back, I flipped it on.

At the same moment the light bulb lit, a flash went off in my mind.

There is no fireman coming for me in the morning because he didn't call anyone.

No one knows I'm here.

Chapter 14
No Way Out?

Tears rolled down my cheeks. *Get hold of yourself.* I wiped my face and took two deep breaths. In this remote location, screaming for help would be a total misuse of my vocal chords. He might even enjoy the fact that I felt scared. So I banged against the door—a metal door. Bam! Bam! Bam! "Okay Bud! It's time to let me out!" *Don't let him hear fear in my voice.* "My parents are expecting me tonight. If I don't phone them, they'll call the police and the police will see where I went off the road."

"Yeah, sure. Don't bet on it. Screaming is a waste of time. Don't strain yourself. I'm going to bed."

I told him that my parents expected me. But they didn't. They also didn't know where I planned to go, or even that I had left school. My friends only knew the person I planned to meet in California about joining a band, not which highway or where I might stop. *How stupid I've been.* In the back of my mind I could hear my mother's voice. "Always tell someone where you're going and how long you'll be."

Okay, gather your wits! Think! There has to be a way out! At the bottom of the stairs I sank to my knees.

"Dear Lord, I don't know why I believe, but I do. I know. I only talk to you when I need something. Please . . . Help me. Stay with me please, dear Jesus. Show me the way."

With my gaze casting about my surroundings, I felt

comfort, warmth, like a hand on my shoulder. I had to look around to see if someone stood behind me. Somehow I could feel Him bolster my strength.

As if I forgot how to breathe, I sucked in another deep breath. *Okay use your common sense. Think! There has to be a way out!*

One light bulb with about 50 watts did little to illuminate the basement. A grungy mattress lay in the corner next to the stacked-stone wall. Newspapers were piled next to one ratty, old overstuffed chair with its upholstery padding sprouting out of several holes. Twelve water bottles filled a flat box that sat on the chair. With the two blankets piled in disarray on the mattress and the one across the chair, I had a solution to one of my immediate problems. Shivering. I picked up the one hanging on the back of the chair and wrapped it around me like my cape.

I took stock of what items in this room might help me find my way out.

In my hair I felt the three bobby pins and my barrette. Checking my pockets, in one pocket I pulled out my mini nail file and my comb. In the other pocket I felt a pen. I quickly hid all of them in the box of rags. Bud might make me check my pockets.

A single toilet filled the corner opposite the mattress. Tears filled my eyes. I gritted my teeth. "NO! Don't get sad, get mad, and get even!" Yelling as I stomped my foot. "Oh how thoughtful, Bud, toilet paper!"

Okay. I kicked the box of rags. *He didn't kill you or hurt you—yet. From the looks of it, he must've done this before. He means to keep you—at least for a while.* I didn't want to think what he did with someone else that might have been kept here.

"Yuk!" Staring at the toilet, I wondered when it last had been scrubbed. I shuddered. I needed to use it now. If it didn't flush, it wouldn't take too long before this room would become a worse place to be. Picking up a rag and a water bottle, I wiped down the seat. *Okay, I might as well.* I sat and used it. I stood for a moment contemplating the rusty handle and my snarky yellow deposit. I grabbed the handle. "Kerplunk," it made a strange sound, splashed up a shot of tinted water and finally swirled down the drain. I let out a breath. *Yeah!*

With a blanket thrown over the grungy chair, I composed myself. Once I placed the water bottles on the floor, I picked up a paper from a stack of yellowed newspapers against the side of the chair.

After I plunked down in the seat, I pulled the cover over myself, and propped the newspaper in my lap. Doing nothing would leave me sitting here crying.

The date on the paper—November, 19, 1999. *Guess I won't be catching up on any news in this old paper.*

I dug in the rags for my pen.

Finally, I unclenched my teeth ready to make a list: what do I have and what can I do?

No ink? I scratched the pen on the paper until it scribbled. My mind searched for ideas to write down.

1. A blanket—used like the old Roman arena fighters used a net.

2. A file or the pen-used to stab

3. Bobby pins, barrette, nail file—pick a lock

Could there be anything to use like a club? No. But I did see a loose baseboard with a rusty nail working its way out. Maybe I could pry off a piece of the wood and use the nail for something.

4. Baseboard

5. Water bottles could be hurled.

6. A glass shard as a desperation tool

My eyes felt dry and tired as I scoured the room for more items. Finally, I slumped in the chair. I laid the paper back on the stack so that my list couldn't be seen. My head began to bob. Though as worried as I felt, I still fought a losing battle against falling asleep.

I screamed as I sat straight up. The flames crackling and leaping around me accompanied Bud's fiendish laughter ringing through the air. I screamed again before I realized the fire filled my dream and I remembered where I happened to be.

Still seated, I pulled the covers around. I shivered for a long time before I fell back to sleep with soothing thoughts of a little white and gray kitten nestled in the arms of Jimmy.

Chapter 15
A Wake up Call

"Wake up!"

No! I don't want to!

My eyes popped open. I jolted straight up. Everything in me cringed as I stared into Bud's red-rimmed brown eyes, lines crinkling at the corners. *This couldn't be the nice man who had taken me in and patched my wounds?* His evil sneer transformed him, but he still wore the same clothes. *A Jekyll and Hyde. He verified I had not been dreaming.*

"I have your breakfast, my dear." His face softened.

While he approached my chair, my mind scrolled back to my abnormal psych class. We discussed an article about a kidnapped woman who talked her way out of her similar predicament by figuring out what the perp responded to. I hope my trembling couldn't be detected under my blanket. I'd have to think about that.

Not wanting to rile him I responded. "Thank you, Bud. Is the fire out?" I eased my arms out to take the tray. A bowl of Cheerios in milk sat next to a piece of white bread toasted. I sipped some orange juice and eyed him as I took a bite out of the toast. "I'll be glad to help you with the dishes."

His cruel smirk froze as he leaned near. "Let's get things straight. **I** make the rules. You don't speak unless **I** ask you something. You earn what privileges **I** give you."

"Is that clear?"

"Yes, but I . . ."

He slapped me hard across the face. "A yes or no question needs no other words. You understand?"

I rubbed my stinging cheek with the back of my hand. Even my teeth hurt. I checked them with my tongue. The were all there.

"When I speak to you, you answer. Do you understand?"

"Yes." *But I don't have to look at him nicely.*

I squinted my eyes and planted my arms across my chest. Pure hatred spread over my face.

He grunted then whipped the tray away from me. I still held the toast in my hand so I gobbled down it in case he came to snatch it from me. The orange juice in my nearly empty stomach seemed to curdle. I gagged but held it back. My eyes fogged. *Okay, obedience is one trait expected.*

I listened as he stomped up the stairs and slammed the door, but not before the smell of coffee wafted in. The aroma just activated my hunger. I tried to get the toast and cereal out of my mind. *Would he bring more food at lunchtime?*

Well, he can keep me silent but he can't turn off my mind.

First, I had to set my creativity loose. *How can I escape from this basement?* I wandered around checking the only two exit points—the door and the window. Either one would take time and much patience with my limited tools.

Sunshine rimmed the window and shot through the cracks capturing the flying dust particles in the sliver of a beam. I pushed the chair over to climb up. I could break the window's glass, however Bud must've nailed it shut then boarded up the outside. I assessed my shoulders and hips. *Even if I were able to smash it and loosen the boards, it'd be a tight squeeze. Besides, if Bud came around before I got all the work done, he would notice glass pieces. If he didn't hear the crash, he'd notice it before I could situate myself for an attack. What reaction would that cause?*

That thought gave me a quiver up my backside. *If he attacked me, I could break the glass to defend myself. Though, I might not have time to wrap a handle around it. Could be deadly for me as well.* I shivered.

Outside, the noise of chopping wood gave me pause. Squinting one eye, I peeked through a slit in the wood slats covering the glass. Bud wailed away splitting logs. He was a powerful man. With the force of the ax, the split logs leaped to the ground. No wonder my jaw still pulsed in pain. Beyond his woodpile, the garage door stood wide open—close and yet so far. Garden tools leaned in a corner with tools that hung over the workbench. *If I could get out there, I would have weapons.* A bike sat next to several shovels.

Getting out of here is where I need to begin my work. I climbed the stairs to check out the door.

Even though the door felt like steel, a wooden jamb edged the door.

What could I do if I couldn't pick the lock? Could I unscrew the hinges with my nail file?

I looked. The hinges folded to the inside, trapped between the edge of the door and the jamb. My shoulders sagged.

Listening for the sound of the axe whacking outside at least let me know his location. The lock! I decided to try for it. I had hidden my bobby pins in the rag box. *If I hurried, he'd still be outside. I could escape on the opposite side of the house.* A rush of excitement and hope coursed through me. I dashed for my tools. With bobby pins in hand, I knelt in front of the lock. After I unbent the pin, I clenched my teeth. I shoved one end into the jagged slot. It wouldn't go. I pulled it out. Holding the pin up, I stared at the rubber tip. I gnawed that off ready to try again. As I inserted it, the chopping stopped.

I froze. My ears twitched. If the back door opened or slammed, *if I hear him, then if I mess around with the lock he would hear me.*

Slumping, I padded back, silent in my rubber-soled shoes. I crept to the chair and pulled it back from the window. I sat down to check my list . . . Footsteps approached. I folded the paper to hide it.

Now what? The steps didn't come to the door. *Would he bring lunch?* I wish I knew the time or how long since he took the tray away.

Could I ever know when he would come? I sat, tried to read a paper and collect my thoughts. *If he brought meals regularly . . . If . . . I'd be mighty hungry pretty soon, if he didn't.*

I shook off a chill.

Worrying what would come next, consumed me with tension.

To accomplish anything, I would probably have to wait until he went to bed. Waiting. Something I always hated. Now —waiting and fear of the unknown were my only companions.

The newspaper gave me something to distract me. Before I read the first section, cover to cover, I noticed the name, Register Guard, Eugene, Oregon. I looked up. *So that's where I am, somewhere close?*

I waited. I read. I dozed.

No lunch.

Hunger began gnawing at my stomach.

I pawed through the stack of papers. Unfortunately the papers weren't all from Oregon. Idaho, California, Nevada and New York mingled together so now I returned to asking myself, *where am I? Did I cross a state line? It had to be Oregon or California. It had to be, didn't it?*

Chapter 16
Pacing

My derrière ached from sitting. I wanted to stay strong as I could. *I may need more than words to fend him off.* After shoving a few things out of the way, I spread a blanket on the ground and ran through some floor exercises I knew, finishing up with nine pushups. I couldn't do number 10. I would have to work into more reps of each of the exercises. I needed to be in shape. Next I began walking then jogging around the small space.

Now I felt real hunger. A glance at the window let me know an approximate time, late, as it seemed nearly dark outside. I picked up another water bottle and quenched my thirst, leaving it half full. I still had plenty of water but I thought about drinking too much and then running out of it. *When would he bring more?* I decided to ration my water.

When I heard steps in the hall upstairs, the door handle turned. I couldn't believe I became excited that he came back. I knew his technique—an attempt to brainwash me. He wanted me to be happy when he showed up with food. *I will not let that happen—he might think so if I play act well enough.*

I stood. *If he were going to hit me, I could at least I could duck.* My empty digestive system reacted to the fact he carried food. *I have to plan.*

"Well, now. Are we hungry?"

My mind led with, *"WE are not anything."* However I

paused, remembering the one-word reply rule. "Yes." I bowed my head. I didn't want him to see defiance in my eyes.

"I assumed you were, so I brought you your lunch. Meals are earned." He handed me the tray then raked a rough hand down my cheek.

Had I not had the tray in hand, I'd have punched him. But my hunger even for the peanut butter and jelly sandwich stopped me. *Mmm, a big frosty glass of milk.*

"How's that?"

Thinking for a moment, it wasn't a yes or no question. "Nice, thank you." I sat in the chair with the tray on my lap. Being young and stupid, thinking before I spoke wasn't my usual practice.

"There now, that's my good girl." He patted the top of my head. *Does he think I'm a new pet?*

Hope he didn't see me cringe.

Milk, I nearly downed the glass in one gulp. It tasted even better than I thought it would. *Mmm, obviously whole milk, not low fat or skim.* Maybe I hadn't eaten a peanut butter and jelly for a long time because I smacked my lips as if it were truly epicurean.

Bud sat on the bed, laid back against the wall with his hands behind his head, smiling as he watched me eat.

Without knowing if I would 'earn' my next meal, I snuck crust pieces and slipped them between the chair arm and its cushion.

All finished, I wiped my mouth with the napkin. I must have missed a bit of jelly on my cheek because he reached over and wiped it off before he collected the tray. "I'll see you later, sweet girl."

What fantasy trip is he on? What did he mean 'later?' As he pivoted and walked up the stairs, my stomach churned.

I took some TP to wrap up my crusts.

He'd see me later? That thought would keep we awake for hours.

After I did a few exercises, I took off my shoes and sat in the chair perusing the November 4th issue of the 1995 paper. Headlines, "Prime Minister Yitzhak Rabin Assassinated," reminded me that not much improvement has occurred in the mid east. I decided that old news is more like history.

I turned the paper to the crossword puzzle, which kept me busy for a long while. I wished I had a watch or something that told me how long I'd been sitting. I finished the New York puzzle all but three spaces, a feat that usually gave me more trouble. "Yeah!" I congratulated myself. *Maybe that exercise could activate my brain cells.*

A picture of an elderly couple smiled at me from the local news section. I read the heart-warming story of the couple who was 97 years old, married in 1915. They'd had been married for 80 years. My throat swelled and tears shot to my eyes. I sobbed into the blanket. *I would probably never escape, never marry, and never have kids.* As I sucked in a breath, a voice in my head said, *"Yes you will. Wipe your eyes and think."* Somehow that calmed me. I stood up, grabbed a wad of TP and wiped my face.

Just then the door handle turned. He stood at the top of the stairs. *What was he holding?* A fiendish grin masked his face.

It chilled me, toes clear up to my scalp.

Chapter 17
New Expectations

Bud descended the stairs slowly carrying what looked like a tray with a bowl on top. "Now my dear, I have a surprise for you. "Aw. . ." He set it down on the chair and moved toward me. "Oh, my sweet."

I drew back.

"Your eyes are all red." He put his hands toward my shoulders. "Have you been crying?"

Backing away, I escaped his grip. "No. Lint in my eye." *No way am I letting him know he had distressed me.*

"Look. Here's your surprise." He took the bowl off the tray and sat the chocolate ice cream on the arm of the chair. I hoped my eyes weren't popping open or that I drooled. The ice cream looked so good.

I moved toward the chair to sit and the take the bowl. I wondered if I should say, "Thank you."

"Ah, ah, ah. Don't touch it. I want to give you another chance to earn this reward. I gritted my teeth. Not a tray, he held a slim box. *What would Bud have me do for the ice cream?*

He handed me the gift wrapped in pink paper with a sloppy pink bow. "A little present. Take it." His twisted grin revealed a mouthful of yellow teeth except for the missing one.

My stomach turned as I took the box from him.

"You can use the pink ribbon to tie up your hair."

With hesitation, I sat perfectly still.

"Well . . . don't just stand there! Open it!"

The force of his voice made me flinch.

I pulled the ribbon off and set it in the chair.

"Be careful with the paper. We can use it again."

Luckily I hadn't ripped it off or I don't know what he would have done. I played his little game and folded up the paper before I lifted the lid. I stared down at a pink lacy thing, probably a nightie of some kind. I just stood there trembling.

"Take it out." He didn't wait. He reached in and lifted out pink baby doll pajamas. "It's just your favorite color." He held the flimsy top.

"Yes." In truth, I hated pink.

"Well, put it on. Your ice cream is melting."

"It's too cold to wear . . ."

With a quick snap, he connected to the other side of my head, back-handing me hard enough so I tripped and fell into the chair. The ice cream bowl fell to the cement floor and shattered. I grabbed my ear to stop the ringing and burning.

He balled his fists.

Waiting for the next blow, I cowered.

"Oh, now look what you've done! What a mess you've made! You spoiled my surprise." He took a deep breath. "Oh well. We'll clean it up later." He reached for me. "Let me help you dress for bed."

As he stepped closer, I shrank back near the wall.

Before I knew it he clamped his huge hand around my throat and slammed me against the wall of uneven stones. He squeezed until I gasped for breath. My automatic self-defense mechanism awakened, hitting my impulses. I jammed my hands up through his wrists and pushed outward as hard as I could. His grip broke. Without thinking, I twisted my fist and snapped in a swift, underhanded punch to his gut.

As he bent forward in pain from my first blow, I rounded a

kick to the side of his head. He collapsed to the floor. It tookme a minute to realize what I'd done.

I didn't wait another second. I dashed for the stairs. When I grabbed for the door handle. It jiggled.

Yeah! Not locked!

Chapter 18
Escape?

The thrill of escape set my hope soaring. I hadn't given a thought as to what my plan would be if I managed to escape in his presence. I would have to outrun him if he came after me. *He has a limp! Maybe I can outrun him.* I didn't have many moments to think.

I threw open the door. Streaking like a rocket, I broke through the back door. The forest! Heading that way, my bare feet found every rock and burr in the soil. It slowed me down. I checked over my shoulder.

He shouted. "Stop or I'll shoot!"

Indeed, he held something in his hand. A rifle? Did he have a site on it? *If I continued to run, I could be dead. Maybe I could zigzag and dodge the bullets. He must have some accuracy as witnessed by his stuffed deer heads hanging on the walls.* In the end, I slowed.

Mutt barked and tore ahead of Bud.

Even if I managed to outrun Bud, I couldn't fool Mutt.

The next thing I knew, Bud grabbed me. His massive hand felt like a vise as he gouged his fingers into the back of my neck. He spun me around and thrust me toward the house. "Uhg, arg!" He grunted some weird, guttural noises all the way back, but didn't say a word. When I tripped, he yanked me up by the neck and hair. I bit my lip without screaming.

Thoughts of karate moves passed right on through my

brain. No way can I outrun a bullet.

Mutt whined.

Back at the cabin, the back door slammed behind us. The basement door still stood ajar.

"Sit Mutt!" His shrill shout against my ear splintered my eardrum.

Grabbing the stair railing, I took a few steps. With a massive shove, I lost my grip on the handrail.

In a blur, I missed. My forehead smacked the stairs.

When I woke up I wanted my recollections to comprise a bad nightmare. In the dingy darkness, I touched my throat. It was not a dream. *Had he left me alone? He must have turned off the switch. Would he disconnect the electricity?* The dim light lined the window through the slits. I could tell east and west from the glow—brighter in the morning. I calculated late afternoon.

Creeping up the stairs I stood for a moment. I didn't want to even contemplate being left down here with no light. I flipped the switch. My breathing calmed when the light lit and the blackness melted. I would, for sure, not let him know one of my worst fears—darkness.

Sucking in a deep breath, I inspected the room.

When I knew he had gone, I let out my breath. With my glance around, I noted that the pink things disappeared. Polished clean, the spot where the dish fell looked pristine next to the rest of the grungy space.

What did he think I might do? Lick it up?

Not knowing if he would return with the nightwear or to administer some punishment, I sat in the chair and assuaged a chill with my blanket. I rotated my neck. Outside of feeling his fingers still imbedded in my throat and shoulders, pain spread everywhere, terribly sore, but nothing broken. From this experience, I learned a couple of things: Always keep your shoes on. Also, he was not a fighter. I actually could protect myself, but I needed to make sure I took him down and out for more than a minute. AND I would have to make a plan if I ever get that chance again. I'd need to have a bag of tricks to grab.

My one big mistake—I didn't lock the door so he'd be stopped. *Could I slam the door quick enough to lock him in? If I did, would he die? Did I want him dead? Even if I had wished it a few times, no I didn't. I wanted him locked up so he knows what it's like.*

For this infraction, I knew the penalty would be harsher way worse than speaking out of turn. I just didn't know how much worse his retribution might be.

After a sleep filled with nightmares, a whale of a headache woke me. A giant thirst had dried my mouth and throat. I drank a bottle of water almost straight down when I noticed I only had five left. I put the bottle back with the water level at about a third. At least the water alleviated my hunger. I thought of the bread crusts I saved—not exactly a feast. I'd have to ration myself with the water and the food if he stayed with the same penalty of withholding them.

Beginning my exercises with a good speed walk, I stopped after a few steps. "Ew! Ow!" Everything ached. *What if I had a concussion? I should probably wait until my headache disappeared.*

"Let your heart not be troubled, neither let it be afraid. John 12:27"

Please, God. I feel you here with me. Help me through this. Give me ideas for my escape. Please, dear Jesus.

Chapter 19

A New Threat

"Wake up my pretty." His voice etched on my nerves. He pulled the covers back off me with a thrust.

He grabbed my shirt and yanked me out of bed. His muscles twitched on his neck and up his face. The glare in his eyes chilled my body scattering twinges down my back. With a mighty force, he shoved me against the stone wall. My head banged back finding the same spot I bumped on my way down the stairs.

"Ow!" I curtailed a scream.

"Oh, I am sorry. Forgive the few bruises on your lovely soft neck." Grabbing my chin, he tilted my head to each side as he inspected his handiwork. As he touched my neck, even though he touched softly, it sent a spasm like electricity shooting through my body.

His eyes squinting in a crooked leer, he stepped back, probably remembering my expertise in self-defense. "I brought you a gift." He picked up a heavy chain and held it in the air. At the end of it dangled a single iron shackle. Its clinking sound screeched through my eardrum.

The dim light from above shone on his grimace making his teeth appear to be fangs.

Suppressing a grimace, I tried to control the expression on my face. I sent my nerve endings a signal to look defiant and not petrified.

"This fits rather nicely right around the ankle and it restrains one from moving freely."

He grinned as he pointed to a place against the base of the wall. "I simply hook the chain through that iron loop over there and Voilà!" He slammed the two sides of the shackle shut. The metal clamp squealed.

Are you drooling? I cringed.

Sweat dripped between my shoulder blades despite the chill I felt.

"So my Dear, just put your right foot forward."

I didn't move.

"Would you prefer it around your neck?"

I grabbed my hands in back of me so he wouldn't observe them trembling. "Look, Bud."

He raised his hand cocked for a backhand. "Okay. I did ask a question. You may speak." He fiddled with the chain making it jangle against the floor.

I jutted my chin in the air. "I uh. . .I understand that with Mutt there is no way I can ever escape and hide from you."

"You're damn right about that."

"You could always shackle me later, if I don't . . .uh. . ." I pushed my hair behind my ears, "behave." Fortunately I kept my loathing in check and didn't use the word 'kowtow.' Instead I gave my most sincere apology followed by an endearing smile. "Lesson learned. Let's start over, Okay?"

I touched his hand.

First looking at the place I touched, he ran his hand across his nearly bald crew cut. "Sit!"

I sat down and tucked back my feet. *You'll have to. . .* I didn't have time to finish my thought, when he grabbed my leg, slipped his hand down to my ankle, yanked and twisted.

"Ahhhhhhhh."

"If you ever try to escape again, I will chop off your foot."

My eyes blurred. *He would not see me cry.*

"Do you understand?" I concentrated all my hatred into one word. "YES!" *Yes, I will escape!*

"And with this shackled to your other foot. Now wouldn't that be a shame?"

When he dragged the chain up the stairs behind himself, I let out the breath that swelled my lungs. Has he decided to leave me loose? I didn't quite believe it until the metal door clanged shut.

"Thank you, dear Lord. Please continue to help me do and say what it takes until you help me escape."

Staring at my shoes for a moment, gave me an idea. Shoestrings. If I could knock him out for a time, I could tie his hands and feet.

Duh! Then I would find it hard to run if one of my shoes fell off. Going barefoot didn't prove to be a smart move on my first escape. *I need to wear my shoes at all times, even when I sleep.*

Then I checked out the box of rags. I tore several of them into strips and tied them together making them into ropes using square knots. I gave my rope a hefty tug. *That should hold him.* I dug out the rags and placed my ropes at the bottom of the box. My burgeoning list included my ropes and a blindfold. Each entry gave me more gumption.

After I put my shoes back on, I looked heavenward.

I believe.

Chapter 20
Undaunted

A sudden idea rippled through my brain sending me to the rag box again. I retrieved my list of weapons, expanding my escape plans. *How did I forget?* After grabbing my nail file, I rushed over to the wall.

Careful not to bend or break the file, I scooted it down the wall behind the baseboard. I pried the board away enough to get my fingers behind and gave it a tug. Inching along until I had loosened about three feet of board I placed my feet on the wall and pushed off as I yanked it free. It splintered away from the wall.

A grin spread across my face. "Aha!" In my hand I held a weapon that resembled a museum art piece from the middle ages. I tied a rag around the blunt end forming a grip to ward off splinters. I admired the sharp end. The three-foot long weapon could be a spear, a sword or a club with several rusty nails protruding near the end.

Dancing up and down the stairs, I played Robin Hood, I parried and jabbed the air around the room. "En Garde! Touché!" Being so delighted, I almost didn't notice my body still bore the remnants of my painful capture. When I did, I sat on the bed registering what just happened. Rather than deter me, his threats just challenged me to be more prepared next time. Hope swelled again at knowing I had some defense.

I took a few gulps of water.

Now, where to hide my sword? The rag box wasn't deep enough. If I hid it behind the bed, I'd have it if he attacked me in bed. If I got to the top of the stairs, the spear would be helpful in warding him off as he chased me. Or I could hide behind the door so I could whack him with it. Glancing up, I noticed the shelf near the door made of the same kind of wood. It would blend so as not to be visible. I added those ideas to my list. I also made note that I need more than one way to incapacitate him.

After climbing the stairs, I had in mind to set my club on the shelf. Grinning as I visualized connecting with his head, I swung my weapon. "HA, HA!"

Time. I always had trouble estimating time. It took forever for the day to wear on. No food, No Bud. I needed to do something. I scanned the room. If there were any other heavy items I could hit him with, I couldn't find them. With a little scrutiny, I spied a single rusty nail lying next to the baseboard. A good traveling companion, I scooted it into the coin pocket in my jeans. I reached back in with my index finger and found that I could scoop it out in a hurry. If he surprised me while I was in bed—I imagined the perfect places to stab.

That made me realize I needed to cover the evidence of my 'night stick'. I picked up a couple of newspapers and folded them next to the wall where I'd removed the baseboard.

Spending minutes with the newspapers, crossword puzzles, and comics, made me thankful that he left me something to fill my time. Even so, I kept glancing up at the door. I suppose that's what he's waiting for—me to feel so grateful he shows up that I'll cooperate with whatever he wants.

Chapter 21
Time

My headache slacked off by the end of the day, so I exercised. That just made me hungry. I made do with a few yoga moves and thought about food. Like they were gold, I went for my crusts. I unfolded the TP and broke off a bit. By then the crusts were dry and crispy. It came to me as I crunched a bite or two interspersed with water: In addition to the body's need for the food and its taste, hunger also consisted of the sense of touch, the feel of texture. Fresh bakery soft bread, toast or dry bread all added to the satisfaction of relieving hunger.

I heard a motherly voice, "Don't play with your food." I felt the warmth of a touch on my hand. "But it's okay this time."

I hadn't been isolated and hungry that long. Had I been hallucinating? The difference between the dry crust and the moist one as I added a bit of water, made a meager meal a bit more satisfying. I wrapped up five more crust tidbits for later.

A while after no more light rimmed the window slits. I understood. There would be no more food today. I reached for a water bottle—now only three and a half bottles left.

I could last about 10 to 30 days without food, but not nearly that long without water. It's cold. Maybe I would have six or seven days. I put the bottle back after a couple of sips. *I'd have to ration. No telling when he'll come back.* As much as I wanted food, he might decide that I needed more physical punishment.

I teetered on the edges of fear and need.

Taking the nail out of my pocket, I looked for a place where Bud wouldn't see it and know that I had a sharp instrument. Behind an empty box, I scratched 10 tally marks in my wall for the days here — a perfect place for my nail.

Could I sleep without a bite of food? I ate one small crust and washed it down with one mouthful of water.

The anxiety of not knowing what the next cruelty might be or when I would eat again or the possibility he might show up at any moment, all that made sleep a stranger.

When I finally nodded off a vision of his fiery brown eyes so close to me made me sit up, gasping. I stifled a scream. It took a long time before I dozed again.

My stomach growled like an alarm clock. I don't usually remember my dreams but this one seemed to come with aromas of hot turkey. Just as I almost took a bite, a hunger growl woke me.

Early morning light streamed around the window cracks. I ran quickly to add another tally mark before Bud came with my breakfast.

He would come, wouldn't he?

I waited.

His footsteps captured my attention. I stopped. I listened. The steps came close though kept going out the back door. The crash of a metal lid clanged when he replaced it on the trashcan alerted me to his whereabouts. The door slammed. The steps continued back into the front room.

I slumped into the chair.

By now I figured that he didn't have a job or he would have been going somewhere, which he hadn't. This would add a problem planning my escape.

Obviously having him gone would give me the best break.

Scratching on the door made me freeze.

Hearing Mutt's whine, I realized the dog had discovered my location. I tiptoed up the stairs and sat at the top. I spoke softly. "Good Boy. I miss you." After sticking my baby finger through the bottom corner of the door, Mutt tickled my finger with his tongue. "Love you too, Mr. Mutt."

"Hey, Mutt. Get over here!" Anger riddled Bud's voice.

Funny how the merest touch, the merest communication, filled my heart with a smile of hope.

I waited for some time before moving. If the dog kept up whining and scratching, Bud would kick him until he moved. *I wish you could come down with me, Mutt.*

Tears ran down my cheeks while listening until the dog's scratchy paws on the slick wooden floor lead his steps away to the living room.

Chapter 22
Beginning the Task

As I sat on the top step, I noticed the hinges. The screw portion of the hinges was not exposed on this side of the door.. *I couldn't just unscrew them and be off.*

However, another brilliant notion presented itself, round metal dowels held the hinges on this side. My dad called them pins. A picture came to mind of me helping take doors down at home so we could paint them. When one removes a door, these pegs come out. These might not be easy as they were quite rusty. My nail could help me to pry these out slowly, which would make the final removal pretty fast. Being a noisy project made night my only time to work.

Occupying my time with exercises then the newspapers, I waited with my one eye checking the window to judge the time of day. I couldn't be sure but I thought maybe afternoon. I'd have to wait until he and the dog slept to start working. I'd know because I'd hear them as they trod up the stairs to Bud's bedroom.

It seemed like forever as I waited.

No food. No water. Crusts long gone.

I waited.

Trying to fill my time with the newspapers didn't capture my attention as my stomach roiled with a growl. I'd been hungry, but never this famished.

Now I knew what they meant by hunger—real hunger. Even though my hunger is quite less than people who have gone for more days than I have, this is one sensation not to wish on anyone—except maybe Bud.

I would never look at someone who is hungry and tell him to go find a job. It's very hard to think of anything else right now. I definitely feel like a weakling at what ever I try.

Would Bud starve me?

Lids heavy, I checked my timepiece. Black surrounded the window edge. *Quite late, probably.*

Settling under the covers, I just dozed off. I dreamt of hamburgers all juicy, stuffed with cheese, lettuce, tomatoes, and pickles. I took a giant bite while the mayo oozed down my chin. I licked my lips.

The heavy steps woke me —how much later I didn't know.

Suddenly, the noise of the door handle twisting made me rear up. *Why is he coming this late? Food? Maybe not. Would he go away if I feigned sleeping? Did I want him to go away? He might have food.*

Chapter 23

One Step Forward, Two Steps Back

"I brought you dessert."

So I can see, Beast. "Thank you." Shivering, I sat up.

"I thought you'd like another chance to earn your keep." He pointed to the bowl. "I'm sure we will not have a repeat of your former behavior." He handed me the box. "Well?"

After opening the box, I found the same damn pink thing. "It's lovely." I stalled by taking both parts out of the box. He didn't hit me so I continued. "It's so cold."

"It won't take long. Make sure you take your play clothes off, before you put it on."

What? "Could I put it on under the blankets? I'm so cold."

"Make it quick. Your ice cream is melting."

After I tucked the baby dolls under the blanket, I put myself under too. I knew if I didn't do as he told me, what it would mean. Would he notice if I put the bikini and the top on backwards with the opaque sides over my front? I poked my head out.

He moved across the room. " Come here." He swooped his hand out and picked up the chair blanket.

I tensed.

"This will keep you warm." He held it up like he held a cape.

I didn't move.

"Come. . . Now!"

I hurried over quick as a darting humming bird, grabbed the edges of the cover and wrapped it around myself. "Thank you." I shook. I hurried so he would not notice the backwards way I wore his little "present" or that I had left my underwear on.

"That wasn't so hard, now was it?"

"No." I wanted to ask him if I could have some soap and water but I needed an open-ended question.

Taking several giant bites, I gulped it down just in case he took it away.

"Do you like chocolate?"

Could I try a little more than yes or no answer just to check? "It's my favorite."

I prepared to duck.

"Then I'll get some more."

Whoo hoo! That means he'll have to go to the store. My inner self cheered. Not knowing when, I would need to start working on the door as soon as he goes to sleep tonight. *Be ready.*

"Could I have some soap and water?" I cringed waiting for the slap, as he reached toward me.

"Let me check your forehead."

I pulled back when he neared the chair.

"I'm not going to hurt you. You have been a good girl."

He pulled back the Band Aid.

"Ow!"

"Now it wasn't that bad. The wound is healing pretty well considering you fell again—a lesson learned, I hope."

Continuing to eat my ice cream as he sat on my bed, I gagged at the very thought of what would come next when I finished, so I slowed to a sloth's pace. The ice cream left had melted to the consistency of a malt.

I could drink it real quick and/or throw the bowl at him

just to see if my karate could take him down.

He was ready. Maybe he anticipated that I might try something. At my last spoonful, he swept the plastic bowl and spoon out of my hands like he had a magic magnet.

When he headed up the stairs, I let out a sigh, another day alive. "Thank you God." I felt Him watching over me.

Well, Bud'll be going to the market soon. I'll be ready. I waited until I heard him climb the stairs then gave him some time to fall asleep.

Meanwhile, that one bowl of ice cream made me feel better even though I could have eaten 10 bowls.

I don't know how long I fought with my eyelids to stay awake. Finally, I dressed back in my clothes first then gathered up my tools in a couple of rags and crept up the stairs. At the top, I listened. When there were no sounds, I started with the lock again realizing I didn't try options with all my tools. I assumed that the lock would be the easiest.

It wasn't.

Chapter 24
At Work

After unwrapping my ragbag of tools, I took out the nail. The lock had a bigger opening than smaller locks so this size nail went into the lock where I could feel something. However no amount of twisting, tweaking or turning worked. I spent a while working with the nail as I kept telling myself, "Patience, dearie!" Trying a bunch more twists at different angles, I quit. I let out the breath I held and sat back on my heels. *Use the bobby pins.* One bobby pin achieved the same results. How about two? At it again, brought a couple of clicks spurring me to believe I had the magic tool. But zip, no luck.

The barrette's underside clipped with a long, slender back piece. "So here goes." *I'm losing it talking to myself.* The curvature of the barrette stopped it from fully penetrating the lock. I stood, pressing down with my full weight. A few tries and the piece lay flat as a knife. It wasn't nearly strong enough. As I twisted and tweaked the lock, the barrette bent, giving me nothing more than a click.

I stopped instantly when the footsteps came down the hallway. I checked the window. Sure enough the light formed streaks around the window—early morning. Like a flash of light, I rolled up my tools, stashed them and sat in the chair holding a paper.

The newspaper rattled in my hands. Breathing slowly to calm myself, I reread the headlines several times.

He unlocked the door. When he stuck his head in, I shivered. "Are you okay?"

"Yes." My shoulders dropped.

"I saw the light under the door. What happened?"

Not a yes or no question so, "I can't see to read in the dark." With my plan, never to turn out the light, I thought this as a positive moment. Maybe now he wouldn't come to check every time he saw a light.

"I'll make your breakfast."

The door slammed. *All that effort for nothing!* I pounded my fist on the arm of the chair. *I'd been here over a month, would I break soon? NO!*

Ah food. That thought drove the edge off my frustration and depression. My hunger had not melted away when the ice cream did. Food! I dreamed it, envisioned it when I closed my eyes, my mind focused on the smell and the taste of a Big Mac. Eyes open, I sniffed. Picturing bacon and eggs lying on a plate with hash browns and toast, I even imagined I smelled the bacon.

When he descended the stairs he held a plate of bacon and eggs (minus the hash browns) a cup of coffee, and a glass of milk. My nose didn't deceive me. I licked my lips.

"Now, my little pretty, that's the first time you've smiled all week."

He set the tray in my lap then flopped himself on my bed. The fact that he sat there with the covers rolled back didn't worry me as much as it had the night before. Eating distracted me.

While he wasn't looking, I stashed pieces of the bread into a rag I'd placed in the side of the seat cushion. The rest of breakfast, I scraped my plate clean. I finished off my milk and held up the glass. He hadn't noticed when I spoke without being spoken to a couple of times the night before. I wondered how he had fresh milk having not shopped since I had been here. "Say, Bud, do you have a cow?"

He stood over me glaring down. "Did I ask you anything?

"No."

I cowered as Bud lashed out like a spring-loaded backhand. Funny though, if he had hit, I knew a way to block it and punch back. *Thanks Dad for teaching me karate.*

"Just watch it." He picked up the tray quickly and stepped away. When he reached the stairs he looked over his shoulder. "And no, I don't have a cow. I freeze lots of things so I don't go to the store very often. Afterward, milk's fine if you shake it."

He mumbled on his way up to the door. "Hate people. I have her now."

At least that's what I thought I heard him say.

My mood sank down with as my body slumped. *How long can he go without shopping?* Of course I expected him to go to the store soon, because nearly two weeks had passed. I took a couple of deep breaths. *Maybe I'm not ready yet anyway. I will have to have a means to leave this basement. I don't. Not yet anyway.*

I ran my tongue over my teeth. *What I wouldn't give for a toothbrush.* I'd been rubbing them off with a rag, which wasn't working so well.

When he'd gone I wrapped up my bread crusts and hid them, then did my exercises. Afterward, my throat dried up with a great thirst. "Rats!" Too busy eating while planning I hadn't noticed I only had one bottle of water left. I drank a small mouthful. After all, I'd just had coffee and milk. I could last until he came back with lunch.

Only he didn't. That's when I really decided to leave the light on all the time. Then he won't know when I'm asleep. *All I'll have to worry about is the light burning out.*

Chapter 25
A New Problem

Time went by like waiting for a turtle to cross the road, while I worked on a crossword puzzle. I knew his plan, brainwash me into appreciating him, being glad to see him. Understanding his tactic didn't stop an emotion arising—anxiety mixed with relief when the food arrived.

When the lock finally rattled, my 'window clock' showed me afternoon light. He came down the stairs with a bucket in each hand with a towel draped across his shoulder.

I stood smiling. *See his trick worked!* I gritted my teeth, mad at myself for letting him trick me. Before I forgot, I pointed to my empty bottles. He ignored me. *Did he actually see that I used my last bottle?* He usually brought more water when there were still a few bottles left. *I shouldn't have waited so long to show him.*

He set the buckets in front of me. "You wash at my command." He reached in his pocket and drew out a used bar of soap. The other pocket contained a toothbrush and paste. Both were used.

"This what you wanted?"

No, I wanted a shower!!! "Yes." I took the soap and dental rescue items.

"What do you say?"

He asked the question you ask when training a child to say, "Thank you."

I think his approach to his treatment of his captive, me, is to turn me into a child-like dependent being.

"That's my pretty." He patted my head. (or maybe worse yet, a pet)

I laid the towel, washcloth and soap on the chair. *Maybe if I am nice enough he will let me upstairs to shower. There's a window in the bathroom I think I could get out.*

He stood with his arms crossed over his chest. "You bathe with clothes on?"

I froze. I knew this had to be too good to be true.

"Come on now, you want me to wash your clothes, don't you?"

The yes or no question. "No."

"Why not?"

"I can do it in the bucket after I'm clean."

"Take off your clothes."

I trembled.

"Now."

Not close enough for me to attack, I stood. With my back turned, I took off my sweater with a glance behind me then handed it to him, covering myself.

"Your pants."

Tears filled my eyes as I unzipped. I slipped them off and gave them to him. *What are my chances he'll take them and wash them?*

"All right. We have plenty of time. We'll be together forever."

When he left, I couldn't believe he actually climbed the stairs leaving me in my nothings.

First, I filled a couple of bottles with bath water. The buckets remained warm. Using the toothbrush, I did my teeth first. When I took a drink of the warm water, I reacted. "Ew . . ."*Warm water tastes awful!* In haste, I spit it in the toilet.

A leisurely bath would have been nice, but shivering, I feared he'd come back. I stripped off my T-shirt, and underwear. As two buckets would not be enough for a thorough rinse, I didn't use a lot of soap. My bath began in parts, starting with my face, body, then my hair. I washed. To remove the suds, I rinsed the cloth and wiped away the soap. I dunked my head in the soapy bucket first then soaped up. While I scrubbed I picked up a couple of empty water bottles and filled them with the clean water. I rinsed my hair in the soapy bucket. I dipped again a couple of times. The last dip in the clean water, I swished around until there didn't appear to be too much soap left.

After drying off, I laid the towel on the chair. When I'd finished everything except my feet, I laid the cloth on the floor to stand on. After I drizzled a little water, I washed and rinsed them in the bucket and dried them. Without the socks, I laced up my tennis shoes.

Before I dressed—in the pinky, backwards of course—I wrapped my hair in a towel turban.

Clean is more than a state of being. It's a state of mind, a mood elevator. My underwear, sox and tee I dunked in the soapy bucket then rinsed in the least soapy. After rolling them in a couple of rags, to eliminate some moisture, I draped them over the boxes to dry.

After taking a drink I put the two filled bottles behind my chair and sat, covered in my blanket.

Waiting a short while, I put on my underwear. Even though damp, my body heat would dry them soon if I hugged my blanket around me.

I hated the way I began calling these things; my pinky, my blanket, my chair, my bed. *They are **not my** things. **They are his things!** I am **not** going to be here forever!*

Chapter 26
What Does He Want?

When my handy 'window clock' became dark, I worried if any food would come for dinner, since I'd had no lunch.

I knew he calculated the way he spaced out my meals to make me particularly glad when he arrived, just like the white knight to rescue me from starvation.

Not wondering long, the door handle turned. He entered with a tray. I could smell it all the way down the stairs, the smell of a hot dog made me smile involuntarily.

"I hope you like hot dogs."

"Yes." I looked at the dog in a bun with mustard and relish on it. Milk and potato chips topped off my epicurean delight. Drooling, I bet that would have entertained him. I wiped my mouth.

Since I behaved myself, I expected he would let me eat. As he sat on the bed, I stashed a pinch or two of bun before he settled and glued his eyes on me.

Enjoying every tiny bite, I nibbled between chips and gulps of milk. Worrying about what would happen after the last of my gourmet hotdog disappeared. I ate leisurely.

When I finished, he asked, "Do you like to dance?"

Pausing to answer, I considered. *He asked a yes or no question and he didn't ask me to dance. Because I love to dance, should I be honest?* Without knowing why he asked, I answered, "Yes."

"Good." He leaned back against the wall, stuck his legs out and crossed his ankles. After he put his hands behind his neck, he smiled. "Then dance!"

"There isn't any music."

"Make some."

I stood for a moment with my back toward him, still wearing my pinky, before I started humming the *"Blue Danube."*

"Now! Dance!"

With a hand across my chest, the other in the air like I had a partner, I waltzed around the floor, trying to keep my front side away from him.

When my arm tired I switched hands and hummed slower. Just before I nearly said, "I'm tired," he started applauding. He stood.

Afraid to stop dancing, I floated around him.

"Okay. This is a standing ovation. When I stop, you can stop."

A little breathless, I stepped around him and flopped into the chair.

"I'll see you tomorrow." He walked toward the stairs with the tray in hand then turned his head back toward me. "I'll have another surprise for you."

So then I had a surprise to worry about before I went to sleep. *At least I'm not hungry.*

When I woke early the next morning, I glanced toward the door curious as to whether I'd be getting breakfast or not. Since he had taken my clothes, I would still have on this stupid baby doll.

I combed my hair appreciating the fact that I didn't have too many snarls.

That's when I noticed a small, old fashioned, pasteboard suitcase sitting on the top stair. *Maybe he brought my clothes!*

I fastened my barrette holding my hair back then scurried up the stairs with the curiosity of my kitty Dotty. A quick remembrance of Polka Dot scooting into her favorite small open spaces or even opening boxes or cabinets to see if there she could play with something inside, she made life fun. *I really miss her. I am not sure I'll ever see her again or anyone I love. Would I ever have fun again?* And suddenly I thought of my phone with all pictures of Dotty, Mom, Dad and my friends. *When I get out of here I sure hope I'll get my phone back.*

The remembrance of three Cleveland teenage girls' held captive for 10 years came to mind. By the time a guy heard some pleas for help, one girl had a child by her captor and the other was pregnant.

I might be in the same situation. This could be happening to me.

"No, please God."

After I wiped my eyes, I ran up the rest of the stairs, to see what the suitcase held. I know it's just another trick of his to surprise me with something nice thinking I'll soften. *I'll just call this curiosity.*

Because I wanted to know if it might be something unpleasant, I returned to the chair to open it. I don't know what I could tell when I shook it. It just rustled softly like cloth. So I clicked the lock open and lifted the lid.

Another clean outfit, a pink and blue plaid blouse, pink sweater with a denim skirt atop clean pink underwear. *Oh, goodie, pink! My favorite. Maybe he throws everything in the washer with new red towels!*

Anyway, it all fit.

Then I trembled. *Who wore these clothes last?*

Chapter 27
It's a Waiting Game

Over two months I'd been Bud's 'guest.' Never knowing what to expect made anxiety become my newest character trait. It kept me vigilant. The clicking and squeaking of the doorknob always made me jump. I hoped he wouldn't look at my handiwork on the hinges. He didn't seem to notice. The rusty hinges didn't squeal as much after I worked on them.

Since I had little choice of entertainment, I did my exercises first, while hoping each morning would mean breakfast. I would try to be "obedient" as long as he didn't cross the line.

Of course, when the door mechanism announced his arrival, I jumped.

My constant fear became water. He might not bring water on time. *Yeah! He carried a tray* on the top of a case of bottled water.

"Ah, I see you like your clothes."

"Yes," *If you like 1950's 'play' clothes.* "Thank you."

Coffee plus orange juice sat next to the bowl of Cheerios and an apple. I started eating right away—just in case.

Shoveling in became a change in my usual fine manners as recommended by Emily Post, my maven of propriety.

"You haven't eaten your apple. Shall I take it back?"

He reached to grab it away, however I beat him to it.

"No." I sounded a bit desperate so I took a big bite. "It's

really delicious!" I had planned to save the apple, but no.

"I have an apple tree in the yard. When I pick them they last quite a while." He took another apple out of his pocket. As he tossed it in his hands, he spoke. "Think I'll join you."

After both of us munched about half our apples. I wiped away my look of revulsion just in time. He looked at me.

Me in his sights made me uncomfortable so I looked away. The expression on his face changed. This one made me queasy. The expectation of a new worse action might come next.

"Look at me."

When he raised his voice, it also raised my fear. I didn't want him to see me weep, so I blinked the tears back.

"I said, look - at - me! " He spoke slow and deliberately. I cowered.

When he stood, he balled his fists.

I looked into his squinty eyes and struggled to hold my hands still.

"Yes?"

"This is fun eating together. Would you like me to join you at meal time?"

Wringing my hands, I tried to decide if he wanted the truth. *"NO! You turn my stomach."*

"There's no way you want me to ask you again."

"No." I shrank back.

The slap came when I turned away.

"Ooow!"

"Sing."

With my ears ringing, my face still burning, I couldn't be sure what he said.

"You are being difficult. This is the last time I will repeat. Sing!"

With my vocal chords tied in a knot, I thought of an old

Faith Hill's song, *"Let Me Go."* Squeaking out the first few notes, I continued.

"No, no, no, not that one."

After I swallowed hard, I cleared my throat. *'Sixteen Tons,'* My tenor voice made him smile, a twisted smirk.

He waited until I finished. "Well, I'll say one thing. You gotta voice. Don't sing any more Johnny Cash songs."

He grabbed the tray and stomped upstairs.

Torn between wanting to annoy the hell out of him, or not wanting to kowtow to him, I thought through what I could sing without being on the receiving end of his wrath. Maybe religious songs would soften him. If they made him feel guilty —he might be mad. *No, hymns will be perfect.*

I figured there would be no lunch. By late afternoon, not wanting to completely decimate my entire stash of crusts, I ate a couple then nibbled on the rest of my apple until only strings remained. Holding a water bottle up to my mouth, I downed half the water. It tasted so good to drink without conserving. I had heard you could die from drinking too much water so I didn't go overboard.

When will my next meal arrive? As I lay my head on the pillow, I tried to think of times, happy times to surround myself with conditions of beauty and of love. Closing my eyes, a quick view floated in my mind like the stream near Jimmy's house. It shushed on by, lit with diamonds from the sunbeam dancing on the ripples. Hunger gnawed at my insides. I glanced around looking for an apple tree but only felt the beauty of the thick forest of spruce jutting like church steeples around me. With no one there, I begin to shiver in fear, when abruptly a figure rose from beneath the water with a tray of food. The scintillating fragrance wafts my way. The closer he came, I recognized Jimmy. "Oh Jimmy! I jumped up. Jimmy handed me the tray, leaned over the tray and kissed me. I almost dropped the tray with his alluring kiss still tingling on my lips. He disappeared like the vapor of steam.

I dropped to the ground with tears stinging my eyes.

"Come back Jimmy, I'm all alone."

At my back, Poppy's deep voice spoke. "I will trust and not be afraid, the Lord is my strength and my song. Isaiah 12:2." Poppy's voice rose ever so whispery in song and faded away into the air. "Poppy?" I sat up, back to my present circumstances.

Even though I didn't recognize the song, I finished the music Poppy sang with my own song.

I laid my head down. "Help me, dear Lord."

Chapter 28
Same Ol', Same Ol'

Days passed by in much the same manner, however, I had figured out how to flatter Bud into thinking he had brainwashed me. The first thing he did? He relaxed the one word rule, so I could tell him things he wanted to hear—how lovely the clothes were, how I appreciated my meals. He began to shave and dress better when he came down. I poured down compliments like a soft rain. When he asked, I danced for him to classical music that he played on a CD player. He'd ask me to sing. I let religious hymns swell like a prayer. Bud sometimes sang along. With a heart full of love songs to Him, I prayed night and morning for the courage to withstand what would happen before the help I needed to escape would come.

After plied Bud with praise, he brought sheets for the bed. Guess what color? Putting them on the mattress is when I found it. A gold locket lay puddled in its chain on the cold cement. The single light bulb overhead cast a slight glint that caught my eye. After I picked up a lovely locket, I snapped it open. A picture of a beautiful blonde girl maybe 18 or 20 years old with a photo of a handsome young guy pressed onto the other side. I slipped it in my pocket.

If I did get to a police station, maybe this would be helpful. I shuddered to think what might have happened to the locket couple.

When late evening came, I clocked in—time to work on the

hinges. Although slow, I finally scraped past the rustiest spots as I continued to work. They were about as far as I could go without him noticing they'd been loosened. So now I had to wait for the right time.

I consented to have him stay with me for a couple of meals. Fortunately for me, after that, he allowed me to say no. I even invited him a few times.

He began to trust me. So I could carry on a conversation without expecting a backhand.

One evening, when the door opened, Mutt dashed in and scampered down the stairs, his toenails clicking like a tap dancer on the cement floor. I ran toward him. We romped and played. I held him and cuddled. Such a small favor brought so much joy to the shell of a person I had become!

"I love you, Mr. Mutt."

We'd been having so much fun I hadn't noticed that Bud had come for Mutt.

"Oh! No! So soon?"

"Get, Mutt." He pointed. "Get!"

The dog charged up the stairs then paused looking over his shoulder at me, like, "Aren't you coming?" Bud stomped up behind the dog and pushed the door open.

"Get!" He pulled on the dog's collar, not without resistance. "I said, 'Get!'" That tone of voice obviously meant a consequence if Mutt didn't move. He put his tail between his legs, climbed up the last stair and out the door.

My eyes blurred. My face collapsed into a pout. "Thank you. Mutt is a special treat."

"Don't be sad. I brought you your bath, my princess. You have a surprise for later." He grinned. "Do your hair special."

"Here." He handed me a brown bag. Here's lunch for after you bathe. It's my favorite."

Following my "luxurious" bucket bath, I did my hair in a

ponytail, but this time at the side so it hung over my shoulder, a different do than the way I usually fix it. Perhaps he would think it more special than in a knot on my head. I checked the door. The suitcase made its appearance again at the top of the stairs.

Better start planning a little better. Hammering a piece of the floor molding on my nail, I had worked to pry up the pegs in the hinges. It would only take a few more taps then I could force the door open. I just prayed that the door wouldn't fall off when Bud opened it. I wasn't entirely sure it would open with all that rust, but hope swelled.

My best plan would include grabbing some food and water. I remembered seeing a flashlight near the back door. Maybe tomorrow night if I had everything ready. Sometimes he left the garage door open. *Maybe I should wait 'til then.* I sat for a moment thinking through what I had seen in the rooms I had been in—things that I could travel with. I would have to stay off highways because he could be trawling with his pickup truck.

I could take the bike part way then trash it before I took off on foot. *Should I take the time to go to my car? Maybe some of my things are still there. If I could get my phone, I could call the police, call my parents and this whole ordeal would be over in a few days. Never mind that the phone would've lost its charge. I needed money and my credit cards.*

Imagine, bologna, his favorite! Something I normally hated. However bologna took an interesting turn in taste when I thought of my alternatives. I felt my pulse quicken. Somehow my escape seemed too easy. I finished off my lunch while I planned.

Since I wasn't too anxious to open the case to find out the contents until I finished off my 'gourmet' sandwich. I assumed it would be clothes.

Could it be something a bit nicer than the others? Or it could be something worse?

So I donned my underwear before I brought the case down. I sat in the chair and clicked open the hasps.

"Oh no!" I lifted out a ruby red dress, obviously a very fancy one. It sent shivers all over my body. *What reward would he expect for this—plus the Mutt visit?*

He pinned a note on top. I unfolded it, penciled on a torn out piece of lined paper ripped from a spiral binder:

Dear Sweetheart,

Please wear this special dress.
I will bring the CD player.
Your Bud

I let out a sigh of relief. I peeked under the dress where a pair of jeans and a sweater lay next to a red strapless bra with matching bikini underwear. I took out the dress. Low cut with a fluid, full skirt, it would probably be fun to dance with such a dress flowing around me if the circumstances weren't what they were. The shoes were dazzling, red, dance shoes that looked as though they stepped right out of the movie, *The Wizard of Oz,* with Dorothy dancing down the Yellow Brick Road.

Maybe he just wants to watch me dance in a pretty dress OR does he also expect to see me in the underwear?

Chapter 29
Escape is Imperative

Red. I hadn't worn much red since my mom made me a red costume for my debut in a play. I also had never indulged in such fancy underwear. Without waiting, I put the underwear on immediately. *Now he wouldn't get a chance to watch me.*

The bodice of the dress dripped with bangles and beads. With a mirror, I could have watched myself as I swirled, swishing the full velvet skirt around the room doing one of my dance recital songs. Instead I wondered if I'd ever sing or dance for anyone other than my captor.

When the latch finally clicked my tension eased, subdued by the surprise. In walked Bud, grinning with a huge bouquet of wild flowers bound with a pink ribbon.

"Turn, let me see how the dress fits."

After a pirouette, I twirled around a couple of times.

"Here!" he threw the flowers down for me to catch. As I jumped up to catch the bouquet, I heard a strange scraping noise. A folding chair with card table slid down and landed in a noisy heap at the bottom of the stairway.

He patted the lapel of his dark blue suit and straightened his red tie on top of a starched white shirt. His hair had grown a little, which he parted and combed to the side. His clean-shaven face beamed. He stepped down. "You . . . You look stunning."

"Thank you. So do you."

The air swelled with the fragrance of Colgate mixed with his cologne. I figured he must've scrubbed his teeth. Anyway, they seemed whiter.

While not stunning, he might've turned my eye if things were not as they were. Instead I cringed.

"Go, go sit in your chair, go on." He waved his hand, sending a whiff of aftershave with it.

Sitting, I watched as he set up the card table pushing it tight to my chair. All the time I am thinking how I can use these as tools.

However he stood jamming his body against the table and set up the chair against it, thereby hemming me in and preventing me from using them against him without a lot of effort.

I could wait.

He dashed up stairs bringing the tray all covered in tin foil. Under the foil, he pulled out a white tablecloth. (albeit stained.)

"Please, cover the table." He picked up the tray.

Unaccustomed to a polite request instead of a command, I paused. Following his direction I laid out the cloth. The scent of something delicious delighted my nose.

He unloaded the silverware and matching ceramic plates. (not plastic ware or paper plates, as per my usual) They were hot. He lifted a large skillet's lid that imitated a fancy restaurant's silver covers. Aromatic steam rose from a platter of two steaks, baked potatoes and a heap of canned corn.

"Would you please dish it up while I pour?"

He took a champagne bottle out of the bowl of ice. I recognized Boyer Blanc de Blancs, French but cheap. Bud poured it into two stemmed glasses, while I distributed the food. *Don't drool all over yourself. The smell—I couldn't remember the last time I ate steak!*

He struck a match and lit the half-burnt candle. The glow spread an eerie light casting sinister shadows around the room and moved with the flickering flame.

Silence surrounded us for a moment. He picked up his glass. "A toast. To you coming here to me."

I tilted my glass. I had my own silent toast, *"To my escape."*

"I wanted to thank you for bringing Mutt to me." We clinked glasses. "Is it possible for him to visit again?" Taking a bite of my steak, I contemplated how I could keep a knife or a fork without his notice. *But when he went to wash the dishes he would find out. Then what would happen? The element of surprise would be gone.* "Mmm! Delicious."

"I'm sorry."

"What? Is Mutt okay?"

"Sorry, because I've been a bit, uh . . . rough on you. Haven't I?"

"Yes." I waited for his reaction. He looked down at his hands. Nothing but sad registered on his face.

"I've tried to figure out why I act this way, why I hurt you. You have returned my bad behavior with kindness then my punitive negativity with . . . force."

"My dad taught me self defense."

We continued eating with little conversation. "Pass the salt," etc.

As I enjoyed my steak, he pushed his food around his plate.

"Were you able to analyze the cause of your negative reactions with your bursts of anger?"

"I think so."

While he took a few more bites, I pretended to sip a little champagne. No way I wanted to be inebriated.

"My mother left me alone with him." His eyes began to fill. He wiped his face with his napkin. "She died."

`"Oh, I'm so sorry." I sipped again and touched his hand.

His fist clenched. "After she died, my dad would beat me for the smallest infraction of his rules, like, 'Speak when you're spoken to.' Then beatings came for no apparent reason and his drinking became worse."

"You hated your father?"

"After a while I figured that my fists worked pretty well. I became the biggest bad boy at school. When I could hold my own with my dad, I beat him bloody. I left. I guess I didn't hate him otherwise I would have killed him."

"Then you would be in jail."

"When I heard he died drunk, I celebrated."

"Have you ever treated a girl the way you've been treating me?" When I didn't get an answer, I studied his face. I knew he had. I wasn't the only girl he'd had here. *What happened to them?*

He finished his last bite of steak. "Well, I'm going to change all that—starting tomorrow."

"Why? What's tomorrow?"

"I'm going to town to shop for groceries. I need to get you the biggest surprise of all?"

"Oh?" My mind went nuts.

"Yes, I am leaving early in the morning." He smiled and stood. "Enough of that." He had brought another sack that I hadn't noticed. "TADAH! For tomorrow's breakfast." Out of it he handed me a brown bag holding a couple of sweet rolls plus a quart of orange juice.

He took out his small CD player.

Clearing the space, he pulled the table and chair away. "I've practiced a few steps, from on You Tube, you know." He laughed nervously then pushed the button. *Claire De Lune* filled the room.

With his hand held out, he bowed slightly. "May I?"

We had never danced together before, so it surprised me. I took his hand. You could not even tell he had a limp when he danced. Since I could dance with my mind occupied by other things, I held down my excitement. *He'd be gone tomorrow— leaving me here alone. I'll have a couple of hours to escape.*

With each new piece of music, he drew me closer.

Resisting at first, I put my head on his chest.

His breath on my shoulders gave me goose bumps. (Not the good kind!)

I had no idea what would come next. I could endure nearly anything if I believed I would be gone tomorrow. He put his hand on the back of my neck, pulling my face to him and kissed me. I couldn't show my revulsion. I had to think. I kept remembering the time he nearly choked me to death, so I yielded.

"We'll take a little outing tomorrow afternoon when I come home with your surprise." He drew back. "I love you, you know. We'll be together forever."

Panic swept through my body like a hurricane.

Chapter 30
One Surprise After Another

After the last piece played on the CD player, he held my left hand. In the other he held a black velvet box. His hands trembled.

With my mind on super speed, I thought through my plan of action.

"Make me the happiest man on earth. Marry me."

I am escaping tomorrow. What's the downside of saying yes? I couldn't think of one.

"I know. It's kind of unexpected. But think of all we have in common.

Like What?

"We both love music . . . And food. Plus Mutt likes you and you like him."

Music, yes. Oh sure, because I gobbled down my food? But I do love it more now that I know what hunger is. Loving Mutt—a no brainer.

"Well?"

Will I rue this decision? "Yes." I croaked out.

"Yes?" He shot an arm in the air. "You won't regret it! Give me your hand. The left one."

I reached out.

"Wile his hand trembling, he pushed his gift on my ring finger.

With great panache, he bowed. When he reached out his

hand, with hesitations, I put mine in his. In a formal dancing posture, he danced me around the room. "You won't be sorry."

When we stopped, I held out my hand to inspect the ring. It looked about like a karat and a half. "It's beautiful." *How much I could sell it for at a jewelers or a pawnshop?*

"Now let's get to bed early. We've got a big day tomorrow."

My nervous system sped into full throttle into seizure. I must have turned ashen as I trembled.

"What's the matter?"

"Uh . . .I can't. I mean, we can't do anything like that until after. . ."

He stood staring at me for quite sometime while I quaked.

"Okay. Okay. You're not like those other girls. They were tramps."

I hadn't realized I had been holding my breath.

He picked up all the dinner dishes, silver ware and glasses, but left the table and chair. With that he bounded upstairs leaving me with my mouth hanging open.

"See you tomorrow afternoon. Your breakfast is in the paper bag, I'll make you a special lunch."

"Wonderful!" Did my ear-to-ear grin look as phony as it felt? "Ta! Ta!" My glee wasn't a fake. *Yeah! Tomorrow!*

Thank you prayers danced in my head as I dropped to my knees. "Thank you, Lord Jesus. Help me get through this with you by my side."

Debating with myself, I stripped out of the red dress. I decided to keep underwear. Wanting nothing to remind me of this experience, I rationalized. I should remember this and never be so stupid again. *This is my winner's prize.* Before I got on my jeans, I pranced around in my snazzy underwear.

Missing 'winning' his next prize, *will I always wonder what he had in mind for his 'surprise'? Better to always wonder than staying here to find out! What luck that you gave me jeans for my escape. Am I that good at my 'attitude' performance?*

After I slipped the sweater over my head, I pulled on my jeans. Already accustomed to wearing my running shoes every night, I climbed in bed with all my clothes on. I wanted to be absolutely ready when tomorrow came. Setting my mind like a clock, I wouldn't over sleep. I took a moment to count my tally marks on the wall. Thoughts about 'the other girls—the tramps,' gave me the feel of icy fingers around my neck. *Bodies could be buried on this property.*

Tomorrow I will have been here for four months.

With my head on the pillow, eyes wide open, muscles tense, I planned what tasks I should consider in the morning. I heard a heavy rain pounding the side of the house. It doesn't matter, I am going rain or shine.

"Dear Lord, Please be with me tomorrow . . .

After quite a long while, I heard Bud tromp up the stairs. Bursting up I kicked my covers off. After I rolled some rag strips I'd already tied into a rope, I put them in the middle of the blanket. With not many belongings, I rolled bottles of water into the blanket. Water's heavier than I thought, so I just took three. Upstairs, I hoped I would find some food to take, maybe a knife.

My pack all set, I resumed the tapping of the pins in the door hinges. *It won't take too long to get the door off. The pins are really loose.*

In the morning, it would only take one more, small tap . . .

Chapter 31
Escape!

Morning came quickly. Fortunately Bud made coffee, the aroma of which crept in like an alarm clock, awakening my nose. I sat right up in sudden remembrance of the day's opportunity. I smiled at the beginning of my forever.

Fully dressed, I pulled the covers over my head, just in case he came in to say goodbye I stayed in bed. Though if he did come in, the door would probably fall off the hinges. That gave me a little something to worry about.

I listened. He went up stairs again. I heard the shower as it came on and as it stopped. *Thank you Lord, for noisy pipes.*

While he busied himself upstairs, I downed about half of the orange juice with the sweet rolls.

When he came downstairs from his bedroom, the refrigerator opened and closed before he clomped down the hallway. He opened the back door and slammed it behind him. With quick steps, he descended the porch stairs.

Mutt whined and scratched at the door. Mutt wasn't going. What would Mutt's reaction when I came upstairs? I think he would be excited. That'd be nice but it would slow me down.

After I pulled the small chair over to the wall, I climbed up and peeked through the window slit. The early morning sun rose to a glow behind the stand of pines. No clouds meant there probably wouldn't be rain. *A good day for an escape!*

From the back, as he walked toward the garage, Bud

walked like a bowlegged cowboy, wearing a western hat, boots, worn jeans, plaid shirt, under an old jean jacket. He unlocked and opened the garage door, hopped in his Ford pickup truck and backed out. *Don't lock the garage door*!

He did.

Stepping out with the truck door open, he hooked on the lock. *Rats, I will have to trek faster, now that I can't speed away on his bike.* Bud took a long gaze toward the house before he jumped into the truck.

I shook until I realized just because I could see him, the narrow window slits wouldn't let him see me.

At least I knew what he looked like, what he wore. If he followed my trail, I could pick him out of a crowd.

After splashing through a muddy puddle, his truck sped down the gravel road pinging up pebbles. Through his open window, I heard his radio, spewing out cowboy music into the cool morning air.

I could scarcely breathe. Taking in a few breaths, I stood like a statue. My heart pounded so hard I heard it in my ears. My hands trembled.

I imagined standing beside myself and shaking me. *Get hold of yourself!*

"I can do all things through Christ who strengthens me. Philippians —4:13"

Still not knowing what to expect, I crept up. I kneeled in front of the basement door. Starting at the bottom, so it wouldn't fall on me, I aimed my nail at the pin. With a tap, tap the pins loosened and pushed up out from the hinges. My heart skipped a beat. "Yes!" I thrust one arm in the air. It really worked! The pins had held back the door. With them out, it didn't fall by itself. As I braced my hands against it, the ponderous door almost dropped on top of me. I willed my adrenalin to pump me up as I held it back.

With great gusto, I executed a Herculean shove.

The door crashed against the wood paneling in the hall.

After picking up my blanket roll, I took a few quick steps, jumping over the fallen door and down the hall to the kitchen.

There he stood.

Chapter 32
UP, UP and Away

A few embers still glowed. He Mutt jumped up from sulking on the rug in front of the fireplace. He raced toward me and leapt up. In one smooth move, he licked my face, landed his front paws on my shoulders, and knocked me clean over onto the couch. After he covered my face in slobber, he backed off letting me sit up. We had a little tussle, hugging, and tummy rub before he allowed me to rise from his turf.

"I think Bud is going to be sorry he left you here after we were already friends! You're definitely not a guard dog against me."

With a 360 take on the cabin, I assessed. What could I take? In the freezer I took out a loaf of bread and a quart of frozen milk. Things frozen were heavy, so I took two dishtowels instead of getting bigger towels from the bathroom. I checked the drawers and found a lighter. One click, "Yup it works!" I packed them in my blanket along with a butcher knife, a butter knife, fork and spoon with a few paper plates.

I patted Mutt's head as he followed me around the room.

A very long plank of wood spread across a couple of file drawers comprised a makeshift desk against the windows. On the top, Bud's shortwave radio faced me. I didn't know how to work it, so I concentrated on the computer next to the radio.

Because I might need a pen to jot down something, I opened the top drawer of the file cabinet that held up the end of the desk. I clapped my hands "Wow!" I whispered in utter amazement. My mouth dropped open. A 22 caliber pistol with a box of ammo stared back at me. I remember now. When I first came and knocked on his door, I'm sure he heard my accident crashing loud enough for him to notice a car in his field. He probably watched me approach. When he opened the door, he reached behind himself something like tucking his shirt into the back of pants. Could this pistol have been what he tucked in? *I should pack this for easy access, but how?* Glancing around the room, I gasped. A holster and belt hung from a peg in the entry hall.

"Good! I won't have to pack my 'medieval' weapon." When I threw the nail-baseboard aside, Mutt chased it. He kept busy chewing for a few minutes, clattering around on the bare wood floor.

Before I closed the drawer I found a curious, lumpy envelope marked 'visitors.' As I felt it, I almost thought I knew what might be inside—plastic cards of some sort. Tilting the envelope over the desk, out dropped the collection of driver's licenses and credit cards–all young women. "Look, Mutt. My ID is here!" I couldn't take long to peruse them in this limited time. So I put the envelope in my pack. To keep them handy, my cards went in my pocket. *Something must be wrong. This is too easy! Next I moved to the computer. Could I get in?*

As I pushed the drawer to close it, I saw a file labeled, **Mr.MuttOU81.** As Mutt pawed my leg, suddenly I knew. His password had to be **Mr.MuttOU81!** Inside the file, I found Mutt's pedigree with shots record. After I sat back down, I tapped a few keys. *Yes! Not very smart!* I chuckled to myself. *No firewall! And just 'sleeping'!* He hadn't logged out!

Obviously he thought he lived so far out here, no one could get in that he wouldn't know about.

I laughed out loud. "I'm in!" I took Mutt's head in my

hands and scratched behind his ears. "Yeah, Mr. Mutt. He loves you. So do I." I ignored a few 'interesting' files: Taxidermy, poisons, clean up materials, police calls, weapons and other ones that gave me the chills.

Checking the screen again, I couldn't believe what I saw before me. "Yeah! BMC Helix Multi-Cloud!" I hollered out loud. Mutt yipped at my exclamation. I used this system at my last job. Its complex security network, very familiar, put me at ease. As a systems analyst, I'd worked on far more complex systems.

Without much work and not many minutes lost, I could transfer money, if he had any, from his bank accounts to my accounts. As I opened his different investments, I realized I didn't have time to do much with stocks and bonds, so I changed their passwords. I grinned. I suppose he could resurrect them, but I giggled while thinking how much fun that would be. Budrey Sherman Dutton, his complete name was plastered all over his accounts. With that name, I hoped it would be easy for the police to find him. Could I give them an accurate set of directions? I hoped so since his address was only listed as a P.O. box.

When my father served in Germany, he had opened a German bank account for me. I drew on it when I went to Germany for a semester abroad. Dad didn't want to get taxed on it, so he left it there.

"Oh my!" Bud had a bunch of money in a Swiss account, $407,308. My German account is where I put the greater part of it. Several clicks later I had $407,691.89 combined with the money I already had in my account. A couple more clicks and I had $7,691.89 in my Banner Bank checking account in Eugene, Oregon. Being ever so nice, I left him $308 in his account. A smidge of guilt settled in my brain for my theft. "Forgive me, Lord." The guilt dissipated in about a second.

I checked the time at the top on the computer screen, 8:30. I had probably wasted only 15 minutes. Though it really hadn't been squandered. I collected just compensation.

Knowing he would probably be back in another two hours or maybe three counting drive time each way to where ever he planned to go, I hoped it took more time. Whatever wonderful 'surprise' he planned to pick up, as well as his grocery shopping, I assumed that Bud would spend some time as he doesn't go too often.

Opening the cupboards for travel food, I found what I needed. "Peanut butter!" I chucked it in my pack with some energy bars.

Something must be wrong. This is too easy.

As I slung the gun belt around my waist, I noticed a pretty nice leather jacket hanging from another peg. I slipped it on, with a gaze upward. "Thanks, Lord. A little big but it'll be fine." When I checked the pockets, I found a wad of something. I withdrew a small lump of bills that I unfolded. "Eureka! Well, howdy Mr. Hamilton." A five, a twenty, seven ones, not that much money, but I'll take it.

I tied my rag rope around my rolled up blanket then fashioned the rest of the rags into a sling for easy carrying.

It just took a few more minutes to be ready to go.

As I went for the door, I realized I had a decision to make.

"Should I take you, Mutt?"

Chapter 33
Going, Going, Gone

When I stared right into Mutt's big brown eyes, I asked him, "Do you want to go with me? You'd have to be good." He reached out his paw. I shook it. "Okay if you follow me out and go with me, I'll take you but first . . ." I grabbed a plastic bag. I scooped some dog food into it along with a bag of dog treats.

"Follow me." He did. "I should go back to my car." So I tied the end of the dog food bag around my rag sling. "Well, I won't know whether you are following me for this food or just to be with me." About half way there I realized that I couldn't see the wreck. The grass grew just about to my thigh, not that deep. I couldn't be that far from it. I could still see some of the broken trees, matted grass and the break in the fence. What had happened to my car?

We had only gone a little further when I saw the burned grass and scorched frame. "He torched it!" I sank to the ground on my knees. Mutt nuzzled me. "No! All of my belongings gone!" I sniffed. "You will not let this little glitch stop you, Natty!" I screamed at the top of my lungs with no one to hear me but Mutt. I opened my arms hugging him tight. "So that's why! That night, he fooled me into thinking the fire came toward us because MY car's flames lit the sky."

Nothing to cry over—so I had no phone, not even one to charge!

"Okay!" *God has given me everything I need to survive. I would need to get somewhere that had a Banner Bank or better yet, an ATM so I could make a withdrawal. How long before I found a town?*

An image popped in my mind—the collapsible fishing poll in Bud's back hallway. Since we needed to head south, it wouldn't be out of the way to return to the house. "Come on Mutt." We trudged back. I laid out my blanket. In went the pole, with a couple of hooks out of his fishing box. After I wrapped it up, we were off.

I figured we would have roughly four hours before Bud would be back. Maybe longer before he realized I was gone. So I didn't hurry that much. Besides I had Mutt.

On the way by the apple tree, I grabbed as many as I could stash. I tossed the last one in the air for Mutt then one for me. I caught it and munched it down almost as fast as Mutt. "Breakfast, Mutt?" I tossed the core up ahead. Mutt raced for it, leaped to bite it out of the air.

Free at last! Thanks, MLK. Living free again! I thanked God as the sun warmed my back. "We are heading southwest, I think."

We stayed fairly close to the road for a short while. "Good having you along, Mutt. I'm not alone." I hadn't talked this much in the whole four months I had been held captive. I held a regular conversation with him. Then I'd answer myself back like I spoke for Mutt. *Was I losing it?* Raising my spirits, I sang, but not by myself. When I hit a high note or belted out my song, Mutt howled. The rest of the time he 'sang' along with me, though I'd hardly call that rumbling whine singing. Mutt seemed to like it when I sang. If I reached a high note or belted out my song, Mutt would sometimes join me with a bone-chilling howl. "Hey Mutt. Will you save that howl for when something attacks us?"

Soon he had me laughing. It had been a long time since I laughed. It felt great.

It would have been such fun if I had my phone to record some of Mutt's antics along with our conversations or duets as he howled along.

I assessed my dark brown leather coat while I patted Mutt's black and brown head. "Let's go into the forest for a while. While it gets dark, we'll be hard to see. Besides we better not sing anymore. We'll draw attention to ourselves."

The forest became denser as we continued on.

When we had been traveling about 20 minutes, I noticed something up ahead.

"What's that, Mutt?" As we came nearer I thought I could see a shotgun. Something leaned against a tree trunk.

Mutt whined a tiny sound.

"Shh! Someone might be hiding around here." My voice came out as a raspy whisper. I squatted down behind a tree trunk, gathering Mutt beside me.

Swiveling my line of vision around, I could see no movement. I listened. Mutt's breathing seemed very loud, but no other sound interrupted the calm. No rustling of bushes or crinkling grasses. Nothing sounded except the bird songs rifling through the air. Birds' songs meant safety. Maybe. If they hadn't ceased their chorus for Mutt and me, then other hikers wouldn't scare the song out of them either.

Crouched, absolutely still as a rock, I waited.

After what seemed like a very long time, I rose. On my tiptoes, I approached the darkened space. Glad it hadn't been later in the evening, or with a couple of more steps, I would have fallen into it.

"Oh, dear God!"

I promptly realized what I had found.

Chapter 34
Not a Day Too Soon

A shovel next to a hole! When I leaned over to check the hole's contents, thank goodness no body lay inside. Shaped like a grave, a mound of dirt piled next to the hole, just waiting to be shoveled over the top of my body. When I realized that he might even have lured me out here to bury me, it might have been a live burial! I shook all over while I thought of those girls, the ones whose IDs I found. Mutt shook too!

"I knew it!" I knew what Bud planned for me by digging this hole. *How much time until he had everything ready? So when would it have been? When I fought back? When I didn't obey him? When I wouldn't sing for him? When I wouldn't kiss him? When we had some kind of weird wedding ceremony? When he . . . If he hunts me down, that's when!* I shook like a violent earthquake had overtaken me. When I sneezed, the goose bumps crawled across my entire body. I didn't want to think about the horrific things that might have happened to me or will happen if he overtakes me.

I composed myself then leaned down hugging him. "I am so glad you came with me, Mutt. "Let's go, boy. We better put some space between us and Bud." To escape Bud's search along the road, I needed to stay off it for a while, but I knew a stream ran parallel to the road. I wanted to keep the road in my sights. It should lead us to a town.

"Let's step up our pace, Boy." Running with a frequent

glance over my shoulder, I panted. "Bud might not be far behind us."

Though I knew we couldn't continue running, we kept going until my heartbeat pounded along with my feet. Even as we slowed, I didn't know how long we could keep up this pace of a rushed walk.

I stopped for a drink. "Sorry Mutt, I should have brought along a bowl or something for you to drink from. I splashed water in my hands for him to lap.

"I know boy. We'll get to the stream pretty soon where you can drink all you want." We were both panting as we continued, but had to slow our pace again.

More tired that I'd ever been, I sagged. How long had it been since I slept more than an hour or two?

As I looked up, I shielded my eyes. The sun gleamed straight overhead—my only way to determine time—that would make it about noon or probably three hours since we left Bud's place. Recalling my hikes with Poppy, I wished I had the odometer he gave me. Then I could tell how far we hiked.

At school, I walked for exercise with my odometer. I kept up walking around Bud's basement to keep fit. I exercised. *I am in good shape!* I figured that I could do a mile in 15 minutes, relatively easy, for sure on a flat walk. Without flat terrain, I assumed that in three or four hours, I probably only traveled about eight or nine miles.

Thinking back to that afternoon at the time I crashed into Bud's fence, I had only driven a few miles after Wolf Creek when I came upon the detour. I put my hand on my brow as if I could turn the wheels in my brain to remember the name of the road I had turned right off the main highway. (That I also couldn't recall. Sun Valley?) I headed west before I came to the fork to where? *No use trying to this location until we find a road.*

The day had warmed up a bit so I tied the jacket arms around my waist.

"Hey, Mutt." He turned back from his sniffing along ahead of me. I sat on a rock in the shade while I admired the pattern the sunbeams made as they shot through the branches and leaves. I patted weeds next to it. "Sit." He came back and sat right down. "Good Boy. We need to rest." I looked into his big brown eyes. "You need a new name. Mutt is not a name for a good boy like you! What do ya think?"

I gave him a few dog food bits. Next I fixed a peanut butter sandwich. We shared a few bites. The milk had melted a bit so I gulped. "Great!" I found an indentation in the rock so I poured a few mouthfuls of milk for Mutt. He lapped it up while I grabbed an apple. I munched while names ran through my head.

Mutt didn't even let me toss the core. He snatched it out of my hand before I finished my last bite. "Hiking builds an appetite . . .I've got it! How about Matt for your new name?" He looked up at me as if he understood. "Matt sounds a bit like Mutt, huh, Matt? Sir Matthew or Matt for short! That elevates you to earldom from the ordinary Mr. Mutt." From then on I mixed Matt with Mutt. It seemed to be working. He tilted his head to the side. "You recognize your new name? We'll see then if it would work. Huh, Matt?"

He looked up!

"Good Boy." I gave him a treat. "That's how I'll teach you."

Matt cuddling up next to me and being as tired as I felt, I leaned back against a tree. I closed my eyes and drifted off to sound of the leaves fluttering in the soft breeze.

Chapter 35

How Far is Away?

When I woke, I couldn't tell how long I had napped. It had to be sometime in the afternoon according to the sun. I had hoped I would make it a good distance from my 'jail cell.' Now we'd have to run again to make up time! "We gotta get going, Sir Matthew."

Poppy's voice again whispered, "I can do all things through Christ who strengthens me—Philippians 4:13."

I stretched tall. "We can do this, Matt!"

Following a quick pack-up, I sped up my pace as I hummed a little tune in double time. Matt pranced ahead still making sure he smelled just about everything. Finally we slowed, continuing at a more reasonable stride. It seemed like about two hours after we moved on from lunch, plus the three hours this morning, maybe we had been on the trail for a total of about five to six hours. We began to speed up again. "We have to cover a little more ground before it gets dark." At our super speed, I found I breathed too hard to sing, so I let the birds do it for me.

Matt sniffed around my roll locating his pack of his food. "You're hungry boy, aren't you?" I slowed. I checked around for a good spot to rest.

"Let's take a break. I'm hungry too." I sat on a fallen log. "At your service, Sir Matt." I gave him a snack while I munched on an apple.

Thoroughly enjoying the forest, I glanced around as if someone watched through the trees. "We have to go, Matt."

He stood with a big shake off. "I think you like your new name, Matt."

Was I imagining? A little bird watched. He chatted with Matt who seemed to answer back.

Matt loved to pass me, which set a pretty good pace for both of us. A very uneventful trek on a path that someone had made brought us into late afternoon, and then on until the twilight set in. Suddenly, Matt took off running. "Hey boy, wait up!" Running after him, I realized how lonely and probably scared I'd be if I lost Matt. He led us straight to the stream. Immediately he plunged his face into the water. "You were thirsty!"

The overgrown path we were on most likely had been made by animals to reach the water. Or maybe there's a ranch around here. When I thought through knocking on another stranger's door—well, I couldn't see that happening again.

Since I hadn't slept much since I planned to escape, I decided to camp where the stream cut through a small meadow of flat ground. Soft breezes made patterns in the flowing grasses. The last rays shot down through a few puffy clouds leaving interesting shadows that highlighted the purple lupine scattered among the grasses. "It's beautiful here. Besides our water is almost gone."

After filling the water bottles, I assessed our location. "Maybe we should stop right here." With a glance upward, I noted the sunset would soon give way to evening. The thick forest cast long dark shadows. "Let's set up camp."

I threw my stuff on the ground, under a tall pine. When the fishing pole rolled out, I assembled it. "How about a fish tonight for dinner?"

Needing to build a fire ring, I gathered stones. We had to

stop to play a little stick-throw because Matt wouldn't let me gather kindling until he got his attention. I broke up several dry fallen branches then lit the fire with my lighter.

I swallowed a chortle. 'My lighter' had been a token taken from Bud. Beside the elegant design, the slight tarnish, it had to be real silver. "Forgive me God." They wouldn't let him keep it in prison, anyway. Would they, Sir Matt?" I rolled the lighter over in my hand. The initials MSD scrolled across the back. It had to be one of the girl's IDs I had. I paused with a shudder.

"Bet peanut butter would work as bait." That took a bit of time because Matt wanted to 'help' me.

After I finally cast my line, I sat down next to a tree to rest my head. Matt went to the edge of the water and waded in. "Now don't you go getting all wet then want to cuddle with me!" He shook himself.

Drowsy, I closed my eyes. I don't know how long my little nap took, but a fish woke me, swimming away with my line.

After a battle of wits, I reeled in the silvery, slippery fish flipping in the air. The biggest battle, though, became the fight between Matt and me. It ended in my win.

I hung the fish over a branch "If we can't get another fish, we'll share. You won't go hungry."

While not watching Matt, I loaded the hook. I turned to see that he waded in, belly deep, intently searching the water, with his nose hovering above surface.

"I'm coming." I cast in my line, resting again. Like a lullaby, I listened to the gurgling steam with quiet sounds of the forest. Before my heavy lids closed, Matt splashed forward practically jumping into my lap with his very own silver fish flopping in his mouth. "Good Boy. You can keep that one." He already started chewing on his. "I didn't suppose you wanted yours fricasseed, fried or roasted? It's sashimi all the way."

The fire leaped over the pile of sticks with the smoke rising in swirls. After gutting the fish, I poked him on my skewer of a sharp stick just as the glow of coals looked right for a BBQ.

"Mmm. This smells really good." Holding my fish over fire, I watched Matt devour his fish. "Ew! My fish is a lot tastier-looking than the raw one you're eating. Watching you eat it is making me lose my appetite!" He promptly finished the entrails produced from cleaning my fish. "That's disgusting!"

Matt obviously didn't think so as he engulfed it like a carpet sweeper.

Sitting Indian style, I finished eating my fish, sort of like a Popsicle on the end of my knife. Surprisingly, Matt lay quietly with his paws crossed, his snout resting on top and allowed me to eat most of my fish. Then he laid his head on my knee, rolling his eyes, trying to make me feel guilty, staring at me with those big brown eyes. I cut off the head. When I gave it to Matt, he consumed it with great dog panache.

We drank the rest of the milk, split an apple and tried to ignore the howl of a wolf or coyote. The wailing animal sounded a safe distance away offering an eerie solo. With my gun and Matt, I felt pretty safe.

The warmth of the fire and Matt cuddled up next to me, brought a little song to mind, but we didn't want a visit from the wolf. So I just hummed while we lay back and relaxed. Matt hummed his own little whine. When my head bobbed as I nodded off, I snapped up with a slight chill. Up then in a drowsy state, I spread the blanket, folded it in half and crawled under the top half. Matt assumed we'd both fit. Settling, I drew his back to me and we curled together. I woke myself up snoring. Then later he woke me with his snoring. Being so tired, though, I slept solidly through the rest of the night.

With daylight savings time, the sun peeked out about 6 a.m. waking us. I felt really grungy after our run-a-thon the day before. When I brushed my teeth, I squeezed out a finger full of the Colgate for Matt. While I tried to finger brush his teeth, I chuckled. "You just want to eat the toothpaste! So go ahead have dirty teeth! See if I care!"

I took one of the towels with my nub of soap to wash up in an icy cold stream. "Matt, this isn't playtime." He didn't understand plain English. Not much escaped the soap and water. To rinse, I plunged under the frosty water, with a slight whelp and scurried back out.

The dishtowel didn't exactly get me dry but I dressed quickly, catching the last warmth of the fire. It took a little time to pull all the burrs out of my socks.

My feet would warm up as soon as I started walking again.

Matt splashed out of the stream and padded up next to me. "Don't you dare . . . Ah!"

He shook himself giving me his own special shower.

Matt caught himself another fish. So I fixed myself a gourmet energy bar spread thick with peanut butter. The sun began to warm the air helping me to dry for the second time!

With several hands full of dirt and a bottle full of water, I extinguished the fire. "Are you kidding?" Matt turned around kicked the fire with his back paws, just to make sure. "You are just the smartest boy!"

I pulled that hulk of a dog over onto the blanket so we scuffled for a while. "Oh! Stop it! My face is clean."

"Another great day for a hike, ol' Buddy." I rolled up our stuff. Looking upward, streaks of morning sunlight beamed through the trees creating a variegated carpet of sun and shadow on the forest pine needles.

As we took off, I began singing, *"Good Morning Merry Sunshine,"* a song my mom used to sing to wake me up in the morning.

"When I get back, Matt, I'll have to send a video to 'America's Funniest Home Videos.' We're really good together." *The Dynamic Doggie Duo* marched along belting out our hilarious duet.

Things couldn't have been better if I had planned this camping trip with my own dog.

"But I guess you are my own dog, huh Matt?"

Chapter 36
Surprise, Surprise

With a song in our hearts, Matt and I kept on a trail that I hoped would soon find someone or some inhabited place. The trail came to a split with a path that wound away from the river, so we stopped at an easy place to fill the water bottles. It seemed reasonable enough to expect that either right or left would take us to the road or back to the river. After taking a big drink before we left the winding stream, we headed on the lane to the unknown.

Back in the forest, I welcomed the cool shade. I picked a wild lupine and stuck the purple flower behind my ear.

Matt inspected the trail at a good gait with me keeping right up with him. He stopped. I almost walked into him. "What are you doing?" He turned his nose on super speed as he sniffed and whined. On guard, I checked around us. I didn't see anything, but that didn't mean there wasn't danger. My heart stepped up its pace until I looked down at him. He held a lizard in his mouth. He came to my side, tilted his head up offering me his catch. "That's okay, Matt. You eat it." I had to look away hoping our situation never got bad enough for me to contemplate having a lizard for lunch. I did let out a relief breath. We continued on for a while longer when my stomach rumbled announcing lunchtime.

Just then Matt took off running. When the chipmunk turned, chirping at him, Matt stopped. "Grrrr!"

Before we knew it, the little fellow disappeared through the thicket.

When I found a little open spot, I spread out the blanket.

"Want a treat, Sir Matthew?"

He sat up with a little whine.

"Silly question."

I held out some Kibble and a couple of doggie treats. "At your service, Sir Matt."

"Well, at least that looks tastier than that lizard." When I uncapped the peanut butter, Matt looked up, but not for long. He gobbled up his creature before he took up his post pointing his nose at my peanut butter sandwich. I guess you do like lizard better than kibble. So I split my last couple of bites with him. I sliced an apple in half. "There you go." I gave it a toss. With a flying leap, he snatched it out of the air.

After lunch, we started off again.

We watched a couple of squirrels chase one another up a tree. Matt gave a small chase but gave up when they disappeared into the branches.

Once my lunch had settled, we jogged forward ever cognizant that we might be followed.

Humming along I checked the sky. The afternoon started to fade. I stopped humming. No longer singing with me, Matt's bark raised hackles on my neck.

The grasses and brush crackled. *Could it be a dangerous animal stalking me?*

My eyes darted from side to side. I caught a shadow. I laughed a minute when I thought of Big Foot. It had been sighted on the coast in Oregon and northern California. *Big Foot never hurt anyone, did he? Anyway, he's not real.*

"Shh." I squatted down next to Matt behind a bush. He sat quiet but alert.

Like a periscope on top of a submarine, I thoroughly

examined our surroundings. Matt continued to bark.

Then I saw what caused the ruckus. "Stop it, Matt." I patted his head. "It's just two quarrelling squirrels. Look they're just scrapping over something."

"Aw guys, you really scared us . . ." They literally turned tail, darted away crinkling through the bushes. "See everything's okay, Matt."

A hush settled in. Eerily quiet, nothing stirred. I started off again at an easy jog.

My calm only lasted a second before Matt demonstrated a vicious growl. His lips retracted, baring his teeth. "You look so fierce!"

What is that noise?

"Stop it Matt! You're scaring me."

Glaring around, I observed why Matt still snarled, with his teeth bared.

Frozen to the ground, I calmed myself and spoke softly as I took hold of Matt's collar. "Nice bear, nice big black bear. Come, Matt." Slowly as if I couldn't quite feel my feet, I inched backward.

The bear reared up on his back legs, clawed the air and roared. So startled, I let out my own roar that sounded like a dying animal. Matt belted out another howl that made my yowl seem like a whimper.

Appearing surprised for a moment, the bear paused. The next moment the bear's ferocious growl echoed through the forest. The fierce baring of his monstrous teeth set my teeth chattering. Matt seemed undaunted as he stepped forward. I reached down and caught his collar. Matt clearly didn't recognize his inability to deal with the huge, black bear.

I couldn't remember if you were supposed to stare into a bear's eyes or not. I did remember my dad telling me to, "Make yourself big, yell, and make as much noise as possible."

Slowly, I drew the pistol. Though I knew this caliber pistol would probably ping off his thick coat. That'd just tick him off. *Could I shoot well enough aim to hit him in the eye or his nose? That would be my only chance to stop him cold.*

Not wanting the bear to be hurt, I paused. *The bear versus Matt and me—it'll be the bear.*

"Ah ha!" At that moment, I saw what the bear clawed at when we got in his way. A beehive hung from the branches in a tree. If we could get away, maybe the bear would choose the honey over us.

"We're going to scare him, Matt. Then we'll escape!" I yelled in a whisper, as if letting Matt in on my plan gave me the courage not to back down.

"Let the Wild Rumpus Roar!!!" I shot the pistol in the air. Matt's vicious bark sounded like launching a deadly attack. I joined right in with my arms spread out flapping. I leaped in the air with Matt. When I screamed my loudest wail, Matt joined me.

As I started to run off to the side, Matt stood firm. So first I had to drag the dog. He earnestly thought he could fight the bear and win.

I made the split-second decision to run away, hoping the bear would stay with the beehive attached to the tree just beyond him. Finally we sped off in the other direction. Matt scampered ahead, while I took a moment to check behind us.

After the bear assessed the situation, swiveling his massive head from side to side, glaring at us then the tree, he chose the hive.

"Come on, Matt. All hell's about to break loose."

The bear lumbered forward aiming himself right at the hive—with us bounding away in the opposite direction.

Chapter 37
Help!

Expecting a swarm of bees to follow us, I kept craning around. I probably never ran that fast even on the track team. Matt wasn't about to let me outrun him. He surged ahead. Fortunately by the time the bear had attacked his hive, we were long gone. Believe it or not, not one bee followed us. Probably more interested in protecting their hive.

Panting ,we came back to the edge of the stream.

The two of us dropped down, plunged our thirsty faces in the water, gulping like we had been in the desert and suddenly found an oasis.

I thrust my hand it the air. "Woo Hoo! We did it, Boy!"

With the sun-streaked rays out from behind a golden-rimmed cloud. I cast a thankful eye toward heaven, since we might have had a little help, "Thanks Big Guy in the sky!" I hugged Matt. "I think we're safe now."

With one water bottle empty, another half full, I smiled. *At least we won't have to ration.* I filled our bottles.

As the afternoon wore on, fatigue set in. No wonder. We had hiked all day in terrain the led us up and down. Trying to make better time, we often ran. We had found a trail, a barely-there trail, that I hoped would lead us to a place, a town, a cabin, but it hadn't—yet!

"Okay, Matt. We'll keep going that way." I pointed then continued singing *"Down by the Bay,"* while my head revolved around surveying the forest for movement.

After that confrontation with the bear, we had to be alert.

"Heel." When he did just that, I patted his head. "Wow, Bud trained you pretty well!"

I stopped a few times to watch some birds. I hung on to Matt, who wanted to chase a deer that bolted through the forest. We followed the trail away from the river. I could begin to see the road above us on a gradual plane.

Getting so used to being with Matt, I couldn't imagine how lonely I'd be without him. I couldn't let him run off. I hung on tight until the deer had disappeared.

Besides, I have no idea what the bear thought when he bypassed us for the honey. Maybe Matt kept the dangerous animals away. "You looked so downright formidable maybe that's why we haven't been attacked!" I stooped for a little cuddling.

After a little run, I needed to rest. The sun transitioned through several shades of peach before the sky darkened. "Let's camp."

Matt's 'help' as we scoured the area for kindling, made me have to grab fast. He clearly would rather we played tug o' war. I dragged over a few bigger, fallen branches. I started a fire then smoothed out our blanket nearby.

"Sorry, Sir Matthew. No fish tonight." I took out the bread and peanut butter. First I made the sandwich then I spread it on an energy bar. Holding the food away from Matt, I poured out some kibble on a plate. In minutes, we were gobbling away.

Adding enough new wood so that it might last through the night, I stoked the fire. The moon shining through trees, created a beautiful, criss-cross pattern of the branches. After a few songs to serenade the moon, I gathered some leaves for a mattress. I had gotten used to wrapping myself around the curve of Matt's back. We tucked ourselves in for the night under the blanket. We watched the stars twinkle until sleep stole them away.

A lovely thought settled into my sleepy mind. I imagined sitting under a starry night just like this one. I shared a kiss, with who? I didn't know. *Could it have been just a dream?*

No telling what might happen tomorrow, but today bolstered my bravado to face another day no matter what happens.

I just didn't know the next problem would show up so soon.

Chapter 38
A Reunion

The next morning, Matt pawed me awake with a slobbery wash of my face. Daybreak barely offered any light. "Are you anxious to get going, Sir Matthew?" I rubbed my eyes. "It must be really early or the clouds are making it darker than usual." He whined. With a stretch and a yawn, I got up. As I started fixing our sandwich then cut an apple in half, Matt took antsy-whiney to a new level. "Okay, Okay. Here's yours."

With Matt barking, I hurried with packing our stuff. "Hold your horses, ol' boy. I gotta go." When I started to pull up my pants, I froze. "Did you hear something, Matt?"

My pants zipped, belted, backpack on as fast as I could, I listened. Something rustled the bushes.

That's when I saw the cowboy hat bobbing through the trees probably about a football field away. *Should I yell out for help? It's probably just a hunter after that deer.* My trust had withered, after trusting Bud.

I watched. I waited. A man! He came closer.

I ducked while I held on to Matt's snout. "Shh!"

Bud couldn't have found me, could he?

Through the branches, I detected movement. Until he came closer I couldn't see. Maybe it's someone who could help me. I curled, still crouched, about to holler out, when I realized it could very well be Bud who wore that cowboy hat so like the one he wore the last time I saw him.

Matt's bark became sharp. He leaped up and down.

Bud! Same clothes he always wore. He tracked us!

His cowboy hat bobbed in behind the foliage. I don't think he even tried to hide. Knowing he kept pace close behind me proved to be a tactic of peaking my anxiety and therefore making me more vulnerable.

I ducked down with my arm around Matt. With a finger to my lips, as if he knew what I meant, "Shh."

I scrutinized the forest. No Bud for now, but he is heading this way.

I will not let you intimidate me! Watch it, Bud! I am a formidable foe!

Matt stuck his nose in the air, sniffing in high gear. When his big brown eyes aimed at the rustling bushes, I knew Matt would react. Matt stood still, barked at the sounds and at the sight of the man who worked his way toward us. Matt watched Bud first then me. I took off running as fast as I could.

Matt vacillated, but he didn't follow me.

That hurt my heart, but after all, the dog belonged to Bud.

Just me against the world! I wiped my blurry eyes. *What will I do without Matt? I have to make it difficult to track me. If there were only a stream where I could drown my scent.*

Dashing here and there through the trees, away from the trail, I hurdled fallen trees. Brush caught my feet. I struggled as I crawled out of depressions lined with sticks. I twisted my ankle as I landed on a rock. I paused. As I looked back, it didn't seem as though I left a trail until I noticed the broken branches. I didn't catch sight of Bud or Matt. Ignoring my ankle, I tried to pick up my pace. Formidable accurately described the woodland's flora I fought through. I climbed small rises then sped up through a meadow. Staying off the path in the forest meant safety zones. I could hide. However, Matt could easily follow with his magic nose fixated on my scent. Hiding would be futile. He'd lead Bud to me.

Matt barked, though I had learned to tell the difference in his barks. I didn't fear him with this play-with-me-bark. It might sound vicious to some, but by now, I knew my Matt.

With my heartbeat pounding, my feet kept moving even beyond my telling them what to do. I checked behind me. Bud closed in with Matt yipping very close.

A hollow log lay across my path.

At the speed of light, ideas glinted through my brain. *If I crawl in that log, would I have an advantage? Should I stop right here? Should I shoot the gun into the air? Would that scare him? Or would he have a gun of his own and shoot back? I pictured the deer heads that decorated his wall. He's probably better with a gun than I am. If I aim right at him and he died, would I be able to live with myself? If I continue, there's no hiding from Bud. Matt will lead him right to me.*

Silence. No birds chirping. No Matt growling or barking. No bushes rustling. No sticks crunching underfoot. Utter soundlessness as though I were in a room with padded walls.

When a soft breeze conjured up a whisper, my body shivered in spasms. *A decision had to be made, fight or flight.*

A slight swish swept overhead. In the periphery of my vision, something moved.

I ducked when I caught a shadow that appeared above me.

Too late, out of nowhere, Bud swung from a limb. He swooped down. His arms clamped around my shoulders. Before I could break his grip, we hit the ground. Bud piled on top of me as though a boulder had dropped on my back. The fall knocked the air out of my lungs like he punctured my balloon. I gasped. I couldn't think. He pressed me to the ground as he sat hard on the middle of my back. No matter what I tried, I could not roll him off. I couldn't move my arms with his knees smashing my shoulder and upper arms. I tried to buck him off. Instantly his hands gripped my throat. When He squeezed, I thought my trachea would collapse.

I gasped for air. Am I gasping for my last breath? *Dear God . . .*

Chapter 39
Hang Tough

Help me, Sweet Jesus! Help me! Silent screams caught in my throat. It felt like my face would explode.

My eyes connected with Matt. If it had to be the last loving face I saw, it would be a comfort, rather than stare at the madman clutching my throat.

Please God, forgive me my sins.

With only seconds before I passed out or he strangled me to death, I tried a futile scream.

All the while Matt's deep growling with vicious barks gave me hope. Excited or mad? I didn't wait long to find out. Matt attacked. He lunged at Bud's neck. When he clamped his massive jaws around Bud's throat, Bud responded with a guttural scream. "Ahhh!"

When Bud's grip around my neck loosened, he pulled back and pointed. "Get Mutt! Get!" Mutt's grip choked Bud's weak command.

My chance! I bucked Bud up enough to get my arms loose. I yanked my gun from its holster.

Mutt sat back. Without Mutt's death choke, Bud wrestled me. With a guttural bellow, he yanked the gun from my hand.

"Get! Now!" The dog whimpered but didn't move.

I rolled away. Mutt raised his head for a moment. As though he had to decide, Mutt took turns looking at Bud then me. *Feeling this faint, how quickly I could move?*

I stretched up to my feet. I took my fighting stance and danced away, light on my feet, but also light headed. The dizziness gradually dissipated.

Bud leaped at me, grunting like an ape.

I couldn't move. Without being close enough to Bud, all my self-defense skills were useless. So I stood still. He faced me. The gun aimed directly at my chest.

Matt barked then bared his teeth. He did not like this fight between two masters. He sensed the danger in our struggle. His growl rolled in his throat, in an attack stance.

Dear God let Matt choose Bud as his prey, not me.

As Matt approached Bud's battle zone, Matt's bark ramped up to ferocious.

Bud drew one step too close to me. A big mistake—up flew my foot in a roundhouse kick that knocked the gun out of Bud's hand. It flew off to the side. The next kick pounded him in the gut. As he bent, my uppercut splayed him on the ground.

Bud stretched toward the gun. With just his finger touching the barrel, I kicked it away. I took my eyes off him following the gun's path. Like a snake, he hooked my ankle.

Down I went, both of us scrambling for the gun.

Up on all fours like a crab, I neared the gun. Bud sidled after me. I kicked Bud's face. It didn't seem to phase him. Blood dripped from his nose. Still, he kept coming.

Just as Bud threw his arm out to grab my arm, Matt flew into the action zone. He chomped down hard on Bud's wrist.

Approaching the gun, I snatched it up. I pointed right at Bud's face. "Stand up!"

I panted until I caught my breath.

Bud gasped a few times.

Matt stepped over next to me and braced as he faced Bud,

with his nasty, snarling growl.

Bud stood slowly. He brushed himself off with a swagger—like he had won the fight.

"Now, Natty. I know you don't want to hurt me." He held his hand out. "Why don't you just hand me my gun?"

"Why would I do that?"

"What do you think you are going to do? Walk me to a police station?" He rubbed his hand on his head.

Bud had a point.

He reached back, like to tuck in his shirt. In a second, he whipped out a gun from the backside of his pants. I faced his pistol!

Just as I decided whether to shoot him, Matt jumped up clamping his teeth around Bud's wrist. The gun blasted. I felt the bullet whiz by my ear.

"Throw your gun down." I took a step back, posed with my feet apart. I aimed at his chest. I held the gun with both hands. I sucked in a huge breath, totally in control. "Hands up! Now!"

Dropping the gun next to his feet, he smirked as he put his arms in the air.

"Kick the gun away."

With that stupid grin, he thought we were playing some sort of game. His boot slid forward.

"Step back or I *will* shoot."

"No! Just hand me the gun, now!" He picked up his foot and took a prolonged step. "You might hurt yourself."

"Last warning." I cocked the gun. "One more move and it may be your last.

He teetered then froze.

Bud had a point. I had four choices. Kill him. Let him go. Tie him up. Or, I could wound him. What could I do that would incapacitate him for the longest time?

My hesitation caused him to believe I didn't mean what I

said.

Taunting me, he grinned and took another step.

The gunshot exploded in my ears. I screamed.

Matt howled.

Bud let out a pitiful screech with a stream of profanities before he collapsed on the ground.

Did I kill him?

Chapter 40

Taking care of Business

Bud laid quivering, whining, and grabbing his leg.

Calm as sipping tea, I smiled back at my fallen opponent. "I win."

"You shot me in the leg."

"Did you really think I wouldn't shoot?"

"Good thing you missed."

"Aw, my, my. It's your good leg. From here it looks like my aim was pretty darned good. Would you rather I killed you?"

"Help me?"

"Those who don't obey, suffer consequences. It's a lesson I learned from you." I fastened one of my rag ropes into a noose.

Too busy noticing the blood oozing from his leg, right through his pants, running down to his boot, he didn't notice what I had done. He squeezed, pressing his pant leg to stop the bleeding. I hung the rope down like I intended to cinch it around his neck. When he looked up, he saw I had tied the rope into a noose. "What the hell are you doing?"

The expression of fear on his white face made me smirk.

"Please."

"What a pitiful face!"

I twirled the noose over my head like a lasso. "Did you think I would choke you, or better yet, hang you with my rope?"

"Come on, Natty."

"So . . ." I scowled at him. "You think you deserve mercy?"

After I picked up my gun where I'd laid it on a rock, I pointed at his head.

"Please, be kind." His eyes squinted shut while he waited for the bullet.

"Well, okay. As you were kind and helped me when I came to you with my injuries, I will help you. I dropped the noose on his chest. "Your tourniquet." I waited until he tied it around and cinched it tight.

"I see you already know how to stop the bleeding."

I picked up all my things where the fracas had spread them.

He pressed on his leg.

Matt just stood there, staring into Bud's face exercising his mini growl.

"Put your wrists together." He held them out in front of himself.

"Not in front." I tied a slipknot in my new rope. "Now do the same only behind your back. Keep them together then reach out to the side. Next to your hip."

As he did that, I did a one-handed lasso around his hands and pulled tight. Here you go. I threw him another length of rag rope. "Tie the lasso rope end to the other one I just gave you."

"What is all this for?"

"Make a knot . . ."

"My hands are tied."

"Feel around. You can do it. Your life depends on it."

I watched his hands. Sure enough he tied a fair knot. "Pull it tight."

"Tie another one."

I crossed my arms with the gun still firm in my hands.

"Pull it tighter."

"What are you doing?"

"You'll see."

I walked over to a small tree with my end of the rope.

With several square knots to the slender trunk, I tied it taut.

"Now, Bud. I will say my farewell." With a little wave, I turned to walk away.

"You won't leave me here to die?"

"You're not going to die. You should be able to figure out how to free yourself. The tourniquet around your leg will stop you from bleeding to death. Use your shirt as a bandage. After that the road is probably about a hundred feet, right up there." I pointed. "The hill is just a bit of a lump."

"Please . . ."

"It's very unbecoming to beg."

With a show of dominance, I stuck my gun in the holster, I continued walking for a few steps. "I'll give you a hint. The knot binding your wrists is a slipknot. Crawl a little then loosen the tension. You will have your hands free. I picked up a stick that reminded me of a cane. I threw it at him. "There. This should help. It's in exchange for the gifts you gave me." I patted my jacket and the holster.

After I collected his gun and emptied the bullets into my pocket, I carefully wiped my fingerprints off the gun. "Here." I threw the empty pistol near him. You can better explain how you got shot. Though I don't really think you'll go to the police. Besides, I don't think you'll want them to find me."

Moving a few more steps ahead, I heard a dragging noise. I turned around. "Uh! Uh! Uh! Don't move until you can't see me any more." I pointed the gun at him. "Maybe you'll make it home before the police get there. Or maybe you won't."

"Please. Don't take Mutt!"

I craned my neck. "I won't. It's his choice."

"Come here Mutt, my boy." Bud held out his hand.

"His name is Matt, Sir Matthew." I touched his head. "Let's go, Matt." I took a treat out of my pocket.

"That's a good boy." *The Dynamic Doggie Duo* marched ahead as I sang, "Onward Christian Soldiers." Matt's warbling yowl was the coup de grace! "You know Matt, we're a pretty good team."

"Mutt! You come here . . . Come, Mutt. Damn you! Come to me. Here, boy."

Matt looked back at him then forged ahead of me.

As my steps took me closer to the road, I heard Bud scream, "I'll find you!"

I didn't answer. Maybe he could find me but I never told him anything about me. He had no information about where I to school or where my parents were. Natty is short for something else, though I never told him what. Other than my name, Wilson, hardly an uncommon name, I told him nothing specific. I would be hard to trace in a large state like California—especially after I took his cash. I grinned.

"I'll get you no matter how long it takes!"

His words did stick in my mind, so I hollered out, "No you won't!"

But how long would his threat haunt me?

Chapter 41
Safety is a Small Place

As I escaped my adversary, I kept thinking about movies I'd seen where the foe is vanquished yet, when least expected, he pops out of nowhere. If that were to happen, dear Lord, please give me a little warning.

"Listen Matt. I hear cars. Let's go." We aimed ourselves toward the civilized world ahead.

Still, in the back of my mind, I worried. *Could Bud possible die before he got to the road? If I do find a police station I don't want to wait around until they check my story out then go to apprehend Bud. Would I need to if I don't want any other girl to go through my experience? How far would I have to walk before I got to a town, a police or sheriff station? Most of my food is gone. So is Matt's. I still have the $28. It's not enough for a room or many meals. I had to find an ATM soon.*

The last few feet as I crawled up the rise to the highway proved tougher for me than Matt. It hadn't rained for a couple of days. So he scampered up like an ant on a sand hill. The loose dirt he rustled up landed in my face. I wiped my eyes and waited for Matt's dust to settle.

When he reached the top, he peered over the edge whining. *"Hurry up!"*

Waiting helped my progress. Stopping at the top, still on my belly, chin on my hands, I closed my eyes. "Thank you, dear Lord. May I do something kind for someone who needs my help. Maybe there's someone or place where you will direct me to share the money I stole. I owe you my life." Relief spread over me like a warm shower in winter, putting the major part of my ordeal over.

When I finally dragged myself up to the road's edge, I stood. Thoughts ran through my head about Bud. *Would he be able to make it to the road before he bled to death? Well, the rise Bud had to climb would be way shorter and less steep than this one.*

Giving myself the once over, it appeared as though I'd been clawing through a haystack for a needle. I brushed myself off. Tapping my head, I felt the rest of the forest, which attached itself to my hair. I shook my hair, picked out some debris before I combed out the snarls. After checking my shadow for hairs sticking out, I clipped the barrette back in.

"Come here, Matty my boy." Without much emphasis on the last syllable, I called, "Matty." I tapped my thigh. He trotted right over. "I'm cleaning you up too." I brushed him down with my hand. "I really like the name Matty. It rhymes with Natty." I took his face scratching behind his ears and kissed him on the nose. "Natty and Matty, The Dynamic Duo! But you're still Sir Matthew for special occasions."

For the first time in a quite a few hours I breathed normally.

After I took a couple of swigs of water, I shared some with Matty. "Okay, whatd'ya think? If I hitch a ride, can we trust that nobody like Bud will stop for us?"

No cars came for a few minutes. The sun rose high and warm. *I hoped we'd get a ride before I got all grungy with sweat dripping everywhere.*

I already looked that way without moisture coagulating all

that dirt. A couple of cars zoomed by. A slow car appeared as Though it would stop. I smiled and waved at the occupants, a sweet gray haired lady next to a balding man driving an older model Volkswagen bug. The old man smiled and waved, a cute smile without teeth, but they drove right on by.

"Geez, I think I could have trusted them."

Then a pickup stopped.

Walking near to the door, I stared in at the man behind the wheel.

Okay, so he's workman. Dirty like me. He's all whisker-faced, all grungy. I don't like the lascivious grin on his face. It unnerved me as he scanned me up and down with his bloodshot eyes.

"Put the dog in the back and hop in."

Matty growled. That settled it. "No thanks. My dog stays with me."

I jogged on ahead with Matty as I checked behind us until the pickup veered back into the road. He laid rubber as he rattled off.

After I figured no one would stop, I felt a drizzle of sweat roll down between my shoulder blades. Next I heard a radio blasting announcing a couple of young girls in a yellow jeep—a convertible called, 'Thing'. They pulled over. With its radio thundering, the girls sat inside, one with blonde curls and the other's black ponytail swishing, they bobbed about in the front seat. Their bouncing seemed more like doing a sit-dance. One of them turned the music down. "You guys can sit in the backseat."

"Okay, Matty, we got a ride." I jumped in and patted the seat next to me. When Matty leaped in, I gave him a quick tummy rub so he'd know these girls were okay.

"What a beauty he is." Blondie reached over the seat to pat Matty on his big brown and black head. "How far are you going?"

I held Matty's collar.

"Well, we live in Grant's Pass, but we're meeting some friends in Merlin at the Riffle Cafe."

"That'll be great. I'm starving. Natty's my name. This is Matty." I hugged my boy, incredibly thankful for him at my side, us in this car, and Bud incapacitated!

The girls returned the radio to its party volume. As it blasted, I knew how Matty would appreciate the music, how he would perform. He didn't let us down. With his snout raised up in, "Roo, roo, ahhh, roo, roo!" Matt joined in.

When I chimed in, we almost blew the doors off the car with the radio blaring, accompanying all of us singing. Blondie hollered, "He's hilarious!"

We all bounced, laughed and sang at the top of our lungs until we reached the cafe. I paused before I followed the girls in. I worried about Matty. *If I left him at the door, would he stay? Would he attack someone?*

"Heel." He padded along at my side. "Good boy."

"Stay." A bit surprised when I asked him to stay, he just sat outside the door with a small whimper. I took a couple of small steps as I approached the woman at the cash register.

She handed me a menu. I pointing to Matty, "He is my service dog." I walked him right in before she could say no. After all he is my helper. I'm not sure I would still be alive if God hadn't given him to me.

As I advanced, the girls sat at a large booth. They had joined their friends, a couple of very handsome young men. They signaled me over. "Wanna join us?"

"No that's okay. Thanks for the ride."

"Don and I are going back to Grant's Pass. If you still want a ride." Miss Blondie twirled a strand of hair while grinning at Don.

"Sure, thanks." After I looked around, I seated myself in

the back corner booth covered in aqua vinyl. The color offered a party atmosphere as I watched the girls laughing with their guys.

Back here in the corner, people wouldn't be walking by exciting Matty. I studied the menu for the cheapest item with the most protein, just in case there's no ATM. *Ah! Breakfast served all day.*

When the waitress stopped by she flipped her long brown braid over her shoulder, she took a pad and pencil from her little black apron. "What'll you have?"

Before I ordered, I looked up at the waitress, "Do you have an ATM machine here?"

"No I'm sorry. The nearest is a few miles down the road at the Umpqua Bank."

Okay. Slim pickin's. No hamburger and fries, not with my budget. Save your money. My thrifty voice reminded me.

"Would you happen to know where the nearest Sheriff or police station is?"

"My dad's a policeman so yes, I do. It's called the Department of Public Safety, a mile or so before you reach the bank."

"Thanks. Any chance for breakfast at this hour?"

The waitress nodded, "All day."

"Okay. I think I'll have a side of scrambled eggs with an English muffin as well as lots of butter. Do you have honey or peanut butter?"

"Sure do. Comin' right up."

"Oh," I pointed my finger in the air, "catsup and coffee too, please." *Catsup must have some calories. Maybe the next time I'm hungry, I'll have lots of money.* I poured most of the cream in my coffee along with a couple of teaspoons of sugar. When I eat out for breakfast, I order scrambled eggs. The cook usually mixes them in a pitcher. Thus when he pours out the mixture, it's hard to tell how much is one egg, so they always over do it.

First came a tray of hamburgers, fries and malts. My food came after the kid's food. The smell of theirs wafted over tantalizing my senses as I smeared peanut butter and honey on my muffin. *Later!* Matty's treats I spread with my peanut butter for his special lunch.

Apparently the girls were making a date out of their outing. Outside after lunch, Blondie and her guy hopped into a Chevy and sped away. Ponytail led the way to her Thing, while I beckoned Matty to join her and Don.

"Thanks." She pulled the front seat forward. We climbed into the back. Don slid in the front seat. "The waitress said the police or the Department of Public Safety is just a couple of miles up the road. Could you let me off there?"

Don checked me out in the rear view mirror. He took the opportunity to brush a black wave back in place as he spoke. "Yeah, I know just where it is."

"You should! You're there often enough." Ponytail slugged Don in his tattooed shoulder, laughing. "Just kidding." She paused as her brow wrinkled and she squinted at me. I didn't have time to get nervous about her joke and start worrying about Don being a juvenile delinquent or worse—another Bud.

"Say, this Thing is way cool!"

"Yeah! My grandpa fixed it up for me. He drove it in high school, 1974, I think!"

After a block or two Don pointed. "The police are right over there in that gray building. I'll pull into the parking lot." Before Ponytail had the front seat all the way forward, Matty streaked out ahead of me. I squeezed out after him.

"Thanks, guys." I waved as I approached the front door of the Department of Public Safety. Matt padded ahead of me.

Chapter 42
A Story to Tell

The only other time I had been at a police department Mom took my friends and I for the tour of the Huntington Beach PD, padded cells and all. This was the last place I really wanted to be. I just knew I wanted to make sure Bud would not repeat his behavior with anyone else. The next girl might not be so lucky. My palms began to sweat before I reached for the door.

The building reminded me of an old army base outbuilding. The painted walls of pale gray green stretched up to a popcorn ceiling. Five metal desks lined up behind an oaken counter showing the wear and tear of a 60 year-old building. The high ceilings made me feel about two feet tall.

"What can I do for you, dear?" A middle-aged, clerk with a stocky build met me at the counter. She pushed her glasses back through her thick, steel curls.

I checked her nametag. "I'd like to report a kidnapping, Louise."

"When did this occur?"

"Four months ago. Well it wasn't exactly a kidnapping— more a capturing."

"A Capturing. Why wait so long to report this?" She took off her reading glasses and laid them on the counter.

"Because I just escaped. Look, I don't want to tell this story too many times. May I speak to a detective?"

She looked me up and down as though I might be making up my story. "Where did this happen?"

"Maybe 10 or 15 miles north of Merlin."

'What's your name??

"I'm Natasha Diane Wilson."

She keyed in my name.

An officer headed down the hallway, his rubber soles quiet on the slick floor.

"Hey, Sheriff Tilden. Would you please speak to this young lady?"

"Sure." He gestured, his hand out indicating the office door. "Please come back to my office and take a seat." Matty followed us over.

As I sat down I noticed the officer's desk had nothing out of place, immaculate. A quick glance around, I saw no other desk competing for Neatnik of the year. Was this ordered desk because of his efficiency, that he solved all his cases? I hoped so.

He rounded his desk, sat, and propped his elbows on top. "So what's the problem?"

"I have too many of them, no car, no wallet, no phone, very little money and I'm hundreds of miles from home. But what I need to tell you is how this happened to me. Kidnapping isn't quite the right word. Captured, er, he captured me."

He leaned forward putting his hands together like a spider flexing on a mirror. "So what's your name?"

"Natasha Diane Wilson, just like I told her." Pointing to the clerk at her desk working on the computer, I took a couple of deep breaths.

"I'm ready when you are." He leaned back in his chair.

"About four months ago I graduated from the University of Oregon with a major in music. I thought I was just the luckiest girl alive. A friend helped me get a gig with a band. They needed a lead singer." I sniffled. *Don't fall apart.*

Sucking in a deep breath, I continued. "Planning a leisurely trip toward California, I strayed off the freeway to take small roads for the scenery. After stopping for a wonderful night at the Wolf Creek Inn . . . " I sat up straight. "Did you hear about a small fire, a few month ago, just past Wolf Creek?"

He nodded. "My two brothers are firefighters."

I crossed my legs and leaned forward. "Okay, well, I had to take a detour to avoid the fire. I think I didn't follow the signs because I ended up on a dirt road.

About to turn back, I hit something. When I ran off the road, my car tumbled off the hillside. I think I must have hit the gas pedal as I bolted over the edge, through a fence and into a field." I took a breath. "My Toyota rolled over on the passengers side." I pushed my hair back. "See there are a couple of scars. Right here on my forehead." I pointed. "Stuck in the car, I noticed a cabin in the distance. So I broke out of the car. With no other options, I headed to the cabin. Not a good choice!"

"Why is that?"

Louise walked toward the desk, interrupting my answer. "Excuse me, Sheriff." She handed him a piece of paper.

"A missing person's report." He took a moment to read it. Miss Wilson, it says here that you have been missing for approximately four months."

He looked a lot more interested in what I told him after he read it.

"That's what I tried to tell you. When I got to his cabin, Bud treated me okay. He invited me in, fed me. He cleaned my wounds." I sat forward in my chair. "That night he told me the fire headed right for the cabin, so that we needed to get to the basement. I think he fed me tea that he'd laced with something to knock me out. Once there, he locked me in."

"Can you tell us the location of this house?"

"If you know where they closed the road just south of 'The Wolf Creek Inn.' The detour I took—there can't be that many houses in that area at the end of a five-mile dirt road."

"Especially ones that have a burned out Toyota in their field." I crossed my legs.

Matty's snout lay on my top knee. "I just waited for the right time to escape. A couple days ago, when Bud left the cabin to go to a store, I knocked the pins in the hinges loose and escaped. Matty is his dog." I patted Matt's head. "Matty chose to come with me. After I escaped, we hiked into the woods. Fairly close to his cabin, we found a suspicious hole in the ground that looked like a freshly dug grave. I figured he dug the hole for me. Maybe I made it out just in time."

Running my hand through my hair, I pushed my bangs out of my face. "You might want to check the local hospitals for a Budrey Sherman Dutton." I sat back in my chair and folded my hands in my lap. "There can't be many with that name."

Sheriff Tilden took a pen out of the drawer. Could you spell Budrey?" After I spelled it, he wrote that name down on a piece of paper. "So why a hospital?"

"Well, Matty and I camped for a couple of days as we followed the stream away from my internment cabin.

Bud tracked us. When he caught up with us, we fought for the gun I stole from him. My dad taught me karate and self-defense. Still I don't think I would have bested Bud without Matty's help. Bit the guy's hand, he did." I crossed my arms over my chest and looked down into my hero's big brown eyes. "I grabbed the gun when it fell out of Bud's hand. He took several steps toward me. I warned him. When Bud came at me,

I shot him."

"How did he get to the hospital?"

"I don't know that he has gotten there yet. Maybe you should go and check. I left him with a tourniquet tied around his leg where I shot him. Then I took off leaving him not far from the road. I figured he could drag himself up. It happened only six or seven hours ago,"

Tapping my neck I felt it. I reached around to the nape of my neck and unhooked the chain. "See this locket. Bud put a mattress where he kept me in the basement. This is one of the blankets he left there." I pointed. "I found this necklace under the mattress. I surmised there had been other girls he locked up in that basement." I dropped the locket on the desk in front of the sheriff. "Oh, I have an envelope, too," I removed my credit card, ATM card and my driver's license. Here." I shoved the envelope across the slick desk.

He squinted as opened the locket.

While he examined the pictures on the licenses inside, and perused the credit cards, I fidgeted in the chair. "Hey, my parents are probably really worried. I haven't been in touch with them for over four months. Do you suppose I could call? Bud burned all my belongings when he torched my Toyota. So I don't have my phone. Or anything else I owned."

My eyes blurred.

Sheriff Tilden pushed a box of Kleenex at me. "You can use the phone in that office over there."

Chapter 43
The Road South

How did that officer know that as soon as I called home, I would cry? Dad called my tears 'waterworks' when I cried. I turned them on as soon as Dad answered the phone.

"Hello."

I dabbed my eyes with the Kleenex before I spoke. "Daddy. I'm okay."

"Uh . . .Natty?" Silence. "Pumpkin?" Silence. "Mother, pick up the phone. It's Natty."

I heard my mother shriek through the phone. "Is it really my Natty?"

"Yes, Mommy." Then we were all sniffling.

"We were so worried . . ." Mom blew her nose.

"What happened? Where are you?"

"Not now, Daddy? Can you come get me, please?"

"Soon as we hang up we'll be on the road." My dad sniffed.

I told them where they'd find the Department of Public Safety. "But I will call back as soon as I get some money, and find a motel. That way I can be more precise with my location." I could hardly gather up my words. "I love you, Mom and Dad."

"Love you too. We'll be waiting. Call my cell that way we won't have to wait to be on our way."

Nothing like a life-altering experience and a separation to help you realize the extent of your love. I had decided not to tell them over the phone about my experience, until we were together.

Wiping my eyes, I returned to Sheriff Tilden's desk.

"Thank you, sir." I set the Kleenex box on his desk. "My parents were so worried." I sniffled then closed my eyes. "I'm really tired."

"I'm going to have Louise take you to the hospital. You need to be checked to make sure you're okay.

"Absolutely not!" Pushing back, I stood up. Matt stepped aside while I did four or five jumping jacks then dropped and gave him a couple of push-ups. "See?"

"Well."

"No 'well'. I am not going." I handed him my ID. "I am old enough to decide."

"Okay. I think what you should do is come back in the morning then we will get a complete statement. There is a motel down the road a ways, less than a mile. Just past pass the Umpqua Bank.

"I can do that. I have to admit I'm going to really appreciate a shower and a real bed with clean sheets."

"You obviously have no wheels. With no purse, I assumed you might need help. I can drive you there and take care of the room."

"Thanks, but that's not necessary. I can go to the ATM at the Umpqua Bank. I think I'd like to walk."

"Meanwhile we'll see what we can find out. I need to do a little research on our perp. I think I know where that cabin is, but I'll have to get a warrant. And maybe we'll have to get your jailer to a hospital."

"Come on Matty." He stood with me and shook himself off. "What time tomorrow?"

"How about 10. That'll give me some time to get a warrant."

"Okay, See you then."

On our walk, we passed local businesses. A smile crossed my face. Stores, sidewalks and people made me so glad to be back in civilization. I felt safe. I whistled as we ambled along. Matty didn't miss a beat. I'd have to describe his accompaniment to my whistle as a wavering whimper. "Okay Matty, a new song for whistling. When I get a new phone I am definitely going to put you on YouTube."

A library across the street peaked my interest. They'd have computers. So I climbed the stairs. The computers were lined up across a sidewall. Nodding and pointing at Matty, I let the librarian know my dog had service dog status. I sat down to think for a minute before I found my way into my bank accounts. I switched my new wealth from Germany to Switzerland, where I set up a new account. I deposited a small amount from there to my Huntington Beach accounts. If Bud checked, the money would be gone from that German bank. He would have no way to trace it to my hometown.

After that task, we left the library to find the bank and the motel. Down the stairs and out on the sidewalk, we moved at a good clip. "Look Matty! The bank is right up there." Matty whined as he looked up at me. It's almost like he could understand me. "Everything's going to be all right, now!"

The thought of money in my pocket set my mind thinking of what I would buy first: a phone, clean underwear, a brush, a new outfit, plus a toothbrush! *I can even be extravagant! I am rich!* I skipped along feeling giddy like a little kid. I'd have to decide whether I should tell the sheriff about hacking Bud's computer and acquiring my newfound wealth. *No sir! I'm not giving it back! Bud could get a swank attorney and weasel out of a prison cell. Besides, it's ample pay for four months of my life. Is there adequate restitution for being detained 24-7 for months in a gloomy basement and experiencing constant dread.*

Since we didn't happen to pass any stores that would have what I needed, I'd have to look for my items later.

I stepped up to the ATM. Since I didn't know when my parents would get here, I figured I'd need some extra money to pay for my room, buy food and shop! A car slowed. It pulled up ahead. Briefly glancing, I punched in the buttons on the machine. Three hundred dollars slid out the slot in twenties. I gathered up the bills.

While I stood there counting them, I watched Matty doing his business in a patch of weeds way across the parking lot. Just about to call him back, a shadow rose above my head.

With the putrid smell of sweaty, body odor, an elbow clamped around my neck, I struggled against a strong body as he clenched his other arm around my chest pinning my upper arms. His hold choked the air from my lungs as I gagged. I tried to scratch his face or gouge my fingers between his arm and my neck. I couldn't—I couldn't even scream. Were there two men?

Matty erupted in vicious barking, racing toward me but still a distance away.

A heavy blow bit into the back of my skull. My surroundings blurred.

I blacked out.

Book Two

Going, Going, Gone

Chapter 44
A Rude Awakening

When I opened my eyes, I stared directly into the glaring sunlight. Then, blocking the light, a huge, black and brown dog hovered over me, licking my face. I screamed. I put my hands up to block his massive pink tongue. His fangs dangerously close to my face, I pushed his wet brown nose away. He scooted his snout under my hand. I stroked down his back. He pawed at my chest. His tail practically wagged his whole rear end. The dog barked, pawing me again. I sat up. "Get away from me, you mutt!"

My throat felt raw. My head ached with a pounding fury. A survey of my surroundings, a weedy empty lot, brought me no nearer to understand what happened. *Where am I? What happened to me? What am I doing here?*

"Dog. What are you doing? Scat! Go away!"

He whined.

Apparently, he's tame.

As he sat, his tail wagged like crazy rooting up dust from the open weedy lot.

"All right. So you're a friendly Rottweiler?" He slinked over to me. When he sat down next to me, with his brown paw outstretched, I shook it. "Do I know you?" He nuzzled against me with his brown snout. "Okay, nice doggie. Maybe you can help me."

I cuddled next to him, drawing comfort from his furry

body, though not enough comfort that I could ignore my headache. Reaching my fingers around, I patted my cranium until I found the source of pain in a raw sore at the back of my head. When I stared at my palm, I faced a handful of bloody, matted hair, dirt and weeds. My neck and jaw didn't feel so good either. Under my chin not only ached but my skin hurt to the touch.

Taking a quick check around where I sat, I found a few items: a comb, nail file, rusty nail, barrette, plus three dollars and thirty-five cents. A little weak at the knees, I rose from the ground. I checked my pockets. My pants were fairly loose since they were ripped. Easily I extracted a lump bulged in my left pocket. I pulled it out. *Bullet? A bullet? Why did I have a bullet? Am I thief, a druggie, worse?* My face crinkled as I stared at it for a moment. I shook my head. Returning those items to my pockets, I noticed my ripped blouse had exposed fancy red underwear. Nothing seemed familiar, not even my underwear. *Were these few things the sum total of my belongings? No identifying purse, wallet or phone.* Whoever robbed me must've torn my pockets. I reached in my small change pocket. *Ooo eee! A 10 dollar bill, two ones and a dime, how did they miss my great wealth?*

Checking the grass and weeds, my line of sight traced the road. There were tire tracks like someone dumped me and laid rubber as they sped away. I stood for a moment. I must've been attacked, choked and hit over the head, loaded into a vehicle. Could I be a police person? Since I possessed an ability to assess my surroundings, that might be why I have a bullet in my pocket. Why could I not recall any other details of my situation?

As a matter of fact, I didn't know much of anything about myself. The dog pawed my leg while he whined. "Where did you come from? You seem to know me. Why don't I know you?"

Across the waving grass, a tractor barreled my way.

"Hey you! Get that mangy mongrel off my property! You're trespassing!"

"Would you help me, please?"

"I have had enough of you druggies causing mischief! Now get! Or I'm calling the police."

My mind spun in many directions as the tractor headed right for us. *Should I let him call the police? He actually is aimed at us! What did we do?*

The dog barked and snarled.

Kicking up a storm of dust, the tractor kept a steady pace steering right at me. Malice disfigured his face into a mass of angry wrinkles with a nasty grimace.

Wiled the dust rose, I coughed and sneezed. I took off racing across the large weedy field toward the road. The mutt ran right along side of me, barking his head off. My head ached with each pounding step.

Chapter 45
What? Where? Why?

Gasping, I stopped, bent over, holding myself up on my thighs, I struggled to catch my breath. Questions battered my brain as I straightened up. I wondered. *Am I running from something beyond the angry farmer? Should I ask someone for help?* After a slow spin, taking a 360-degree view, nothing around me seemed even vaguely familiar? *I had to be headed somewhere? Am I wanted by the police? If I am then I don't want to call them. Am I not noble enough to own up if I committed a crime? What kind of person am I?*

Something in the back of my mind whispered a place. Huntington Beach, California? I know where that is. *But why? What's there? Is that where I am supposed to go?*

I wandered ahead with this big black dog sticking to me like gum in my hair. "Where did you come from? Why don't you go home? Get mutt, Get! "I shooed my hand at him. He tilted his head to the side with a simple, tiny whine, as if to say, *"What have I done? Don't you like me?"* He padded away with his tail tucked in.

He sat down, facing me, dusting the road with his thick tail. Then as soon as I checked on him, he trotted right back to me. "What am I going to do with you? How can I take care of you? I don't know what I'm going to do. I don't even know where my home is." Abruptly, I stopped. The sudden reality hit like the pounding of my headache.

"I don't even know who I am. I don't have a name."

A gas station up ahead caught my attention. *Maybe I can find out something there.*

A woman came out of the rest room at the side of the station. "Here." She passed me the key dangling from a worn block of wood then slicked her hair back. "Return it to the office when you're finished."

"Sure thing."

Realizing that I did, indeed, need a restroom, I took the key. "Thanks." I entered the bathroom. *Not too clean but also not too dirty—typical gas station restroom, tiled with dirty grouting. Rust stains rimmed the sink's drain.*

"You wait here, Mutt."

He sat.

"Maybe you'll go home if I take lots of time."

After I shut the door I caught a glimpse of myself in the mirror. Doing a double take, I studied my reflection. I touched my red neck and jaw, bruises starting to form as I turned from side to side. I wiggled my nose. *At least nothing is broken. Wow do I always look this dirty, this disheveled? Am I really a bum? Homeless?* I pulled my sleeves up. No needle marks. *I guess I'm not a druggie.*

Following my use of the facilities, I scrubbed my face and tried to clean the blood off my clothes. After washing my pits, all my pits, I dunked my head under the cold water. The greenish yellow hand soap burned my wound as I gently massaged the back of my head. "Ew." As I rinsed, a flood of brownish pink, bubbly water drained down the sink. A bunch of paper towels didn't exactly work like one terry cloth towel would've. After cleaning up myself, I worked on leaving the restroom with no trace of a mess, cleaner than it had been. The rinse water drizzled down my back. A chill ran down my spine, from both the cold water and the circumstance.

Beside the headache, I didn't seem to have any symptoms of a concussion. No dizziness, no tingles and my eyes could follow my finger as I tested myself. *I'm okay.*

Following my 'chris and pits' bath I felt a bit better.

Remembering the key, I picked it up and exited the restroom. Mutt lay in the sun resting his shiny black head on his fat paws. "You still here?"

Entering the office at the service station I noticed some snack foods that made my hungry stomach growl. Walking toward the desk, I held out the key. Mutt followed.

"Hey! Give me that." He grabbed the key practically ripping my fingers off. "You homeless people! Don't think you can come back here and use the restroom for a shower! And get your grungy dog out of here!"

"Okay, sir. I'm sorry." I pushed my wet hair strands behind my shoulders and put the dog outside.

"May I buy a snack?"

"Okay, but make it quick. Having you people around deters the decent customers. As it is, I'll have to sanitize the restroom."

No wonder he took me for a bum. One look at my clothes told me why. *How long have I been wearing these same clothes? Blood, dirt stains and rips all over the pale blue, checkered pattern of my shirt. My jeans aren't in any better shape.* The knees were ripped out exposing the newly scabbed kneecaps.

After picking up a small bag of nuts, a pint of milk and a bottle of water, I returned to the desk. I chose a Snicker's bar from the counter. I laid out five dollars.

"That'll be four dollars, ten cents."

"That sure shoots my wad." I didn't think I had spoken out loud.

"None of my concern. Now go! Join that other bum who

just left. "Thank you for your kindness."

"Wha'?" A quizzical expression froze on his face as he stowed away the last of my money in the cash register.

"Would you at least tell me where I am?"

"This is the outskirts of Grant's Pass."

"Oregon?"

He nodded. With a sneer, he pointed at the door.

"See you later!" I knew that would rile him.

He started to speak.

I left before he could finish.

"Come on, Mutt, guess it's you and me."

I could swear he smiled when I gave him some nuts.

I saw a south sign on the road labeled with the number 23. "Okay Mutt. We're going south for the winter."

After I said it, I realized I didn't even know the month. *With the lovely warmth from the sunshine, its late spring or early fall.*

"Let's go Boy. California, here we come." I looked up at the puffy, white clouds drifting across the blue, blue skies. "Dear Lord. Help me find my way home." *If I have one.*

Chapter 46
On My Way Where?

"I wished I knew your name, Boy. For now your Mutt." Mutt tipped up his snout up for another treat. After I rewarded him, I rewrapped half the Snickers, put it in the half bag of nuts and stuffed it into a slightly ripped pocket. At least my stomach quit growling. "Don't know when we'll have more food. So I'm saving some." Mutt tucked his tail in when I showed him my bare hands. My eyes opened wide. "You understood, didn't you?"

We trudged on not exactly sure of our destination. Whistling as we walked along, the mutt joined along with a crazy whine I hadn't expected. "I guess I'll just call you Mutt." His ears perked up. "You seem to answer to it." I resumed my tune, whistling in the breeze. Mutt took up his whimpering song. I wiped my forearm across my face. Mutt's whine continued.

"Oh, my. You two scared me!" A voice came from behind a wild rose covered picket fence. On our left sat an adorable white cottage farmhouse set a bit off the road and bordered by a white picket fence. Vines of purple flowers wound their way up the posts of the front porch. A small white haired woman rose up gracefully from her flower-filled garden like a visiting butterfly. Her small, white Pekinese (who remarkably resembled the lady being small white and cute) coughed a tiny bark. Mutt padded forward along a winding stone path to the gate. The little white dog poked her pink nose through the fence only to meet a huge black nose.

I wished I had a camera. The two dogs lay down nose to nose while they exchanged little whimpering whines. The little one patted Mutt's big brown paw with her tiny one.

"Well, honey, since our pooches are so attracted, why don't you come on in. Let's have some lemonade? Just going to have some myself and maybe a cookie or two." She opened the gate. "Come on now, don't be shy. Pookie won't bite." Mutt wasn't a bit shy. Pookie certainly wasn't a watchdog. The two dogs raced around the yard sniffing each other.

Mutt followed Pookie up on the porch. They both lapped up a drink of water from Pookie's small bowl.

Waiting for us to follow, picture-perfect, they lay down with their paws draped over the edge of the top stair with their tongues hanging out.

Pushing my hair from my face, I wiped the sweat from my brow with my forearm.

"Go ahead, Missy." She grinned at me like a long-lost friend just arrived. She hugged my shoulder. "Sit here on the porch. "You look thirsty. I'll just be a minute." She tucked a couple of loose curls into her curly, white up-do as she opened the screen door and went in. I glanced up at the hanging, purple, Wisteria vine entwining the pillar posts as I headed for the matching white wicker chairs sitting next to a round, glass-topped wicker table. Atop a white crocheted doily, sat a pink vase of daisies with pink roses sprouting out in various stages from buds to full blossoms. The aroma made my nose twitch along with the dogs' sniffing noses.

My lips curled in a smile as Mutt sat next to me. Pookie laid her snout on Mutt's paw. I didn't know why but I wanted to store this lovely little memory of pink, a color I usually didn't like, or did I? A moment later, the little lady returned with a wooden tray filled with etched, crystal glasses and a matching pitcher. The icy lemonade, cool against the warm air, frosted the pitcher.

She sat a full plate of peanut butter cookies in front of me. They still carried the fresh-baked smell. My stomach reacted. "Mmm."

A fragment of remembrance of making cookies like this rolled through my brain. I could almost see myself pressing the fork down making a crisscross pattern in the top of the cookie. Its familiarity tugged at my memory, but nothing clearly materialized.

"Now, help yourself." She poured the two glasses. "Somehow I knew something special would happen today." Her lips curled into a quaint smile.

Following this morning's interaction with the farmer and his friend, the gas station man, I partially recouped some trust in my fellow humans. Her warm hospitality with Pookie's charm gave me a sense of family.

"My name is Mable. But most everyone calls me Auntie May."

"Auntie May suits you very well." I know she wanted to know my name. I squinted. Though, hard as I could think, I didn't know my name. A sudden recollection of the bullet in my pocket made me think I shouldn't share my plight with this special lady. I might frighten her. Or worse yet, maybe she'd tell the police. With my appearance, I could be wanted for something terrible.

When I studied the vase, it gave me a suggestion. "Rose."

"Nice to meet you, Rose."

"You too, Auntie May." Taking a cookie, I looked into her twinkling blue eyes. "Do you think Mutt could have one too?"

Mutt's upturned twitching nose seemed to understand.

"Well . . .I don't usually feed Pookie at the table. But today is special. Give your dog one. Pookie can have a half."

Mutt's height put his snout about the perfect place to snatch a cookie right off the plate, but he didn't. He sat quietly waiting with his eyes begging. I chuckled as the pooches snagged their treats from me. Mutt snapped his right out of my hand before Pookie had finished her sniff. Pookie took her cookie from me gently like she didn't want to break it.

Mutt's cookie disappeared by the time Pookie ate her half using dainty bites.

"Your yard is just like an English garden."

"My mother was a Brit. She taught me all about keeping a garden. If those gall-darned weeds didn't try to take over before I yank 'em out."

"You do have a bunch of weeds, in great variety."

"Yes. Well, I'm done for today. I'm ready for the rocker." She pointed at the wicker rocker decorated by two pink flowered pillows. She stepped over and flopped into the chair. "That's better. There's always tomorrow."

"Yes, but by then more weeds will have grown back."

"Sure could use some help."

As the thought hit me, I laid it out. "I don't suppose you'd like me to help. I am kind of down on my luck. I could use a few bucks. What if I work for you? Pay me whatever you think I'm worth?"

She reached out a gnarled hand. We shook. "It's a deal!"

As I headed out to the flowerbeds, I picked up her trowel and continued weeding. The helper dogs lined up waiting for me to stack a pile for them to nose up in the air then snort about.

By late afternoon, I made the front yard weed-free! I raked them into pile and dumped them into the trash bin. Before I noticed Auntie May's head slumped to the side with her eyes closed, I stretched up my arm, "All done Auntie May!"

Her head reared up. "Sorry I disturbed your nap. I

shouldn't have startled you almost out of your chair!"

"Oh my! What a great job! I don't see a weed! But look at you! You're all sweaty. I bet a bath would feel good!"

"That's okay. The angle of the sun tells me I need to get going before it gets dark."

"Now you come in here right this minute. No need to argue." As we stood on the pastel-colored, braided rug, I wiped my feet.

"Wipe your feet too, Pookie." She did.

"Wow! What a good little Pookie" I patted her head.

As soon as I did that, Mutt wiped his feet too.

"What a surprise." Mutt got a petting too. "You are so smart, copy cat."

Auntie May held the door. Like a parade I followed her with the dogs right into her cottage full of wonder, just out of last century. Uh oh, I didn't know the date or the century for that matter. Though I did remember something, the word 'amnesia.' I guessed that's my problem.

When I perused the room, Auntie May scurried off. The stone fireplace held pictures of a family with kids and grandkids lined up across the mantle. A couple of wing back chairs matched pink and green chintz pillows along the green couch. The furniture invited you to sit and sink into the overstuffed comfort.

"Here, now." Auntie May returned with a stack of fluffy pink towels with a washcloth on top. "Take these and go right into the bathroom. Clean yourself up."

I paused.

"Go on now. I'll get your pay."

Her vintage bathroom was spotless. "You go right ahead. Use that bubble bath."

She didn't have a regular shower in the 'green room'. With a green bathtub, a green basin, and the green toilet sat in the corner. The trimming of black tiles rimmed the green tiles in shiny black. I started the bathwater entertaining a bit of guilt with the amount of dirt I wore on my clothes and body.

One whiff backed up Auntie May's suggestion of needing a bath. So I climbed in. "Ahhh!" I sank into the mound of bubbles carefully as I didn't want to splash the pretty pink and green wallpaper that had a hint of black to match the tiles rimming the green tiles.

Pure luxury described my lounge in the mound of bubbles.

A knock came. "Yes?"

"It's Auntie May. Please let me put your clothes in the washer. There's a robe hanging in there."

"Just a minute." I dripped out of the tub then picked up my mess of clothes on top the fluffy pink bathmat. One glance at that pile of grunge, told me to take the offer. I grabbed the stuff out of my pockets. I could only say, "That'd be nice," as I handed my clothes out to her, feeling better that she wouldn't find the bullet.

I got back in and rinsed before I donned Auntie May's petite pink robe being careful not to rip the sleeves.

Chapter 47
A Reprieve

Wrapped in Auntie May's rose-colored chenille robe, I stepped out into the living room. I am sure I created an amusing picture with my huge body poked into her tiny robe.

Auntie May sat in her chair knitting with the triangle of light from the overhead lamp shining down on her halo of white hair. What luck to find an angel when I most needed one!

With her tiny wire-rimmed glasses perched on her nose, she glanced up, chuckling at my appearance. "I guess we aren't the same size!"

"I guess not." I pulled the robe together.

"Well, I got to thinking. It's pretty late to start out on foot anywhere. I kind of hoped you'd stay one or two more days. Now that the weeds are gone, the dead stuff needs to be trimmed up a little. Also I have some things in the back yard too. What do you think? Could you stay for a day or two?" She stood up to remove a rolled wad of bills from her apron. "Besides, your clothes aren't yet dry."

I tapped my nose. "I suppose I could." *Perhaps my memory might come back if I take my time. I might know better where to aim myself.*

"Then it's settled." As she sidled past me in her small steps, she handed me the money. "I hope that's enough. It's what I pay the handyman."

"Oh, I'm sure it is enough." I twisted around searching for a place to tuck the bills away.

"Let me get you some clothes to put on." She disappeared into the hallway.

I half expected she'd bring me some of her clothes. Imagining me squeezing into her diminutive size and ripping them to shreds would be great for "America's Funniest Home Videos."

On her return, however, she held up a cute tunic T with a pair of cropped pants in dark blues. "These are my daughter's. You look about her size. She hasn't been up to see me in a while. She didn't wear any of these clothes while she stayed. I'm quite sure she won't mind at all." An elfin look crossed her face creating a spray of wrinkles that made her whole face smile. "I'm sorry we don't have any of the fancy underwear like your red lacy ones." Blushing, she winked at me. "At least not since I married and wore my pink ones for my honey."

When I checked my earnings, I counted out $50, about $25 an hour. "Wow!" I grinned.

So I stayed for the next week. We laughed. We worked. I trimmed her garden, painted her back patio set. (guess what color?) We cleaned all of her closets. We baked cookies and made jam. She loaded a bag with snacks and fruit not only for me, but also some kibbles for Mutt.

When she brought me a stack of my old clothes all clean and folded, she appeared sad.

"Auntie May? What's wrong?" I put my arm around her.

"Other than I will miss you when you're gone? Look. This was a wad of paper I left in your pocket when I washed the shirt. I hope it wasn't important." She handed it to me.

"Well, now don't you think another thing of it."

I pried the paper apart carefully just in case it might be important. Most of the ink was washed away, but I could make out the number 3 and the words, "Huntington Beach."

My face registered concern, however, nothing to be done now. "We can't cry over spilt milk or washed notes, now can we? Let's just throw those old clothes away." I took them to the back door. With a flare, I thrust them in a trash barrel. On the way back, the screen door slammed. "Besides, I just made enough money to buy some new clothes."

She grinned.

So did I.

Still the note made me right about my decision to go to Huntington Beach. Maybe the number could be a clue.

Auntie May brought out a backpack, which she packed to make sure I had a few tools and matches for camping. She wanted to give me a sleeping bag though I opted for a blanket that I rolled tightly squeezing it into the backpack. I now wore a pair of her daughter's jeans with a sweatshirt. I saved my 'dress blues' in my pack.

"Are you sure you won't stay?" She tucked another wad of bills in my pocket and plunked a Giants' baseball cap on my head.

"My daughter lives in San Francisco."

I adjusted the cap on my head then pulled my ponytail through the hole at the back.

"Just in case you need this." Auntie May handed me a collar with a leather leash.

"Yes, thanks. I might."

"This is for Mutt. I made it last night. My sister has one of these for her service. You might be somewhere they won't let you take Mutt." She handed me a folded blue service dog jacket. "My daughter left this jean jacket. You need a jacket too."

"Thank you so much. I didn't think of that." After I buckled the collar on, I rolled the leash and stowed it into a zipper pouch on the backpack with the dog jacket.

"Here's a couple of essentials." She offered me a new toothbrush plus a tube of paste.

"My parents will be worried if I don't get home soon from my adventure." I hated to lie to her as much as I hated to leave. "It should only take a few days to get to Huntington Beach." That city came to mind even before we found that slip of paper, though I had no memory of being there. No other cities came to mind. If it's the only one, it must have some significance. I set a mental destination course. A sudden chill ran up my neck. "Oh . . ." I took Auntie's hand. "I would really appreciate . . . if someone asks you about me, please don't tell them where I've gone."

She did the old-fashioned zip-across-the-lips trick. "Here's a couple of maps. My address and phone number." She reached in her pocket. With three or four safety pins pinned together, she had made a string of them. "I always found a use for these when I used to camp."

After I slipped on my jacket, I tucked the maps and address in the backpack. With the backpack slung around my shoulders, I put the safety pins in my pocket.

"So you be sure to write me, Rose, or call and tell me you are okay, you promise?"

I paused. *Rose is as good a name as any.* "I will. I can't ever thank you enough for this time I spent with you. I really appreciate my seed money! I love you." When it slipped out so quickly, I knew I truly did love her. I wrapped Auntie May in my arms and hugged her tight.

Looking up, I thanked The Man Upstairs.

"Love you, too." She wiped a tear, as we separated. She picked up Pookie. With a parting pat of paws, the dogs whined as we stepped back.

She wasn't the only one who had to wipe her eyes.

"Come on, Mutt."

As I closed the gate, I looked over my shoulder. "Goodbye, Auntie May."

Mutt also peered over his shoulder and whined.

Pookie answered with a soprano whine.

Auntie May smiled and waved. "You be careful now."

As circumstances dictated, I couldn't contact her for a long while.

Chapter 48
Back On the Road

As I ambled off toward the main highway, it occurred to me that Auntie May never asked about my appearance, my ripped clothes or even the blood on them. She sensed my need. Her kind heart saw into mine. I guess she knew if I wanted to tell her, I would. She read me like a magazine.

So did Mutt. "I guess you're my dog now since I didn't find a collar on you. You're wearing Auntie May's now. Anyway, you came with me. You didn't try to stay with Pookie as much as you liked her." I felt warmness around me—the warmth of knowing someone cared about me, a sense of family and belonging with my new-found dog.

A voice inside warned me not to take money out of my pocket while anyone could see me. My situation suggested that someone already knocked me over the head. They took my belongings—if I ever had any.

It'd be helpful to know how much money I had earned. If I hitched a ride, I wouldn't want to count the money while the driver watched. Off the road, I sat down behind a tree. I glanced around until I could be sure no one watched me. I unrolled the bills and counted them. Whew! Three hundred seventy-five, I tilted my baseball cap back. My precious new found wealth wouldn't buy that much but, if I watched it, I'd survive.

I tucked two twenties in my shoe, a couple of twenties with tens in my bra, a ten and some change in my pocket then zipped the rest into my backpack.

Whistling, I carried on. Our duet floated in the breeze as we marched along the frontage road. When we came to an intersection of Highway 199, Mutt sat next to me while I stood wagging my thumb out at passersby.

A snazzy long, black Cadillac slowed, pulled over. As it stopped next to me, the chauffeur rolled the window down on the passenger side. He tipped his official black cap. "My boss would like to offer you a ride."

Since I couldn't see the boss through the dark, colored windows, I gave him a roll-it-down gesture, which he did understand. When the gentleman gave me the once over, I evaluated the man. His sophisticated appearance put me at ease. Every graying hair in place, he straightened his striped tie. With a southern drawl, he spoke. "It just looks as if you are down on your luck, pretty little lady. I'd like to help you out."

As his door opened, I took a step back.

"A little mutual help . . . " He pinched his chin. "if you know what I mean." With one eyebrow raised he gave me a broad lascivious grin.

Mutt rolled a small growl.

"Come right on in, Honey."

The way he ogled me with that smirk, I knew precisely what he meant. His expression, appearance and demeanor perfectly illustrated the word, "lecher."

"Thank you, but no." I stepped away.

"Well Mutt, we seem to think alike." I smiled when the man rolled up his window. The Cadillac disappeared onto the highway.

My thumb out again, a clean-cut young guy pulled up in Toyota Hybrid, window down and asked, "Where you headed?"

The words, "handsome and trustworthy" entered my mind.

"South to California."

"Oh, sorry. I'm just going to Cave Junction."

"I guess I could walk that far."

"Good Luck."

"Thanks. Do you know how far it is to Crescent City?"

"Maybe 50, 75 miles. Not sure. Hope you get a ride."

"Me too."

Being thirsty, I knew Mutt would also need some water. Auntie May had given me some water and a bowl. I sat down guzzled down a few gulps before I filled Mutt's bowl. After using my last bottle I'd need to find a refill soon.

Before I even stuck out my thumb, a Frito truck stopped for me.

A waft of wind blew into her window, as she rolled it down. "Hi, where you headed?" A pretty Hispanic driver pushed a strand of curly dark hair back from her round face. I noticed a nametag on her uniform, "Sophia Hernández."

She had a picture of two little girls pinned to the sunshade.

I liked the way she smiled. "I'm going to Southern California, but if you are going as far as Crescent City, that'd do."

When Mutt stepped up, she looked him over. "He friendly?"

"Whatd'ya say Mutt? Are you friendly?" Wagging and whining, Mutt sat beside me. "Yes he is." I rubbed his head behind his ear. I think that smile of his captured her trust.

"Si. Okay, you come up. Crescent City we go."

We exchanged big smiles as Mutt and I climbed into the cab. Mutt crept behind our shoulders leaning his big head between the seats. "Thanks, Sophia." By using her name she might not ask mine. She didn't. Though Rose sounded pretty good, I could call myself Girl. However, I needed to be somebody. "I'm Rose."

I settled in, putting my backpack on the floor.

Chapter 49
On My Way

Sitting high in the cab of the Frito truck, I peered around at the other cars, the mountaintops and the forests of spruce. I couldn't ever remember getting this great view of the world around me. Not surprising though, since I can't remember much of anything.

I grinned as I craned around.

Getting the driver to talk to me by asking her questions made it easier to keep her from asking me questions for which I had no answers. Pointing to the two girls photo on the sun guard flap, I asked about them.

"Mariana, she loose two teeth this morning. This is Isabel. She is quiet one." She touched the picture. "Fifteen is hard age. She studies. Gets good grades. She babysits Mariana after school until her papa is home from work."

"I hope some day that I'll have a little girl as lovely as yours."

"So where you go for me to drop you off?"

"If you drop me off at the bus depot in Crescent City. I am going south to Southern California."

"Oh? Mi hermano, my brother, he lives in L.A. Maybe he helps you. I give you his name and number."

"I don't have a phone yet, but maybe I will soon." I almost told her that I don't know anyone to call, but decided not to.

Even though I met Auntie May, who was more than

wonderful to me, I still didn't know whom I could trust.

We stopped once, a pit stop for gas and a restroom break. Sophia went inside to buy some candy. Since I had my own snacks, I let Mutt take care of business. I filled the water bottles before we climbed back into the cab. Since he ate most anything, I wasn't surprised that he ate raisins. Mutt also munched down some doggy treats.

When it became a little stuffy, I rolled down the window or maybe I did it because I also like the smell of gas. (I hate to admit that but I do) I waited for Sophia to finish her phone call. Not that I tried to listen in, she spoke Spanish. Therefore I wouldn't have understood anyway. I noticed she turned her phone my way to take a picture of me.

Sophia climbed in. "Here." She handed me one of the two fudgesicles she held. "This my favorite."

"Gee, Thanks. I'm fond of them, myself."

"It's quite warm today. I couldn't eat one while you watch."

"Mmm. Perfect for a day like today." I licked fast to catch the drips. Mutt sat so nicely waiting. As I came to the last few hunks I held the stick toward him. Mutt's first lick surprised him then it didn't take him long to finish the last of it as he licked and bit furiously. I had to snatch the stick away quickly before he splintered his tongue.

Sophia told me about her dog, a stray named Pablo. His picture showed a scraggly black and gray pooch hiding his eyes behind a lock of white fur.

A ways down the road, we fell into a quiet, comfortable silence. Mutt panted over my shoulder then circled around. He coiled into his favorite snooze position. His gentle snore made me sleepy. The rock of the cab with the noise of the engine didn't help. I scooched down in my seat, closed my eyes until I didn't just pretend to sleep.

Chapter 50
A Long Ride

Waking from my nap suddenly with the squeak of brakes and the jostle, I sat up with a stretch. "Where are we, Sophia?"

"Crescent City, mi amiga. I think we're almost to the Greyhound Bus Depot."

"Wow. I can't thank you enough, Sophia."

"My pleasure, mi amiga. Stay safe." She handed me a paper. "This is my brother's information. Maybe he help you."

I unfolded the paper. "Alejandro Menendez, 424 228 1494." I tucked the number into my jean's pocket. "When I get a phone, thanks."

Sophia drove into the parking lot. "Here." She passed me a couple of bags of Fritos.

"Thanks, my favorite."

After I gathered my belongings, I opened the door. I slid down with Mutt right after me.

"Thank you, I really appreciate the ride, Sophia." I pushed the Fritos into a zipper pocket in my backpack. "Thanks for the Fudgsicle—Fritos, too."

With a quick wave, I closed the door. Turning, I walked toward the station. Outside the door, I bent, hooked on the collar and strapped Mutt into the blue service dog jacket that Auntie May sewed for him. He licked my face the whole time while I fastened it around him and clipped on the leash.

He promptly shook himself. Maybe he'd try pawing to

shake himself free, but he pranced around like an English gentleman, head high and tail pointed.

As I stepped into the depot, it surprised me. Clean, freshly painted, the 1940s decor had been accentuated but updated. Like a kid, I felt like sliding across the slick, shiny, gray flooring.

"An older woman came toward us with her gray curls bobbing out of her magenta beret. When she reached out to pet Mutt, I quickly held him back, gave him a pat and whispered an assuring purr.

"My what a big dog. I know I'm not supposed to pet a service dog . . ."

"Oh, I think it'll be okay this one time."

She gave Mutt's fanny a scratch with a few pets down his back. He loved every minute of it plus whined for more.

"My son." She smiled as she pointed. The little lady joined a pleasant looking young man. He ran a hand through a mop of red hair. He waved at us then the two sat down.

Above the counter spread across the wall, the Greyhound logo of the racing dog made me smile. *I guess I'm a dog person.*

At the counter the young blond guy looked over at Mutt. "Has he ridden on a bus before?"

"He's very well trained."

The guy smiled, took my $200 making most of it disappear. I'd have to transfer once. But I'd arrive in L.A. at six a.m. the following morning. Even though that took almost half of my money, I smiled. It meant I wouldn't have to find a safe place to spend the night or thumb a ride.

"We'll sleep on the bus, huh, Mutt."

I felt safe except for the uneasy feeling of not knowing much of anything, especially what I would do next. I couldn't get a job without an ID. How would I get that?

There didn't appear to be any homeless people lounging around. While most people didn't appear to be very affluent, they were ordinary people with a few from almost every age bracket. Two teens, ears plugged in, messed with their devices. An older man bobbed his head back, snorted then continued to snore, which made the teens giggle. A couple of little boys got into a tussle over Hot Wheels cars when their mother pulled them apart. With a shake on both their shoulders, she took the cars. "Now sit!" A small girl saw Mutt. Hiding, she withdrew behind her mother's leg. In full uniform, a good-looking sailor sat a couple seats away from us and smiled at Mutt. I couldn't blame people for noticing mutt. He is a rather large specimen of a Rottweiler, a dog not known for its gentle nature.

"Thank you for your service." I put my fist over my heart as the symbol of appreciation to members of the armed forces.

In less than an hour, they announced boarding. I felt lucky that I didn't have to wait long for the bus. Just long enough to chow down on the snacks Auntie May packed for us. When I filled the two water bottles, I took a couple of paper towels to clean up a little.

As I sat down on the dark blue, plastic, chairs, I realized this place made me feel safe. I let out a large breath. I only sat for a few minutes, before the time came to board the bus.

I waited while the sailor helped Mrs. Magenta Beret up the stairs. At the top of the stairs, her son reached for her hand.

The sailor insisted I climb in ahead of him.

"Thank you." I blushed. When he grinned at me, I smiled back at him.

"De nada."

Pausing, I glanced around inside the bus before I moved ahead. I must have been clogging up the entry because a cowboy let me know. He tipped his scruffy cowboy hat back on his head. "Hey, you, girl with the dog. Move on in."

About half way back the aisle, I sank into a comfy, high back, leather chair. The decor in the bus surprised me being so handsome in its design. Since the bus still had empty seats, Mutt took the one next to me instead of sitting on my feet like the counter man directed.

The last man got on the bus pulling his small fedora hat down. He slid artfully into a seat about two rows in front of me, so I couldn't really make out his appearance.

I guess anyone can tell I'm a people-watcher.

Kudos to the bus designers who made the interior of the bus appear much like a nice aircraft. At least the height of the seat back created quite a bit of privacy.

The driver eyed Mutt for a moment then shut the door and prepared to roll away.

Leaving the station I took a deep breath. At least I wouldn't have to worry about anything until 6 a.m. tomorrow. Noticing the Frito truck, I waved at Sophia who hadn't yet left the bus terminal parking lot. She smiled and returned my wave.

With all the different people who boarded the bus and the change of scenery, I had hoped something would tap my memory, but no. I leaned back reading a newspaper I'd bought at the station. The front page headline read, "*Trump plans meeting with North Korea*," little scary, but at last I knew the happenings in the world, things like what day it is and the year.

Mutt fell asleep with his chin and paws in my lap, making it a bit difficult to turn the pages, so I found the crossword puzzle. After I took out my pen, I scratched in a few letters. Mutt made a nice table. I guess I hadn't forgotten everything as the words came easily. I scribbled for a minute before the pen started to work properly. There were several puzzles to keep me busy for a while.

The bus stopped at a few different depots where Mutt and I could take a stretch. The breaks gave us just enough time to make sure we had a walk and a drink of water. This time Mutt raced around. *I guess big dogs need to have some exercise.* "Huh, Mutt?"

Just before the sun disappeared behind the clouds, I changed to the L.A. bus. A few people on the first bus changed with me. Some got on, some off at different stops, but an express bus goes almost straight through. The last part of the trip the stops were few.

While eating some of our snacks, I checked our food supply. Maybe there would be enough for two more days.

After I unrolled Auntie May's blanket, we cuddled beneath it, letting our sleepy eyes rest.

The bus driver lowered the lights. With the sway of the bus, most of the passengers' heads bobbed while they snoozed.

Chapter 51
A New Day Dawns

Sadly, we left the land of spruce, pine covered mountains, forests, cloud decorated azure skies, lakes and streams, lush green farmland, all left behind with the memories of my past life in Oregon—whatever they were.

As the sun glinted tinting the deep sky with hints of gold near the horizon, I sat up. The bus rocked as it stopped, sped up, slowed again, stopped, then sped up in an open space. The L.A. traffic had a reputation. It lived up to it as we moved along. It would probably worse in a couple of hours. The sun rose probably about 6:15.

My ears were immediately assaulted with traffic, horns, sirens and screeching brakes. The driver of the pickup truck driving along beside the bus had the windows down. Even the double panes of the bus windows couldn't block the invasion the acid rock music fouling the airwaves.

Rubbing the sleep from my eyes, I took in another attack of my senses at the scene through the windows. Ribbons of cement-lined freeways filled with belching trucks and cars that moved along like turtles past garish billboards with buildings stacked like boxes that lined the way. Overpasses, fly-overs and off ramps of concrete walls covered with murals of spray-can glyphs, caught my attention.

Mutt stirred next to me. As the sun peeked in between the mass of buildings, I sat up. Mutt stretched with me. The look in his eyes, rolling around taking in the unfamiliar scene that activated his senses brought a smile to my face.

Mutt raised his head. He seemed to sense we were stopping as the bus pulled into the parking lot. He hopped down in the aisle with a quick shake. His leash restrained him while I repacked.

When I stepped down from the stairs, the fumes of the bus mingled with the body odor definitely woke me up. Some homeless people leaned against the wall smoking. Others sat slumped around on the ground with bottles clothed in paper bags. I turned away when one bearded old man retched, staining his white beard. With that smell joining the fumes of fast food from the place across the street I almost lost my intake of snacks. The whole place reeked. I had to yank Mutt away from investigating the menu of stenches that activated his olfactory nerves into high gear as he sniffed around.

Two other small stray dogs sat with a tattered man whose greasy ripped coat dwarfed him. With his grungy hands bound in rags, the man reached reach out to restrain his dogs. The yapping dogs braced. Mutt gave them the once-over, barred his teeth and growled. The two bedraggled dogs shrank back.

"Good boy, Mutt." Appreciating that I had company, I stroked his back. Mutt made me feel safe. *With no place to go, no identity, no job, will this be me some day?*

Sincerely I asked God to help me get me to Huntington Beach. With a city name like that, it had to be better than this.

Slipping on my backpack, I stepped around those who had stored luggage on the bus.

As I was about to go to the counter to ask about a bus to Huntington Beach, a man came up beside me. A clean smell of aftershave filtered the questionable aromas. He slipped his hand through the space between my jacket and my arm. He took hold of my elbow.

I stiffened.

"Excuse me, Miss Rose?"

Shock spread across my face as I jerked my arm. Turning my head, a handsome young Hispanic man smiling at me.

"Sorry." He loosed his grip on me. "I didn't mean to startle you. My sister, Sophia called me to meet your bus. She said you could use some help." He grinned forming deep dimples.

"Alejandro?"

"Yes."

I took a moment to assess the young man. When he ran his hand through his dark wavy hair, he let me see his dimples again. With manicured hands, he rolled up the cuffs of his blue Calvin Klein dress shirt. His striking light brown eyes sparkled in the morning light. Altogether he reminded me of a model in GQ magazine.

"Sophia gave you my number, right? However, since I had some business to take care of right near the depot, I thought I'd introduce myself. May I assist you in finding your way around L.A? Alejandro Menendez, at your service. My friends call me Al." He bowed.

Charming too. I paused as I glanced around grasping for a last name I could use to introduce myself. I stole the Grey from the Greyhound sign behind Al. "Rose Grey."

"A name in color." His dimples creased as his lips curled. "Could you be ready for breakfast?"

"Breakfast sounds really good."

"My car is right over there, Miss Rose Grey." He spread his arm out.

My eyes opened wide. *Surely not the black Mercedes right ahead.*

It was.

Chapter 52
There—In Style

Al opened the back door first, took my backpack shoving it onto the back seat then, simultaneously, he shut that door while he opened the front door. "Miss Rose." He gave a slight bow.

Mutt growled.

"Wouldn't it be better if my dog sat in the back?"

"Oh. I thought he belonged with the bums. Sorry." Again he opened the back door.

Mutt paused. I looked back at the homeless. *Sadly, there but for the grace of God go I.*

I patted the seat. "It's okay, Mutt." He jumped in, circled then nested his head on my backpack.

"Good boy." I slid in front across the smooth black leather seat. As I inspected the black and gray interior, I decided not to act like I'd never been in a luxury car. I might very well have been. I just didn't remember. Still the opulence of his car surprised me considering his sister drove a Frito truck. *Sophia had an accent. Why didn't Al?*

"What is your destination?"

"South of here."

"Okay. We can talk more specifically over breakfast." Nearby, Al found a parking place near a famous old restaurant called Philippe's. We walked ahead to the entrance where I put Mutt's service dog jacket on.

"Oh! Philippe's! I'm not sure, but aren't they famous for beef dip sandwiches?" *Was this something I remembered?*

"The best beef dips in town. However they also serve a great breakfast, with the cheapest coffee ever."

As Al pushed through the doors, a large sign verified Al's low coffee price, forty-five cents.

I stopped to take in the interesting ambience. Mutt sat dusting the ground with his tail. Sawdust covering the cement floor made me wonder how much Mutt would take with him when we left. Long tables and tall chairs filled the large room—most of them already full of customers. At this time in the morning, I didn't expect lengthy lines. Four to five people cued up in a number of lines along the high counter. Multiple cooks moved like a well-oiled conveyer belt serving up various meats, eggs, pancakes, French toast and biscuits. The aroma started my empty stomach growling.

A couple of people eyed Mutt. One man bent and gave him a rub around his ears. Mutt's behavior couldn't have been better on this trip. He must have had a good trainer.

We joined a line. "Order what ever you like. Breakfast is on me."

"Oh no. I have a little money. This place is pretty cheap."

"I insist."

"Well . . ." I checked the menu above on the wall. "Could I have coffee, French toast, scrambled eggs with crisp bacon? Extra butter, too, please."

"Sure, that sounds pretty good." He ordered two. The lines moved pretty fast. Soon the orders came across the counter. Steam rising with a rich scent aroused my hunger.

Al opened his wallet. He pulled out a fifty from the thick row of bills lining the dollar slot. That's when I noticed the wide gold ring holding a sizeable diamond. He checked his watch, a gleaming Rolex imbedded with diamonds.

The clientele at Phillippe's came from all walks of life. Workmen sat next to men in three-piece suits. We fit right in.

Women in jeans sat next to women in haute couture. Next to us sat three young guys, well-tanned, wearing shorts, with well-stuffed rucksacks. All three smiled at me.

My cheeks felt hot. I think I blushed.

The blond lowered his voice. "Elle est assez. Trop mauvaise qu'elle est avec ce gars."

"Oui, tres joli."

Even though they spoke French, I understood they were talking about me.

I winked at the dark haired guy. "Merci Beaucoup."

How did I know French?

"Votre chien?"

"Oui. Son nom est Mutt."

They chuckled when I reached down with a small plate holding bits of bacon, eggs, and French toast for Mutt. Ten seconds later I picked up a bare plate as clean as if I ran it though the dishwasher.

After I drowned the rest of my French toast in butter and syrup, we all went back to enjoying Philippe's good breakfast.

When Al and I finished eating, we talked for a minute or two about my destination, however I didn't let on that I had any memory problems. I didn't want to be specific with the city.

"I'm going there to see my parents. I have the directions in my backpack."

"Are they expecting you today?"

"Uh . . . Well . . . No."

"I ask because I have to drive to San Diego tomorrow. That's pretty far toward southern end of California. Where you're heading may be right on my way."

"It might be. San Diego's close."

"So if you wait until the morning, I can drop you tomorrow."

We walked to the Mercedes.

"I don't have any place to stay."

"Well, if you don't mind staying in a kids' room. I have my spare bedroom set up for my nieces to stay."

"Beautiful little girls, Sophia told me about them. I guess I could stay."

"Oui, Oui. All set then. "

I slid in.

"The Mercedes awaits to take Mademoiselle where ever she wants to go."

"Mais non! Parlez-vous Français ?

"What?"

"I thought your 'oui, oui' very masterful, so I just asked you if you spoke French."

"Just four words." He grinned and used his best French accent. "Oui, madam, mademoiselle and monsieur."

After I saw to Mutt, I buckled my seatbelt. Al whirled away on the fairly uncrowded early morning streets. Wheels squealing, he turned down this street and that, right on one and left on another. I couldn't have gotten back to Philippe's even if I wanted to. I grabbed the side door grip as he screeched around another corner. "Could you slow up?"

"Sure. My place is just in the next block."

The neighborhood where he drove was obviously in a Hispanic area with an array of bright colored signs in Spanish. When we left a few newer high-rises, the neighborhood looked like a place I wouldn't have wanted to be alone after dark.

He made a quick turn. The sunrays disappeared as the car sped into a dark, underground parking structure, squealing its tires before he skidded into a parking place near the elevator.

When we got out, he grabbed my backpack and scooped

up Mutt's leash.

Mutt resisted when Al tugged on his leash.

"It's okay, Mutt." I touched Al's shoulder. "I can take him."

"I got him."

We stepped into the elevator. As the door slid shut, Mutt stuck his head only part way in. Suddenly Al kicked Mutt in the snout, forcing him all the way out as the door closed.

Al dropped Mutt's leash.

What if the leash gets caught in the door?

Flashing through my mind, I saw Mutt strangled as the leash caught in the door. The elevator rose. If I did nothing, Mutt would hang. I gasped. Instantly I bent and threw the leash out.

My head spun a moment before I screamed. "Help!" Al pushed a button. I sprang forward and pushed all the buttons so the elevator would stop on every floor.

The elevator closed tight.

Mutt's vicious bark disappeared as the elevator climbed.

Before I could process what had happened, Al dropped my stuff and grabbed my wrist. He twisted it up between my shoulder blades. I fought back attempting to free my hand plus keep the other from his grasp. No luck.

Al zip-tied my hands behind me.

"What would Sophia say about this?"

"Sophia? She sends me girls like you all the time."

His grimace sent chills shooting through my body.

Chapter 53
Now What?

The doors opened on the second floor. No one waited there to rescue me. The same thing happened on each floor, until we reached the fifth floor.

Al shoved me ahead of him down a dimly lit hallway. Spray canned images decorated the dark gray walls. The black doors and jambs lent doom to the atmosphere. I strained against the zip ties, but at this moment I couldn't do anything to loosen them. "Help! Help me!"

Al kicked me hard in the middle of my back.

"Ahhh!" Thrust forward, I tripped. I fell on the rough office-grade frayed carpet. The rug burned my knees as I dropped to the ground.

"Ahhh!" A sharp kick to the kidney sent spasms of pain through me. Breathless, I curled on the floor.

"Don't bother to scream. I own this building." He grabbed me just above one elbow and yanked me to my feet.

Even though it felt as though he ripped my arm from its socket, I bit my tongue. No way I'd let him see me as weak. I turned swiftly and kicked him in the groin. He released me then dropped to the floor. By his tone, I assumed he swore at me in Spanish as I sped back toward the elevator. He caught my heel. Down I plummeted, my head pounding with a loud thud against the wall.

Al hoisted himself like a crab and staggered toward me.

Pain throbbed, but I lay perfectly still, faking that the fall had knocked me out. I let my head flop forward so he couldn't see if my eyes fluttered.

"Get up!" Rage filled the air.

Knowing what's coming, I braced.

He landed another kick to my stomach. "Get up!"

Wincing slightly, without responding to another jabbing pain, I fell over on my side. I caught a quick glance, apartment number 506.

He hauled me up.

Letting him react with my dead weight, I fell back down totally relaxing, I flopped around as he attempted to lift me. His annoyance caused him to answer with another string of Spanish invectives. I did understand a few of his expletives.

After unlocking the door, he threw his keys on an entry hall table. He grabbed me by my feet. While he dragged me in. my blouse rolled up. The metal doorjamb raked my back as I bumped over it. While he kicked the door shut, I thought it safe to peek around. A dingy apartment strewn with women's clothes, booze bottles, some half full, others emptied—would this be my jail? I closed my eyes turning my brain on. *How will I get out of the?*

Roughly, he twisted my ankle. My back burned as he dragged me across into the bedroom where he piled me on the bed. As I rolled over, I faced a semi-conscious, young woman. With eye make-up running down her cheeks and the remains of lipstick smears, she appeared as though she made herself up as a clown. Her outstretched arm revealed track marks from shooting up.

My brain sped up to super speed. I recognized this method of getting young women into a sex ring—get her hooked on drugs.

Not me! As Al left the room, I knew I didn't have long to extricate myself.

He went back to the entry door. A series of clicks and jangles told me that he locked up several dead bold locks and chain hooks.

Fumbling around, I reached into my back pocket where I stuffed the safety pins from Auntie May. I don't exactly know how I knew, but I did know how to free myself, like I'd watched a YouTube or something. I dragged the string of safety pins out of my pocket.

No! I dropped them!

Listening to Al walk around, his footsteps alerted me as to his whereabouts. He walked away from my direction.

When I determined his location in the bathroom, it reminded me that I had to go. Trying to ignore that thought made me hurry. I finally got hold of the pins. Trying one or two of them I got one open. A single pin released from the other pins. I aimed the pinpoint for the tiny space between the hard plastic strap and the resin roller lock of the Zip Tie. Poking around, the point caught in the space. *Yeah!*

The flushing sound from the bathroom reminded me that I only had seconds.

I pushed down hard on the pin. The pin missed the crevice.

Al's steps came louder down the hall.

Again the pin slipped into the space.

I jammed the pin downward.

The key to the bedroom door clicked in the lock.

Sweating, I yanked against the strap.

Loose! I let out the breath I was holding.

As I pulled, one hand came free. When I jerked again, the other loosened.

He concentrated on his task. Apparently he didn't see me jerk my arm. In his hand, he wielded a syringe. He poked it into a vial with something that could only be some sort of narcotic. He didn't seem to notice that the zip ties were undone. As he rolled me over, I went limp as though still unconscious.

When he grabbed my wrist, goose bumps raised all over my body.

The Zip Tie fell away.

"Bitch!"

I knew if the needle shot into my arm . . . I cringed.

If I'd ever been more scared in my life, I chose to forget about it.

Since the needle neared my arm, I had to believe God would help me. "Oh, Lord." I said a quick prayer.

Chapter 54
How Can I Find an Advantage?

Al's raging face grimaced, clenched teeth exposed. His wrath couldn't be any greater than mine. I clenched my own teeth ready for the onslaught.

I thrust my arm upward forcing his hand away. He still clutched the syringe of narcotic. That action caused the needle to drip.

Good! Drip all the way out. I shot up my other fist and planted it, an upper cut to his jaw.

Losing his balance, he stumbled backward. Shaking his head, he recouped.

With adrenaline pumping away the pain from Al's previous kicks, I leaped from the bed.

Not letting loose of his syringe, he stepped away. He repositioned his weapon in his fist, more like a dagger with his thumb on the plunger. We circled each other waiting for the right moment to strike.

His fury seethed, turning his face crimson as he took a step. Like a gorilla, Al vaulted up. He charged at me with the knife-like weapon aimed directly at my chest.

His forward momentum knocked me back to the bed. My head bumped the unconscious woman. Her eyes opened wide. She groaned. For a moment we stared, eye to eye at each other almost as though our connection became a collective scream for help. She collapsed.

Al pounced on my stomach, straddling me. He attempted to pin both my arms under his knees. Fortunately, he left one arm unimpeded. The syringe above me now aimed at my neck.

I gnashed my teeth. My free arm shot up to block his weapon. When my arm didn't collide with needle, I bucked my body up like a rodeo horse. That threw my attacker up but not off. When he came back down, he landed with all his weight on my chest.

The air collapsed from my lungs. I gasped as I clenched my fingers around his wrist. I thought of myself as a strong woman against a small man. Though when Al's muscles flexed, he forced the syringe inching toward my neck. I felt my weakening muscles twitching. He forced my hand down close to my body, the needle just inches from my neck.

When the needle touched my neck, I screamed. I reacted by thrusting up again with my body. This time I also threw all my strength into hoisting my arm. Thus his arm raised as I slowly drove the syringe steadily upward. Every muscle in my arm tensed and quivered.

A shadow rose above me. I took my eyes off the syringe for just one moment. A loud scream ripped through the air.

A heavy weight crashed down on me.

Chapter 55
What are Friends For?

Angels come in all forms. The shadow was the stoned woman laying lifeless on top of me. Still breathing? I placed my fingers on her neck. I felt her pulse. "Good girl! Thanks!" I grunted, groaning as I shoved her aside. Her dead weight inched off of me.

I didn't see Al as I looked around.

The woman sat up leaning on me as I came upright. Her voice sounded like her last breath, "Help me."

Al lay heaped on the floor. His forehead oozed blood. Next to him sat a large glass ashtray with one of its sharp angles smudged with blood.

Standing, I almost stepped on the syringe, I caught myself. I picked it up, knelt next to Al. He twitched when I jabbed it into his shoulder.

When I stood, my swirling headache pounded.

As I turned to the young woman, I smoothed a thatch of her bleached hair away from her face. I pointed down. "Well, I guess you knew how to take care of him!"

On the bed, I put my arm around to keep her from falling over. "What's your name?"

Like in slow motion she answered. "Uh . . .Sil vi a."

"All right Sylvia, I am going to get us out of here. You stay still while I get something to tie him up. Even though I shot him with whatever narcotic the syringe held, we can't know if he'll stay contained for very long."

After I emptied his pockets, I undid his pants, yanked his shoes off then the pants. The drapes darkened the room. I drew them back enough to open the window. I gazed out first then threw his pants to the alley below. They landed on top of a big blue refuse bin.

I took stock of his pocket contents: a bill-stuffed wallet, a small address book, a silver money clip with more bills folded into it, and a black Montblanc pen. After I pocketed the wallet and money clip, I spotted my backpack slung on a chair by the door. I stashed Al's pen in the outside zipper pocket and stowed his little black book in my shirt pocket.

From the clothing strewn around the room, I glanced around for something to tie Al. A pair of pantyhose draped over a chair in the corner caught my eye. I rolled Al over onto his stomach. I slipped his Rolex off onto my forearm. His diamond ring I stuffed in my pocket. After I encapsulated his fingers and hands with the body of the hose, I tied them behind his back with one hose leg. With the other leg of the hose, I drew his legs up securing them to his wrists. "Okay." I patted him on the rear. "There you go."

The Rolex slipped down to my wrist. I stowed it in my other pocket.

"Might as well put him at a disadvantage." I wasn't sure Silvia heard me, but I spoke to her anyway. "Now we have to get you sober and get you dressed."

With her arm around my neck, and me hugging around her waist, I dragged her naked body into the bathroom. She fought me a little as I tried to get her into the tub. "It's all right, Silvia. I'm taking care of you, Honey. You need a bath." I spoke to her in the soothing voice of a mother to her child. Silvia relaxed. I don't suppose the showerhead turned on cold felt like a mother's touch but it did arouse her some. After I warmed the water, I gave her a quick scrub, washed her face, her hair then rinsed again with cold water. This time she did react.

"Ew! Stop it!"

"Whew!" I had the image of me dropping her slippery body. Her head striking the tub had the potential of killing her.

I threw a couple of already-used towels on her. "Can you dry yourself?" I took a second look at her all cleaned up. Obviously she was much younger than I previously thought.

"Uh . . ." Without more words, she massaged the towel around as though she wiped a countertop, but that did help. Just try to maneuver a slick, wet body in a bathtub.

After the multi stimuli of her bath, she began to awake from her stupor. She helped me to sit her up. One-handed I propped more towels behind her. I fluff dried her hair. Slowly I eased her down letting the towels absorb the wetness on her back then I wiped down her legs and feet.

Al moaned. I peeked out of the bathroom to check on him. "Whew! Still immobile!" I smiled.

While Silvia air-dried, I scouted to find an outfit for her to wear.

The room sported several layers of clothes thrown about on the furniture and the floor. They all looked like hookers' outfits; gold lamé leggings, ultra mini skirts, sequined low cut tops with thong underwear. I found some bikini ones with a pushup bra. I selected the most conservative dark blue mini dress.

By the time I came back to Sylvia, she put her arm around my neck and made an attempt to help me get her out of the tub. I don't think I ever dressed anyone before, not even a child, at least not anyone of this size. I found a pair of black leggings, which took a bit of 'finesse' in yanking them over her knees, hips, and ample derrière, while I grunted and groaned.

She flopped a bit, though she did try to help me. The task, quite awkward, took time I didn't know if we had.

"Hold your hands up, Silvia." She teetered for a minute as she waved her arms overhead. The silky mini dress with a dipping décolletage slipped easily over her head—backwards. She almost looked decent without her cleavage hanging out in the front of the dress.

The shoes? I cast about the apartment finding nothing but stiletto heels, not ideal for walking a semi comatose girl heavier than myself. I spied Al's shoes that I hadn't thrown out the window yet. I had to practically unlace them to shove them on her feet. Surprisingly though, they seemed to fit. I re-laced, tied the strings tight and double knotted them much as I would a child's.

All the while, I felt the minutes tick by. I checked Al for signs of emerging from his induced slumber.

If this situation hadn't been so serious, I'm sure all the fumbling about would have made a comedic scene in a movie or on YouTube.

On my final check of the room, I noticed the keys on the table.

Chapter 56
A Way Out

While I wiped away all the fingerprints I might have left, Silvia began to come around. After I cleaned the syringe, I clamped Al's hand around it and squeezed.

On the one side of me, Al moaned. On the other, Sylvia mumbled, "What's happening?"

I picked up the keys from the entry hall table.

"Well, Sylvia. It's time for us to get going. Okay? Swing your arm around my neck."

Leaning on me for stability she did quite well in the flat shoes, just a little wobbly as we made our way to the elevator. She tripped as we entered the elevator. Unfortunately, catching Silvia made me hit the button for the second floor. When I punched the garage level, I knew we would stop at the second floor but we were lucky that no one waited on any other floor.

When the elevator door slid open on the second floor, I peeked out. About half way down the hall, a guy with multiple tattoos snaking down his chubby arms and up his neck ran toward us. Arms raised, waving over his head, he hollered, "Hey, espera!" With his girth bouncing, he ran or rather waddled, "Espera!" His speed, or lack of it, gave me a chance to hit the close door button. Just as the man reached out to put his hand between the doors, the snapped shut and the elevator chugged down to the garage. With no one else about, I stepped out smiling as the elevator closed behind me.

"When the Lord closes one door he opens another one."

Al's shiny black Mercedes, parked amongst heavily used, dusty or rusty cars and trucks, stuck out as if someone got lost in the city. It's a wonder in this neighborhood that it hadn't been stolen. One dirty car window wore a saying, "Lavar me!" Even I knew that must be, "Wash me!" Amazingly it seems you can always find something to smile about if you just observe.

On the passenger side of Al's car, I grabbed the door handle. I helped Sylvia in. When I settled inside, I checked the side of the steering wheel for the ignition. I don't know how, but I did know how to operate the car. I pressed the ignition button thus lighting the various dashboard features. I removed the button over the starter, stuck in the key, pressed the brake and the car started. Backing out, I pressed the button to activate the interior locks.

"Who thinks up these things anyway, little tricks you have to know before you start up?"

Sylvia, wide-eyed, gasped as I backed out.

"What. . . ?"

The same guy that I shut out on the second floor stepped out of the elevator. Only this time his gun, a Ruger GP100, aimed directly at me.

He rushed the car.

My heart pounded.

Quick reflexes kicked in. As I stepped on the gas, the car whirled back barely missing one of the cement pillars. Unfortunately, it took a minute for me to think through getting the car into drive. I heard the man slap the fender and reach for the handle of our door. That's when I gunned it, up the ramp. A check in the rear view mirror found 'Tattoos' wind milling forward then landing splat, all sprawled out on the cement floor. Checking the mirror, I noticed the man behind still on the ground and a black dog racing toward us.

"Could it be my Mutt?" Stepping on the brakes, I screeched to a stop.

The man looked up from his sprawl, grabbed the side of a parked car and pulled himself up.

"Come on Mutt!" I raced around to get the back door open, Mutt leapt into the back seat. Slamming that door, I landed back behind the steering wheel, just as the man reached out. He seized the door handle on Silvia's side. The door swung open.

When Silvia and I screamed, Mutt barked in high gear. Silvia pulled against the door. When I suddenly hit the gas, the momentum plus Silvia's pulling sucked the door closed. More alert than I thought she could be, she locked the door. With his legs dangling, the man hung on until I swerved out the driveway.

"Splat!" Down he went as we cheered.

Once onto the street, I had no idea where I should go. The GPS would help me but this was not the kind of neighborhood where I wanted to stop to figure out how to use it, much less ask someone on the streets for directions. I checked the street signs and the building address so I could direct authorities back to find dear Al.

I took Sylvia's arm. "Are you doing okay?"

She rubbed her chin. "Not sure." She shook her head as though trying to clear her thoughts.

"What's your whole name?"

"Uh, Silvia Ackerman."

"Look Sylvia, I'm going to have to let you off. Where do you live?"

"I don't. That building is where Al keeps his girls."

"Do you want to get away?"

"We have rules. You have to take me back. It's my family. I

have to check in with the Bottom."

"What?"

"Al's right-hand lady. She keeps watch over us."

"I am going to drive until we get to a safe spot where we can stop. Then we'll decide what to do."

"Al's going to be very mad. He'll . . ."

"He'll what?"

Tears rolled down Sylvia's face. "He's a gorilla pimp. He'll beat me."

"Not if we get you far enough away. Besides, I am going to leave you with enough money to help you figure this out."

When I saw the Harbor Freeway sign, I followed the arrow to the ramp going south. "How did Al get you into this mess?"

"Hitching a ride to my cousin's house after my mother kicked me out. A lady in a Frito truck picked me up."

I hit my palm against my forehead. "That's how he does it! How old are you anyway?"

"Does it matter?"

"Yes it does!"

"I'm sixteen next week. He told me he had a job for me." Tears ran down her cheeks. "Look." She pointed. "I'm branded." She held out her arm where a weird tat scarred her alabaster skin. "Everyone knows who I belong to."

"You don't belong to anyone except you. I'm pretty sure we can get him off the streets. Do you know where we are?"

"Los Angeles . . . somewhere?"

The way she posed it as a question, I knew she hadn't told me everything. "Where did you live, I mean before?"

"Minneapolis."

"Is that where he kidnapped you?"

She nodded.

I think he has more than one Frito lady or she just goes everywhere, even all the way to Minneapolis.

"That's illegal to transport a minor . . . If you got back to Minneapolis, is there anyone who would help you?"

"You know I'm going to need a fix real soon. I want to square up but I can't while I'm hooked."

Chapter 57
Where, When, How?

Constantly checking the rear view mirror, I scrutinized the road behind. No one followed us.

Without saying much to Silvia, I took a moment to think. *How do I know all these things about zip ties, fighting, operating a fancy car? What about the fact that I knew what kind of gun that man carried, plus I am pretty good at finding clues. The bullet in my pocket makes me wonder. I have to be either a police person, or a veteran. If I'm a service person, am I AWOL? Or the very worst— am I a criminal? Until I know, I am going to have to be very wary of trusting people, even the police.*

Putting my hand down on the seat, I felt a regular smart phone. I had been reluctant to use the car phone in case it could be traced.

Picking up the phone I dialed 911. "Hello! I can't talk very long. I'm in danger."

"Where are you?"

I gave the woman a very brief explanation with the location of Al's apartment. "You might have to beat door down." I screamed. "Have to go." I hung up, rolled the window down and tossed the phone out bouncing on the pavement. About half an hour past the airport, I saw the golf course at the side of the freeway. A quick turn and we drove down the off-ramp.

Before I drove into the parking lot, I stopped for gas then

let the calm rolling green of the golf course soothe my tensions. I checked over my shoulder. Clearly, by now I could see that no one followed us.

Sylvia leaned against the passenger window. I gave a small shoulder shake. She jumped awake staring at me as though she had forgotten what happened. "Where are we?"

"Sorry. I didn't mean to scare you."

"Where are we?"

"I'm not quite sure. Carson, California, I think." I looked up at the sign and pointed. "Victoria Golf course."

Confusion covered her startled youthful face. "Why?"

"Remember Al?"

"Yeah?"

"We knocked him out. Then we escaped."

"Oh." She scratched her head. "Yeah, it's kinda vague though." She sat up straight. "You gotta take me back."

"Well I'm going to take you somewhere, but not back to good old Al. He needs to be in custody." I took hold of her shoulders. Facing me, I bore my eyes straight into hers. "Do you believe I care about you and want to help you?"

"Uh . . . Yeah." She looked away.

I pinched her chin and turned her face toward me. That got her attention. "Do you want the rest of your life to be on the streets?"

Tears filled her eyes. "No."

"Then do I take you to the police or to rehab."

She wiped her eyes on the hem of her dress. "Rehab."

"Okay." I used the car phone to talk to Siri. "Where is the nearest drug rehab center in Carson, California?" As she gave me the answer, I programed the GPS. "The next thing I need is your mother's phone number."

"No! I can't."

"The worst that can happen is she hangs up."

"She hates me."

"Well if she does, we'll go from there, but there is going to be a positive outcome one way or another."

"Okay . . . 267 3070."

"Area code?"

"161."

I dialed. After three rings a man answered. "Hello."

I gave the phone to Silvia. "Hello Daddy."

"Anna! Pick up the phone. It's Sylvia!"

Silvia breathed heavily into the phone until I thought her mom would think the call 'a heavy breather's' call. "Mama?"

"Silvia?" A long pause, "Is that you sweetheart? Where are you?"

That wasn't what I expected.

"Can I come home?"

"That depends. Where are you? We'll come get you?"

"I'm in California . . . I promise. I'll be better . . ."

"You will have to try because I can't stand to see you waste yourself."

Silvia dropped the phone as she began to sob. "Hello. This is Silvia's friend. Look, we just escaped from her kidnapper. The slime ball addicted her to drugs. I am going to take her to a rehab center. I can pay for it. Are you able to pick her up when she completes her stay?"

"We'll be there as soon as we can." Her father's voice elevated with excitement.

"Okay." I checked my phone. "Gotta a pencil?"

"Just a minute."

Speaking slowly, I explained. "I am taking her to Discovery Center, 350 West Wardlow Road in Long Beach, California. She can call you from there."

Sylvia reached for the phone. "I love you, Mama."

"I love you too, Honey. See you soon."

"You too, Daddy."

"Me too, so much! We'll be on our way soon."

Sylvia sniffed. "I can't believe it! I thought I'd never be able to go home again . . . You know . . . I prayed for this."

"Yeah, so did I."

"You know what else? I don't even know your name."

I don't either' on my lips. "Rose . . . Rose Grey."

I wanted to let the police know about Al. He could probably extricate himself when we left him tied up, but I didn't want him to die before someone found him. I didn't really want to talk to any police until I knew my identity. But I did want to give the police Al's little black book. I didn't want to spend any time at the rehab center. They would probably call the police.

Glancing over at Sylvia, eyes rimmed red, she looked even younger than her almost 16 years.

Reaching across the seat, I pulled her over with my arm around and hugged her. "You're going to be okay. You're going to graduate from high school. You're going to do something good with the life God gave you. Pay it forward. You promise?"

She sniffed. "I promise."

"I'm going to check on you, you know."

After I checked the GPS, we took off.

The situation for Sylvia couldn't have turned out better.

Now If only I could find my mother and father —if I have any.

Chapter 58
On My Way Where?

When we got to the rehab center to drop Sylvia off, I wanted to spend as little time at that place as possible. I gave Mrs. Johnson, the supervisor, all the pertinent information about Al's sleazy operation, and how we both came to be his victims. She made a copy for me to give to the police. I also split Al's money. I kept five hundred and gave the rest to Silvia to pay for rehab. "Save some of it for yourself." I told her as I counted it into her hand, but stopped at a thousand.

Noticing a box of manila folders on a desk behind the counter, I asked to borrow one. "A few sheets of paper, too, please."

While the supervisor got information from Sylvia, I quickly jotted a note to the police, placed it with the papers plus the little black book and stuffed them into the manila folder.

I left as soon as I could with a quick kiss on Sylvia's cheek, a prolonged hug, while I reminded her of her promise. "Don't forget. Give your mom a call and update her!"

Sylvia's nose turned red when she waved goodbye. Skeptical that this place could be another sham, I watched through the lobby window to make sure Sylvia made the call. By her body language I could tell. First she cried then she beamed with excitement. When she waved at me through the window, I knew that she talked to her parents. *When would I ever trust anyone again?*

While I drove south on the 405 Freeway, I contemplated what I should do with the Mercedes. Could I sell it without the proper papers? What if I broke a traffic law, if I got stopped? I have no ID. I could be arrested for stealing. I didn't think Al would call the police, but he could just to spite me.

Siri told me where I could find the nearest police station. With a quick stop, I added a small note to give the enclosed money to Silvia. I had no idea if the rehab place would take her money. I stuck the note and a couple of hundreds in the envelope. I caught a policewoman just as she pulled open the door. When I handed the envelope to her, I asked her to give it to the chief.

Gone in a flash, I decided to pull over where it was safe to access my belongings and my net worth. After I exited the freeway, I parked in a mall parking lot close to the door of Bloomingdales. With number of people swarming around the parking lot, I felt safe. The Rolex watch! I'd almost forgotten about it! And the ring!

I let Mutt out to stretch. I laughed when he walked over to Al's rear tire lifted a leg and watered it down. No use making an assessment of my belongings until I could sell my valuables. Not trusting my backpack left in this snazzy car, I grabbed it then ran inside Bloomingdales. With Auntie May's service dog jacket I had no problem taking him in with me.

Checking in a mirror to see if I appeared classy enough, like I should have this kind of watch. I didn't. Instead of heading straight for the jewelry counter, I took a trip to the women's clothing department. I selected a silk tunic blouse, slacks and a pair of loafers then stashed my old clothes in my backpack. That outfit just needed a wash. In the handbag section, I admired my new outfit in a mirror. I walked past and bought a black handbag to store my newly acquired valuables.

In jewelry, at the men's watch counter, I stood on one foot

then the other while the clerk finished with a woman already festooned with expensive gold rings, bracelets and a necklace to die for. When she decided not to buy, I approached the counter. A beautifully dressed clerk, with a pretty nice diamond wedding ring as well, stepped toward me. Her blonde hair piled together at the nape of her neck completed her classy appearance.

"Would you be able to tell me what this watch is worth?"

She took the watch to examine it.

"Grandpa gave it to me before he passed away. He said it would help me pay for college. I don't know where to go if I wanted to sell it. I sure don't want to have some shyster gyp me."

"I can't tell you for sure, right now. I would have to give it to the jeweler." She gave it back.

My face fell. If he'd stolen it, I couldn't hang around and wait to find that out. I began to second-guess my decision to do this.

"However, I could make a guess and give you ballpark figure. I just got a new Rolex catalog."

Ah! I smiled. *The highs, the lows of my predicament!* "A ball park figure would be good. Thanks."

She reached under the counter and withdrew a shiny catalog. As she flipped through pages I wondered. *With so many electronic gadgets to tell time, could people like Al just wear these beauties to impress people?*

"Here. These watches are similar to yours." She pointed as she turned the catalog toward me.

I suppose my eyeballs popped. The cheapest price tag read $12,000 but it had a leather band. Al's had a thick gold bracelet with several diamonds. The all-gold ones made me dizzy with prices in the six figures.

"Maybe you could also find a price for something like

---

this." I pulled out the ring.

With another catalog we found similar rings priced a little higher than the watch. "But Honey, the only way you'll get anywhere close to these prices is at the jewelry district in downtown Los Angeles on 4th Street near City Hall."

I think my face melted again. I couldn't ever go back there, especially in Al's car.

"I suppose you could go to a pawn shop but . . ."

When her voice trailed off, I knew that would be my only option. "Thank you so much."

At least knowing the real price offered me some bargaining leverage.

Boy! Racketeering pays well!

Back in the car, the California map that Auntie May gave me helped me orient myself with the communities surrounding Huntington Beach.

I called my best friend. "Hey, Siri." She answered, "Go ahead, Al." I smiled. I guess Siri doesn't have voice recognition!

"Where's there a pawn shop near Huntington Beach?"

She responded with an easy map to follow. I exited the 405 on Bolsa Avenue then turned south on Goldenwest. I parked. *Bet this area was safer than the jewelry district in downtown L.A.*

"Come on, Mutt."

Entering, I worried. *What if he thinks I stole it?* His bright red hair made me stare for a second.

"Welcome. Whatever you need, I've got it." I caught him eyeing my Mercedes and then Mutt.

"What'll you give me for this watch?" I held it out.

With a jeweler's eyepiece, he thoroughly examined it. "I could go as high as $5,000."

"I'm sure you could. However, I know what my husband

paid for it. I need some money, but no." I turned away, toward the door.

"Just a minute." He tilted his head and touched his cheek with an index finger. "How about I double that to $10,000?"

"How about $15,000 in cash?"

"I don't have that much in cash."

"So?"

"Take $12,000?"

"Well . . . Okay. My husband will buy another. He doesn't really like this one, anyway."

I'll wait on the ring. I might need it later.

As he counted the cash in my hands, I felt quite sure that I never held this much cash before.

With a leap and a click of my heels I made my way back to my other asset. I patted the hood as I rounded to the driver's side. Mutt responded with a happy bark.

My next step: purchase a nondescript car of my own. As much as it pained me, I had to get rid of this flashy one.

Someone could have seen me with my roll of cash. So sitting in a car next to a pawnshop to refresh my planning didn't seem like a good idea. I kept checking the rear view mirror making sure I hadn't been followed. Then I drove to a Ralph's Market parking lot. However, to buy a car, I'd need a plausible address and phone. I made one up for my watch transaction.

I called my friend. "Siri, what is the zip code for Pasadena, California?" That city prompted a memory of the Rose Parade. Perhaps my memory is coming back. Then I did the same for area codes, streets and addresses. *Boy! I'm going to miss the phone when I leave this car. Maybe I can get a burner phone.*

When Siri gave me the address for a car dealership in Santa Ana, my other friend, GPS, gave me a better map and her voice that tells me where to go or if I make a wrong turn.

Funny how talking with these devices made me feel a little less alone. Mutt cuddled up. No, I am not alone.

Chapter 59
Spend, Spend, Spend!

With Siri and the GPS, I found my way to Long Beach and a used-car dealership.

"Well hi there, young lady. What can I do you for?" With a giant smile and matching belly, the salesman rushed toward me. "Let me show you this little beauty I just got in." He held out his arm toward a late model burgundy Jaguar. "Only has 24,000 miles. This little sport suits you better than that Mercedes sedan." He ran his hand across his thinning gray hair as the wisps caught the breeze.

"Well thanks, that's almost like my mother's Jag. But I am looking for a little cheap model I can keep at the beach house when my parents go back home to Pasadena. Daddy's afraid my Beamer will be stolen parked on the street."

"Well, we got plenty to choose from. Take a look." He spread his arms wide.

"Silver is my favorite color. I just love that little Ford Focus SE."

"Come right on over." He patted the fender.

Making a walk around inspecting, I also peeked inside.

"Just got a little over 40,000 miles on her."

"May I check inside?" I reached for the hood.

He looked a bit wide-eyed as I inspected the engine.

"Appears to be okay." I wanted him to believe I knew something about the jumble of parts that comprise an engine.

"The tag says $10,899, but I can give you a really good deal."

"May I sit inside? Mutt too?"

"Sure, little lady. Come on over." He opened the driver's side. "Wanna take her for a spin around the block?"

"Yes, I would." I slid in under the steering wheel, set my backpack in the back and adjusted the seat. Mutt sat in back.

Dropping in like a block of granite, the salesman flopped into the passenger's side.

I scrutinized the interior. Clean, non-descript, I think I knew how to operate everything. We took off with me driving extra carefully.

"We have a 60-day guarantee."

After my short drive, I felt comfortable in it. It seemed to drive pretty well, though not as smoothly as Al's car.

"I think this will do. I have cash, so let's see what you can do for me."

His grin seemed more genuine than before.

"Cash, huh?" He pinched his chin. "Well then, come on into my office." Mutt and I followed him into a small generic office with a metal desk, neat and tidier than I would have thought. He withdrew a contract from one of the file cabinets. We sat opposite each other with him behind the desk. He slipped on his reading glasses with them perched on the end of his nose. He looked at me over the top of the black rims. "Let's make the price even, $10,600."

"Well, Daddy told me, 'Don't you pay over ten thousand.'"

He rubbed his chin. "Let me see, now. Let me ask my boss." He walked to a back office. When he returned a few minutes later, he gave a "thumbs up."

"It's a go!" While he started filling out the paper work, I took out the wallet.

As I counted out the money, I answered all his questions

about my address, phone, etc. without even checking my notes. I made up a Social Security number with a silent prayer that I wouldn't get caught for my little ruse.

"Would you like the year's warranty?"

"Not necessary. I think the 60 days will work. But can you supply me with insurance?"

"Of course."

More paperwork. He showed me the final price after insurance and taxes.

I traded the money for the paperwork and the keys. "Good there are two keys. Daddy keeps the other. Thank you. Dad said he'll come back with Mom to pick up his Mercedes, tonight or tomorrow. I'm going to leave it in my Auntie May's driveway for them. She just lives up the street. Then I'll walk back to pick up my beautiful silver bomb."

"Nice doing business with a savvy little lady like you."

We shook on it.

After I transferred all my stuff to my new Ford, I drove the Mercedes around a block then pulled over in front of the dumpiest looking house I could find.

After I checked the GPS one final time I found out how to get to the beach, to Highway 101. Ultimately I would aim for Huntington Beach, only a couple of beaches south from Long Beach.

Purposely I left the keys to the Mercedes conspicuously on the dashboard. If the Mercedes were stolen, that's all the better. It would be harder to trace me if it turned up in a different area.

"Okay, Mutt. Another detail taken care of." I skipped along. Mutt enjoyed me picking up the pace. While I made my way back to the Ford Dealership, my mind went almost blank. The last few days of my life had been filled with purpose and so many things to do.

As the beautiful sunshiny day faded to an end, I assessed my accomplishments. I had managed to save Sylvia as I made some normalcy out of my abnormal life. Even though knowing her for only a few hours, we bonded. I would miss her and miss being needed or important to someone.

Also, I had just lost the only two people I had left in the world, Siri and GPS, but I owned my own car.

With Huntington Beach still my goal, I realized I did not know the roads to get there. Would being there jog my memory?

As I turned on Lakewood Boulevard heading into the rich sunset, sadness for my losses crept in. When God makes something as beautiful as his sunset cast over the horizon . . . At last I smiled, though my eyes dripped.

Now What?

Chapter 60
Keep on Spending

When I found myself on Long Beach Boulevard, I stopped to ask. Apparently all I had to do was come to East Ocean Boulevard, go south. Just follow it to the Coast highway.

With money in my pocket I noticed a Walmart that called my name. (What ever that is.)

I pulled into a parking space in the shade and rolled the windows down a ways. Mutt whined, prancing around like he expected to get out. Anyway the beach fog rolled in. "No you're staying here. With no sun on the car, it is not too warm." I hugged him. "I'll be back soon."

On the way to the electronics department for a burner phone, the cutest black sundress caught my eye. When I tried it on, it fit perfectly. With a price tag of $19.98, couldn't turn that one down. On the way, I pulled out a shopping cart. Using Al's I. D. didn't seem like a good idea. Swinging my small black leather shoulder bag, after I chose a lady's wallet. *Into the cart and on to the next!*

Now I couldn't wear a snazzy dress with my scruffy tennis shoes or my new loafers. Next, in the shoe department, I picked out a pair of black sandals. Underwear? *Lingerie, here I come.*

I picked out a couple pairs of bikinis with matching bras. *Should I?* A black lacy set tugged at my wallet.

With a sales table piled with socks in my view, I visualized the two pairs I owned. *Yup!* I grabbed up three for $12.

Another sale rack, labeled, "Beachwear," reminded me of my beach destination! With several try-ons, I picked a turquois bikini, a blue-stripped beach towel, topping off with a bottle of suntan lotion. *All set for the beach.*

Tennis balls. Hmm, I don't know if Mutt likes to play ball. I picked up a sleeve. *We'll find out.*

By the time I chose the burner phone and checked out, my bill came to $265.87, the 87 cents coming from all the weird amount of cents they tack onto their prices plus California's sale's tax. I smiled. *Now that was fun!* I hurried to the car afraid of leaving Mutt for too long.

I let him out for a break. He ran wildly around two or three cars. To pack my purchases into the car, I opened the trunk. *Good, a spare tire.* I had forgotten to check. I piled the bags in. "Hey Mutt, come here, boy. Poor Mutt, I left you too long!" He came racing back and jumped into the trunk on top of my treasures, rolled around crinkling in the Walmart bags. I laughed.

At least I didn't feel like crying. I had a lot to be thankful for. "Not the least of my blessings, Mutt, is you!" He used all the Walmart bags as toys. I had to get him into the back seat to save my new things.

When I came to Ocean Boulevard, the big Westin Hotel sprang up ahead. Over the bay, the sun nestled among a few clouds close to the horizon, sprinkling diamonds on the water, while a frosting of gold and peach rimmed the clouds. A perfect place to stop for the night! *With my limited funds, Could I allow one more extravagance? A thing like being practical is not going to stop my immediate gratification.* I drove into the circular check in driveway. *I probably should count my money first, but I deserve this. Just one night couldn't hurt.* Mutt trotted into the lobby right behind me.

Before the clerk could ask, I informed him about my service dog, Mutt. Finding it only cost $150 a night, I asked for a water-view room. Apparently, I got the last one.

When asked if I wanted a bellman, I thought that a little over the edge. Anyway, I deemed my array of grungy backpack and scads of Walmart bags not too impressive in such a swanky hotel. After I took the card key, I led Mutt for a tour of the gardens. Then I found a tall brass pushcart where I stacked on my belongings. Mutt jumped on the top causing a lot tittering in a lobby full of guests as he rolled along. *What a ham!*

I headed for room #202. Sitting on the bed, Mutt moved right on in trying to nestle his big ol' body on my lap. Watching the sun sending its goodbye rays, I gave Mutt his hugs and pets. I forgot how long he must have been without food. I took the last of the kibble out of my backpack then Mutt gave it his disappearing trick.

"Okay Mutt, I'm going swimming. You'll have to wait here."

After I took my swimsuit out, I dressed then headed downstairs to the pool.

Wow, I just spent over $10,000 dollars. I knew I had quite a bit left.

Had I over spent? I avoided taking stock of my money. *What would I do when it ran out?*

Chapter 61
On to the Rest of my Life

The swim felt great but not as good as knowing when I walked through that door, I wouldn't be alone. My favorite being would be wagging his tail, excited that I came back. He didn't disappoint. I knelt down and hugged him for a long moment before we wrestled around on the carpet. With me giggling, Mutt whined for more. I recognized that whine as his brand of giggles. I had to thank God for all the good things that have happened while not dwelling on what I didn't have.

Since I took a shower in the swimming pool dressing room, I came in back to the room to dry my hair . . . *ah the luxury of a dryer. How silly!* I forgot to buy some hair products. As I clipped the barrette at the back of my head, I wished I had a prettier one, *but this worn-out one works.*

I found the tennis balls. When I took one out, Mutt sat up straight, his eyes glued on the ball. I threw it. Mutt scrambled after it racing back with it in his mouth. "Drop it. Mutt." I couldn't believe he did drop it right in front of me. Twitching around, he pointed his nose at the ball. "Well okay, one more." I tossed it. Mutt gave me a repeat performance. When he brought it back, I tucked it in my purse.

"Mutt, stop it!" I pulled my purse away from him.

"We can't play catch in the room. Let's go outside." I hooked on his leash with his Help-dog jacket. "Okay, Mutt, you're going with me."

In my new black sundress, new sandals and purse, I felt invigorated. It all put music back in my toes as I skipped down the hall heading down to the elevator. Mutt loved my rapid pace.

As we waited for the elevator, I bent, held his head in my hands for a scratching behind the ears. "Okay when we get back to the hotel, we'll take a little run around the grounds. We can play catch. Big dogs need to exercise!"

We meandered to the lobby restaurant to check the menu. *A little pricy, I'll start saving money now.* I asked the desk clerk what restaurants were walking distance.

"A nice little Greek place right up the street." He pointed.

"That'll do nicely." I touched Mutt on his head. "Hope you like Greek. I'll go shopping for dog food tomorrow."

Inside, I made excuses for Mutt so we were seated at the back, where I liked to fade into the scenery.

After perusing the menu I gave the handsome young Greek waiter my order. "I'd like Dolmadakia, Choriatiki and Kefrethes with Baklava for dessert, please." I seemed to know how to pronounce those dishes.

What a surprise! I knew all about these foods. With dinner, a fractured memory came back. *Maybe? I have been to Greece?"* Anyway enjoyed my grape leaves, salad, and meatballs in a great sauce with fabulous, sweet, honey, pastry for dessert. Mutt loved the feta cheese from my salad.

When the waiter brought Mutt a plate full of scraps, he whispered, "Shh. Don't tell anyone." Mutt faced into the corner to devour them. The waiter's grin, full of bright white perfect teeth, made me smile. However, when he asked me out for a drink when he got off at nine, I realized I probably wouldn't trust anyone giving me iced tea let alone liquor that could be laced with Rohypnol.

Would it take me a long time to trust anyone? If ever?

"My boyfriend wouldn't like it." I counted out my cash to pay my bill. The waiter got a pretty good tip but I didn't want to go overboard after I turned him down. I hoped my straight face would not be taken as a "no" in a flirty way. He might think I meant yes to a date.

Being rather full, I enjoyed walking it off before I took Mutt for his run around the courtyard. He loved it, especially when the tennis ball came out to play..

That night I slept with Mutt in my arms until I awoke with a horrible nightmare still in my head. Sitting straight up, I screamed.

Poor Mutt howled.

I shook with chills. Could this dream be part of remembering what kind of life I escaped? If so, I didn't want to remember something so terrible.

After tugging the blankets over us, I hugged Mutt. However, every time my eyes closed, I found myself in what looked like a basement, cold, dank with a large, bald man choking me. His hideous brown eyes rimmed in fiery red bore into my brain. I'm sure my eyes bulged open when I sat up hyperventilating and gasping for air.

The image seemed so real, I couldn't go back to sleep.

Chapter 62
A New Day

After my nightmarish sleep, I got up early to exercise Mutt, take a swim then wash my clothes. I decided my breakfast in the coffee shop would be my last financial expenditure.

As I packed up I took out all the money I had stashed away in my shoes, bra, backpack and my new purse and wallet. With all the money laid across the bed, I put all the fives together, all the tens together, etc. In total, I had almost $1,000. I had some time to think about what that meant while I drove to Huntington Beach. I re-stashed it in various places, back in my shoe, purse, bra and zipper pockets.

Al's wallet bothered me. Eventually his car would be found but not close to Huntington Beach, I hoped. I cleaned out his wallet of all identification then I tore it up. Mixing the pieces together, I wadded them up after I crammed the bits into several of the Walmart bags, crunching them into the wastebasket. I'd throw the wallet away later.

Hundred dollar bills would be hard to break once I left the hotel. I decided to pay my bill using two of the hundreds. I didn't get much in change with taxes and breakfast.

On Mutt's walk, he raced around in circles until I grew tired of watching him. Because his energy was still in high gear, we played ball. I rested in a lounge chair while I threw. He chased. Panting, he laid the ball at my feet.

Down in the parking basement, I packed the car. I opened

the door for Mutt to hop on the front seat. Once I was in, he promptly put his head on my lap.

Okay, what are you going to do with the rest of your life? I'm going to put one foot in front of the other, get this car in gear and drive south. That's what I did, until we came to a market. I shopped for some snacks, a bag of dog food, a couple of plastic bowls, with some bottled water. "Hungry?" In the parking lot I fed him. He lapped water from his bowl, splashing it everywhere. "You were thirsty!"

I checked my maps to memorize the beaches I would drive through before reaching Huntington Beach. When I got to Seal Beach, I smiled knowing I'd be there soon. Past a nice stretch of sandy beach, a small section of businesses, and a motel, I found Main Street. A sign near the pier announced Huntington Beach, Surf City. I cruised the three blocks of the cute little town. I hadn't given up on the idea that as soon as I arrived, my memory would be jogged by familiar surroundings.

Nothing, not one thing seemed even remotely familiar. I drove up, down and around several streets. As my whole body, slumped behind the wheel, I pulled over to the curb in front of a little Catholic church. I felt so fractured, like a female Humpty Dumpy. With my arms across the steering wheel, I sobbed.

The priest came out and knocked on my window. I rolled my window down. "I'm okay."

"Is there something I can help you with?"

"Could you say a little prayer for me? I need to find my way."

We prayed for a moment.

I smiled. "Thanks, Uh . . . .Would you tell me where the high school is?"

"Yes, but I am right here to talk to if you . . ."

"I'm fine, but I would like the directions."

I still had the same issues. *What would he do if I told him the truth?*

As it was Sunday, when we came to the school, the few kids around were playing basketball or baseball.

When the car door opened, Mutt jumped out of the car with my purse in his mouth. "Give me that!" We had a little tug-o-war. When I finally rescued my purse, we played with yellow tennis ball bouncing and rolling through the grass under the Eucalyptus trees. "Okay, enough. " I hooked on his leash. "I want to check out the campus. I think I might have gone to school here."

After I walked amongst the buildings, the strip of lockers and watching the kids on the field for a while, if I'd been here before, I didn't recognize anything.

Back in the car, I sat for a long while deciding what to do next. Mutt tried to influence me by nosing at my purse.

Since it was a weekend, I couldn't do much about finding a job. Using my new phone, I found that the Main Street library closed on Sundays. I could use the computers there and search the local paper for jobs, but not until Monday.

Okay, today is for familiarizing myself with Huntington Beach. While I rode around, I found a market and bought a local paper, some sandwich stuff, fruit, not forgetting the doggie treats. The Best Western would be a good place to stay for a couple of days. Maybe if I talked to the management, I could get a job cleaning rooms. If not, at least I'd look fresh for job-hunting the next day.

After driving around for a while, I made sandwiches and packed Mutt's treats in one of the grocery bags. I decided to spend the rest of the day on the beach.

A doggie beach lay at the northern end of the promenade path. After I spread my towel, I smoothed on suntan lotion.

Lunch came next. After, we played ball alternately with a swim.

Mutt romped, played and loved the water as much as I did. If only everyday could be like this. But it wouldn't be.

Chapter 63
Youth Hostel or Hostile

First thing that Monday morning, I realized I needed an address while I looked for a job. I dressed in my sundress with sandals, in case I could find some kind of interview.

First, I stopped at the post office, a tiny little place that looked as though it had been there for a hundred years, sporting things like brass fixtures and bars in front of the clerks' windows. Lots of well-worn oak planks lined the floors, matching the wood trim around the windows. I paid for a post office box, number 321 and located it.

Around the corner, I entered a gift store full of beach trinkets. I bought a key chain. I promptly attached my car keys and my mailbox key.

In the library, I sat for a moment and constructed a résumé in my mind. For once something felt familiar. The grand old library seemed to awaken some small memories when I looked at the checkout desk and glanced at the children's section, but nothing settled with any great clarity.

After explaining my service dog, with the name, Rose Grey, I applied for a library card. My wallet now had a form of ID however weebly for identification.

The library had a couple of rows of computers. First I fabricated a résumé, dates and places where I worked including restaurants and Motels in Oregon. I found the Huntington Beach Independent newspaper and jotted down a couple of places that rented rooms. I perused the help wanted for possible job opportunities. I collected a list of phone numbers.

Before I went outside the library to call, I borrowed a book, *"Cold Mountain,"* to keep myself busy at night.

Mutt sniffed around then sat with me under a palm tree. My list of numbers kept me busy for about an hour.

However, the only interview I got was with a temp agency. Located not far, I drove straight there. The interview was pretty short. Sure enough, a library card didn't provide enough ID.

Back at the motel, I talked to the manager about a job. I tried not to plead, but there was nothing at that time. "Come back in a couple of months when the summer traffic picks up."

All the motels seemed to have the answer that I'd heard before. "Come back in April or May." Restaurants as well, faced slack time.

What about tonight's lodging? I had written down the number of a Youth Hostel and found it not far away. At a drug store on the way I bought a towel and washcloth.

The early 1900s clapboard style, three-story, hostel stood partially obscured under a huge draping tree that I couldn't identify. The guy at the desk checked me in and warned me. "Welcome. Keep all your things together so you don't lose anything. The room is down the hall, last on the left."

"Okay." It reminded me of a dorm with narrow hallways lined in dark well-used wooden floors with lots of doors. A middle door indicated the shared bathroom. The door key was an old-fashioned key with a heavy brass knob soldered to it. I suppose a number of missing keys prompted that addition. The decor of the room probably had been furnished by a used furniture store and the drapes reminded me of bandana material. With a bathroom down the hall, it serviced the six rooms on the same floor. Mutt was welcome, so what more could I want?

After I'd filled the water bottles and fixed Mutt and my lunch, a girl from Bern, Switzerland checked in. As she made herself comfortable in the bed next to mine we had a short conversation.

She changed into a tank top and shorts. In front of the mirror, she brushed through her short blonde hair. "My hair used to be long like yours. I am glad I cut it for this trip. Too much trouble."

When I offered her a peanut-butter sandwich she thanked me in very good English. "I'm going to meet some fellow travelers at a bar by the pier. Would you care to join us? It'll be fun."

It seemed tempting but I had Mutt and I couldn't waste my money on beer. "I'd love to, but I have Mutt to take care of."

"Tata!"

After she left, I tucked my money away, stuffed my backpack under the bed and my purse under my pillow. I read for while, took Mutt out for a walk then I came back and read my book. Getting sleepy, I padded down the hall, washed my face and brushed my teeth.

The next morning, Mutt woke me early with his pawing and yelping.

"Shut that dog up!" a gravelly voice roared down the hall.

"Shhh, Mutt." I sat up soothing him with long strokes. Glad to be awake early to look for work, I got up and stretched. I made ready to shower by taking out my clean undies in my backpack. I dug under the bed. It wasn't there! Not a large space to search, I tore apart everything. It was simply gone and so was the Swiss girl. She seemed so nice. Did she take it, or did someone else when I went down the hall last night or this morning? I grabbed my pillow and threw it across the room. "Ahh," my purse was still there. Checking inside, my burner phone also rested under my wallet that still had $150.

I tried to thank God I wasn't left penniless, but the tears kept rolling down my face, anyway.

With most of my money gone, I decided I would need to sleep in my car. I rolled up the beach towel with the belongings I had left; a toothbrush, bath towel, washcloth, bikini, and a library book. Wearing my one set of undies, and my tee shirt, I grabbed my rolled up jeans and everything else.

I headed for the shower. "What? An extra bar of soap in the shower! I'm taking this!" *Forgive me, God.*

In the shower, I washed my hair and my underwear. After toweling myself, my towel did a lousy job of drying my underwear. I put it on wet.

My makeup being gone meant I had no choice but to look clean, freshly scrubbed.

On the way out, I did thank God. At least our food wasn't taken.

I told the deskman about the robbery.

"Hey, sorry about that."

"Yeah, me too."

Most people in this world I suspect are good. *Right now I just don't know any of them.*

Chapter 64
What Could Happen Next?

With my meager belongings wrapped up, I stowed them in the car. A quick check of the money I left under the seat revealed I now had the grand sum of $310. Things could be worse, I guess.

The only clothes I had left were my jeans, a shirt and a jean jacket. They might have taken the jacket too, but Mutt laid himself on top of it. "Thanks, Mutt. They didn't take your service jacket either."

The morning sun just peeked over the rooftops, too early yet to job hunt. I stowed my meager belongings in the car. And grabbed the bag of food. "Whatd'ya say Mutt. Let's go to the beach. They left us one tennis ball. Come on, I'll race ya!" The cool morning air breezing my face, billowing my hair, made me feel like flying. *I had nothing before there was Auntie May. I'm practically rich in comparison.* "And my best gift is you, Mutt."

At the beach, we rolled around wrestling on the grass before we went down on the wet sand to play catch. I know I wasn't supposed to have Mutt on this part of the beach, but I didn't admit that when a good-looking, bronzed lifeguard drove his Jeep by and asked us to leave. I just pointed out Mutt's service jacket.

We stopped at a picnic table and ate our scant breakfast. "Okay Mutt, today is going to be better." *Yeah sure!*

As we approached the good old Ford, I noticed our car listing toward the street side. *Why?* The rear left tire billowed out at the bottom, not quite flat but trying its best. I really had no choice. I had to drive it somewhere and have it fixed. Being broke and alone doesn't give you many options.

Fortunately, I had seen a gas station a couple of blocks away and I got there after I shredded the tire but before I the rim collapsed. By the time we rolled into the station, the tire relaxed on its rim. Apparently the tire was shot, so the service man put on my spare. Spending the last of the $12,000 was not quite as much fun as spending the first of the $12,000. After I filled the tank with gas, I peeled off some bills and paid my tab.

"On to the rest of the day, Mutt ol' boy." I spent the morning knocking on doors of some ritzy looking, three-story houses asking for work.

One place had lots of weeds. So I stopped to ring the bell. In only his pajama bottoms, and scratching his spiky hair, a bronzed man answered. "Yeah?"

"I noticed your front yard could use a bit of weeding. You could hire me pretty cheap to solve that problem." Mutt whined and I patted his head. "He's tame."

"Twenty bucks?"

"Yeah, sure. Do you have a spade?"

"No that's why I haven't done it."

"Okay, I can do it anyway."

Dropping down I started pulling out weeds. Without a trowel or a spade, I only topped a lot of pulls. I ruined what fingernails I had left, if any. Mutt sat with me until the sun heated things up. He moved into the shade. "Yeah, girly boy, you can't take it, huh!" I took off my jacket and pulled a few more weeds. When I saw the hose around the corner, I turned it on. Splat! I squirted Mutt. Quite surprised and wide-eyed, he got right into the game, chasing the splashing water. When we were both soaked, I held the hose over my head.

"That's it Boy, back to work."

About an hour later the yard looked a lot better. I washed up with the hose then I knocked on the door.

The man stood in his open doorway wearing only a very skimpy Speedo with a lot of muscles.

I did not look down.

"You finished babe? Would you like some ice tea?" He leaned one arm up the door jam and crossed his ankles. "Or something a little stronger?" The way he looked me up and down I knrw what he had in mind for something stronger. With his sideways smile on his handsome face, he looked like the kind of man who wasn't used to a woman telling him no.

"No, thank you, just my $20." I took a step back when he reached for my shoulder.

"Aw, come on."

Mutt growled.

"All right, I'll get it."

While he went back in, I moved Mutt back, so if he tried something, I'd be ready.

When the man returned he had a twenty folded between his first two fingers. He flipped the bill out toward me.

As I reached for it, he flipped it away. "You sure you don't want come its where it's cool?"

I stomped on his toe, grabbed the money, leaped over his short fence with Mutt on my tail. We didn't stop until we got to the car.

Twenty dollars richer and twenty dollars smarter.

Chapter 65
Where to Now?

Quickly, I became aware of the complications of being homeless, one of which would be where to stay. I am more fortunate than many homeless, I still had some money and a car. Where would I be if that changed? I couldn't risk going back to the hostel. *I can't afford for the rest of my goods to disappear.*

I tapped in 411. Information gave me a number for a sporting goods store. On my way, I tried to mentally list what goods I would need. The first notion popped in my head—a knife. Before I went in, I checked my purse. I still had my sunglasses and a lighter. Once there, I picked out a spring-assisted knife with sheath for it, backpack, flashlight, plus a can opener. Still having Mutt's bowls, I just needed a pan, paper plates and plastic silverware for me. They all fit in the small ice chest.

Back in the car, I tried to think of how I could get work doing odd jobs, house cleaning and such. Mutt kept pawing me for attention. I looked at the position of the sun. "We missed lunch. Sorry Mutt." We finished off the last of our food.

At the library, the librarian recognized me and spoke to Mutt like he was an old friend. I asked her about churches that might serve a meal and or allow overnight parking. She gave me a couple of ideas. She also let me plug in my phone to charge. At the computer, I created a one-page flyer advertising myself as a hard worker, ready to tackle garden clean up, weeding, housework, etc. and put my phone number on it and ran off copies. I handed the librarian one of my flyers. She smiled limply—not the best send off for this hard worker. "If you know anyone who needs help, Please give it to them." I walked out of the library.

"Sure thing."

Finding a nice neighborhood, I passed them out.

That afternoon we went shopping for food. I got some ice so I could keep some things cold. I wondered how long it would be before I got tired of peanut butter, cheese, celery, carrots, apples and yogurt. I wheeled the cart around. *What a deal! 99cent bread!* Mutt watched while I picked up his Kibbles and treats. I hope I wouldn't get down to bread and water.

In the restroom, I washed my face and hands. "Okay, Mutt. Let's go see where we sleep tonight."

I went to a church with huge parking lot. After I parked, I went inside to ask permission. With that all settled, Mutt and I walked to the beach to catch the sunset. With my shoes strung around my neck, I strolled along as I threw the ball. Mutt scampered ahead retrieving it.

Near the pier, I brushed the sand from my feet, rinsed and put my shoes back on. I turned on the faucet at the outdoor beach shower. "Yeah, warm water!" So at least I knew where I could clean up.

A bike path, running along the beach brought out skaters, bikers, joggers and other dog walkers. A cute older couple sauntered in front of us holding hands.

I didn't feel so alone on the path with a "Hi," or "Great evening!" Most everyone made friends with Mutt and greeted us.

That night there were other cars in the church parking lot,

safety in numbers. I fixed my towel in the windows for privacy.

However, on the third night, a man pounded on my window. Startling me wide-awake, I screamed. He stayed for a minute until Mutt clawed at the window with his savage growl followed by vicious barks. I think the man's hair stood on end while he darted away.

I got a couple of jobs with my flyer but they were hardly worthwhile. One little lady gave me five bucks for changing some light bulbs and taking out her trash. One old geezer wanted me to take a bubble bath so he could watch. I turned that one down. I weeded another yard and tried to get a couple of permanent cleaning days. That didn't happen—yet.

The church only allowed five nights so I moved around looking to find another temporary home. I found a different church that allowed a two-night stay plus they offered evening meals on Tuesdays and Fridays!

At dinner, I met some homeless people who gave me times and places where some markets put outdated food in the alley. With my money running out I'd have to figure some place to park my car. It'd be too late when I ran out of gas. I found a place behind a small, white clapboard house whose shades had been drawn ever since I'd been in Huntington Beach. The garden sprouted a variety of weeds. A few yellowed newspapers were on the porch. By weeding the yard, I felt as though I paid for parking my car in the alley behind their garage. That worked for a several nights and I had something to read with their light casting on the alley.

With a motel down at the end of the street, my idea was to sneak in early, finding a room before the maids arrived. I'd shower and wash my hair before I could be noticed. I could always wash Mutt at the outdoor shower at the beach. For a couple of weeks, that's where I stayed.

Thanksgiving came and went. Thank you Lord for those

churches that serve meals. The turkey dinner table reminding me of a dream I kept having of a family together around a table. I did get a pocket full of turkey that lasted a couple of days.

But the owners of the house returned a week later and I needed to move the car. When the maids caught me one morning in the motel, my morning showers ended.

With only four dollars and 10 cents, I am sinking further into the abyss of homelessness.

I just didn't know how it could get worse.

Chapter 66
Gone

When I returned to my car, a tow-away notice, tagged to the windshield, warned me. *Where would I park now?* Many streets had limited parking; no overnight, three hours only, etc. I found one for all-day parking. "Okay Mutt, let's just have a fun day today."

It was an unseasonably warm December day so after packing up the food, my towel, my suit, his ball and a water bottle, we headed down to the beach. I changed in the rest room then we settled on the beach. We swam, sang, rode the waves, and played ball. I read the yellowed paper while I watched Mutt chase the sea gulls. When it started to chill, I packed up. At the pier, I took a quick shower. Mutt pranced while I rinsed him.

We headed back to the car. Skipping along and singing softly (even Mutt had a softer whine for my subdued voice.) I smiled with my mind wishing every day could be like today.

On the way a man rolled out his trash. Next to the can, there sat a red wagon. I began to think trash day might be a good day for "shopping."

A small market on the corner tempted me. I paused for a moment. "Mutt, what do you think? Do we deserve a treat?" He sat with his nose turned up, whining. "Treat?" He became antsy, circled to sit again, licking his lips. "My oh my, Mutt. I think you have learned the word 'treat!' " Again he gave a tiny whine.

With a prance to our step, we danced into the store. I bought a fudge popsicle with a chewy rawhide treat for Mutt. We sat on the bench to finish my extravagances. When the last piece of my Popsicle fell off, Mutt snatched it before it hit the ground. He looked quite surprised. "Too cold?" I smiled.

When we arrived at the spot I was sure I had parked the car, I didn't see it. With a little heart flutter, I knelt down. Mutt received a tummy rub. "I must have the wrong street. Let's do a little hunt."

After searching about an hour, up and down the surrounding streets, I finally accepted the fact that it was gone. Lightheaded, I sat down just staring. I couldn't even cry. My car had been impounded. Even if I had the money to pay the impound fees accruing daily, I couldn't reclaim it without an ID. As if in a cloud, I dragged Mutt and myself back to the beach. On the way I saw that red wagon. As if my beach stuff with our meager food supply was too heavy to carry a step further, I dropped everything in the rusty wagon. Mutt helped out by gingerly prancing along. He took a graceful leap, landing on top for his ride to the beach. With a sad limp smile, my eyes blurred and tears dripped down my cheeks as I continued on.

As I reached Coast Highway, I saw a tall woman walking up from her day on the beach. She dragged some kind of homemade rolling beach cart. I thought her homeless like me, but she carried a set of keys jiggling in her hand. We watched her walk up Eighth Street.

It seemed as though I lost my ability to think. This moment had come a lot sooner than I expected. I plodded along with Mutt down at my side making footprints in the sand. We settled down close to the water. I looked heavenward. Dear God, if there's a plan for me, please help me find it. If I am any use to you, help me find my way."

That's when I let loose. I bawled loudly with no one but Mutt and the seagulls to hear me, I thought.

As big as he was, Mutt climbed into my lap and licked my cheeks. I glanced around and saw a family down the beach a ways. With some embarrassment, I noticed they were guarding the sun from their eyes, noticing my loud distress. I pulled myself together.

Sniffling, I wiped my face. Interrupting the swoosh of cold ocean air, I felt a warm breeze surround me. I closed my eyes with the thought of praying, when a sudden burst of light shot through the sun-rimmed gray clouds. The wind whispered in my ear, a very familiar voice, "Oh ye of little faith! And do not settle on what you will eat or drink; do not worry about it . . . all these things will be given you . . ." Did I know this thought? Luke 12: 30-31, I did. The voice was so familiar however I couldn't quite put a face with it. The snippet gave me hope that my memory would soon return.

I sat for a moment feeling my worry lifted away, vaporized with the wind and I took in the beauty of a late afternoon sunshine coating the water's surface with golden glints.

"All right Mutt, let's eat."

After I laid out my towel, I spread out what was left of our food. When I raised up, a man stood near the water. As I studied him, I also made note of the fact that there were still people on the beach. If he meant me any harm, I could scream.

"Little Miss. Could you share a bite with an old man?" Mutt eyed him. Mutt wasn't growling or barking. Even if I felt a chill of fear at the sight of the man's scrufty salt and pepper gray hair with matching beard, I figured Mutt was a good judge of character. I'd just decided to overlook his appearance. I didn't have that much food, but I did know that a church served food tomorrow. I nodded and raised my jar of peanut butter as a question. He wiped his mouth as the wind brushed through his straggly beard.

"That looks absolutely gourmet. Thank you."

He flopped down, fluttering a breath of sand flying with the breeze. His small grunt allowed for how far down the sand seemed to an old man.

As I handed him his sandwich he spoke in a kindly voice. "I see your eyes and nose are all red. Are you Okay?" He took a big bite. "Mmm . . ." his cheeks bulged out.

"Uh huh."

Mutt waited while I poured Kibble in his bowl.

I nibbled on my sandwich. When the man's sandwich disappeared, I gave him the heel of the bread, and the jar of peanut butter. When he'd scraped away the last of it, I threw the jar to Mutt. His long tongue reached all the way to the bottom.

"Well Girl, that was mighty fine. I thank you."

I nodded.

The man rose with some difficulty. He fought his way across the soft sand until he stepped down to the wet beach, where he picked up his pace. As he wandered away looking dark against the setting sun, I wondered if he didn't know about the shower on the beach. I didn't want to offend him by holding my nose.

As Mutt dropped the peanut butter jar, it took off with the wind. Mutt chased after it, biting at it, he pawed the slippery jar. That popped the jar up in the air. End over end, it escaped. He pounced on it and finally stopped it from rolling away. He seized his newfound toy in his teeth and trotted back to the towel. He pushed the jar into the sand so it wouldn't get away from him again then held it with his two paws licking with gusto.

"How smart you are, Mutt!" I had decided, whatever came my way I would enjoy the small gifts in life. I smiled at Mutt as I tousled the fur behind his ears. Off he went leaping in the tiny waves and chasing the gulls.

With arms wrapped around my knees, I drew them to my chin, watched the sun sizzle into the horizon while I wondered what new challenge tomorrow would bring.

Chapter 67
Day to Day

That evening after we left the beach, I wandered up an alley. Some residences illuminated the alley with overhead lighting. The triangles of light made it seem safer. I could see if any one came.

When I found a niche between the three story houses, I waded in through some tall grass where I found a spot. The grass had been matted into a soft 'mattress'. I hid my wagon behind a bush. "Perfect, Mutt, come settle down with me."

We still had some Kibble and one bag of peanuts, a Spartan meal, but it subdued the growling of my stomach and quieted Mutt's whine.

Without a toothbrush, I shredded the end of a stick until it turned into a small brush. I cleaned my teeth best I could. I noticed a hose bib where I could fill my bottle, rinse my teeth and wash my face with the end of my towel.

I whisper-sang a couple of songs with Mutt blending in, like singing a lullaby to help us fall asleep.

When I lay down, Mutt cuddled in with me under the towel. My backside against the wall with Mutt in front of me, I felt almost warm enough. A prayer eased my mind along with the vision of a small girl kneeling by her bedside. "Now I lay me down to sleep. If I should die before I wake, I pray the Lord my soul to take." *Could that be me in that familiar blue room?*

Warm as toast, the prayer comforted me as I closed my

eyes.

I shook when a loud voice roared. I grabbed at the towel as it whipped away from my clutch.

"What are you doing in my house?"

"What?" I sat up holding tight to Mutt, who took his stance growling at a grubby man in dark clothes and long hair. The wind with the moon behind this man made his stringy hair seem ominous. A grocery cart full of his belongings headed straight for me. "Get out! I say, Get out!"

I jumped up holding Mutt's leash tight.

Just as the man lunged for me, another man hauled him back and literally threw him to the middle of the alley. When Mutt got in the fray I called him to settle him down.

The second man introduced himself. "Jonathan Rousseau at your service." He lifted his floppy hat, swished it around before taking an elegant bow. He turned toward my attacker. "Now if you will be so kind as to vacate the premises. This is Girl's residence."

Even in the dark alley, I recognized him as the man who dined with us on the beach.

Attacker hauled himself up on his grocery cart. With an, "Harumf, " he pushed his squeaky cart down the alley.

"My humble abode is just here, he pointed behind a wood pile, a couple of houses down.

Walking over to him, I reached out my hand. "Thank you."

He swept it up and kissed the air above my knuckles. Not at all, my dear. I think you'll be safe in this spot if you are of a mind to stay for a while." He waved. "See you in the morning." He donned his hat using it to give me a singular wave."

Mutt licked the man's hand then followed me back to our humble abode.

Chapter 68
A New Day

The sun dawned bright, waking the two of us at the same time. Mutt licked my face. I sat up rubbing my eyes and stretching my stiff muscles.

"Ah, you're awake." Jonathan threw me an apple. "Got the apples at that little market on 18th, I think. May I join you?"

I spread my hand, a gesture toward an open space next to me.

Jonathan dragged out a stump and sat on it. "The ground is a long way down for an ol' geezer like me."

I offered him my half bag of peanuts.

With his palm toward me, he declined.

Chomping right into it, I smiled large. "Mmm." Even an apple with a few soft spots tasted like a gourmet treat. I savored the rest with small bites interrupted by a few peanuts. Mutt begged for our cores. Jonathan tossed his first. Mutt leaped up and caught it mid-air. Then he snagged mine the same way.

"How talented you are, Mutt!" I gave him the rest of his Kibble.

Jonathan stood. "Just remember to stay with your belongings wherever you go. With a single open hand fan wave and a slight hitch in his hip, he wandered off down the alley. "If you go to 11th Street after 4 o'clock, dinner will be served at the Catholic Church." Wishing would not make it so—but as I tucked in my makeshift toothbrush, I wished for my memory, which might mean I'd return home. If not, I'd have to leave the rest to Him.

I packed up my stuff a little slowly hoping the cool marine layer would burn off. Though still foggy, I leashed Mutt. When we headed for the beach the November wind came up so by the time I reached the shower, the fog became thicker. There wasn't another person around that I could see. An eerie chill shivered all the way to my wet toes. I simply washed my face and armpits. The cold water helped me brush my teeth but the taste, "Yuck!" I spit it out. Doesn't compare with Oregon's crystal clear water. I sat on a bench drying my toes when a skate boarder whizzed by. Both Mutt and I yelped. My feet warmed up once in my shoes and socks.

I could see why those scary British movies always plunged the heroine into a foggy scene.

Mutt barked while he chased the dancing Ziploc baggy as the wind carried it along. He returned with the bagdangling from his mouth. I reached down for it a bit surprised he let me have it. Washing it as best as water could, I hoped nothing toxic had been stored in it. Actually I knew what I'd do with it.

With the change I had left, I could get a bar of soap and maybe a comb if I went to that little store,

Making choices hasn't been my best attribute. At the store, I had to choose. Did I want a bar of soap, a bag of Corn Nuts and a dinner mint or a brush? My stomach decided.

As we left the store, the sun burned away the fog into wisps of vapor that disappeared.

Chapter 69
Merry Christmas

Days passed. It proved to be a full time job just trying to keep warm and sheltered, feed myself and survive. I did pick up an odd job once in a while. Christmas decorations noted the passage of time. California's weather isn't like other places with definite seasons. I really looked forward to Christmas dinner at the church. Days rolled closer to the 25th.

This was a time when I saw the goodness in people, the sharing of those who didn't have enough for their own needs. Without the two giant trash bags, Jonathan's Christmas gift to me, I never would have survived winter.

Jonathan and I waited in the long line up. The huge Christmas dinner at the Lutheran Church brought even more homeless than I realized lived around me. We are invisible.

Inside, a church lady stooped to pet Mutt. When she disappeared, I didn't expect her to return with a Ziplock filled with kibble. And a blanket, "Thank you!"

Mutt's nose sniffed and twitched. When I sat down, I finished off my plate, leaving Mutt his due mixed with kibble. Thank goodness the ham, turkey and mashed potatoes filled the air with the aroma that covers a multitude of other odors. In my pack, I managed to stash a few rolls and turkey and ham. The Church gave us all a bag with a tube of Colgate and a toothbrush delivered by Santa. So, much as I hated to discard my stick brush, I now had two Ziplocs and could keep my tasty soap separate from my toothbrush.

Our voices sounded great when the whole meeting hall full of people sang some Christmas carols. There were more smiles than I'd seen in a long time.

With nothing else to give Jonathan, I composed a song for him. I hummed an intro and then sang:

Sometimes comes a dragon

It rises in the dark of the heart
It captures your fears
And fills your heart with dread

It blocks your instincts
It steals your confidence
And obscures your world

It darkens the light in your eyes
It floods your soul with waves of angst
And robs you of your trust

When all seems lost
When winning seems beyond the gate
Find courage through the Spirit

Then comes the white knight
To help you slay your dragon
He helps you find your song

And lets you recover
Your mettle, your fortitude
Your strength of character

Yet remains
To help you
Slay your Dragons

Sometimes comes the Knight

When I hugged him, his eyes filled.

"I'm sorry. I couldn't give you a gift, Jonathan, but thank you for being my knight."

"No, my dear Girl, my dear friend, you are the gift to an old man. You put the song into my heart. You gave me a reason for hope. Next Christmas we will be in a better place."

Could that really happen?

Chapter 70
Moving On, Staying in Place

The weeks sped by quickly and along came Easter Vacation before I knew what happened.

As the day warmed up people began populating the beach, more than I'd seen before, mostly teens. That dissipated my fear. I certainly had plenty of company on the shore. There is something to be said for living in a warm climate.

On the way to the beach, the dark-haired woman that I'd seen some months ago, held out a sandwich in Saran Wrap. "Here, I have an extra. I'm not very hungry today." I hesitated.

Eying her beach cart, I spotted a laptop.

For some reason, Mutt didn't bark, just his 'I'm hungry' snarl. Maybe he smelled food.

My stomach gurgled.

"Go ahead. Take it, I hate to throw it away."

Mutt whined a bit. It probably scared her but I knew his way of talking to me.

"I reached for the sandwich. Opening it, I saw that it was cheese, so did Mutt. I tore off a bite for Mutt then took a huge bite for myself. When I had rewrapped it, I stored it in my towel. Walking on without saying, "thank you," *did I not want to acknowledge that I had become homeless? Maybe if a kindness happens again I should be more polite.*

Mutt and I settled close to the water's edge and lay down. Even though the cool wind swept over us, the wagon acted as our windbreak. The sun broke through and warmed the sand.

Mutt cuddled up next to me. Upon waking, the wind died down giving us time to enjoy our cheese sandwich. There were dill pickles on it. I let Mutt try a tiny taste. He shook his head with his eyes scrinched shut. I laughed. "Okay, I'll eat the pickles from your half." Things turned out just as my dream told me. I hadn't really been very hungry today and Jonathan had invited me for dinner on 11th Street.

I took a wide view of the puffy white clouds drifting across the sky. Looking skyward, I whispered, "Thank you, Lord."

Chapter 71
A Way of Life

By afternoon, the warmth invited us for a swim. I wrapped my towel around to change into my suit, a real trick with all the teens out of school. Located on the beach, the up-scale model of a green outhouse didn't offer a viable option. Beside the obvious olfactory aversion to such a structure, I'd lose sight of my wagon. Besides, there wasn't much more space in there than under a beach towel.

After I removed his service vest, we sped to the water's edge and dove in. Swimming in the icy water felt great—after you got used to 62 degrees! Riding the waves and racing back warmed me up. I couldn't believe Mutt learned to catch a wave! He also loved to stand over and jump on the small waves. The kids stopped to watch him, laughing and pointing.

As it got nearer to 4 o'clock I packed the wagon. I could take my shower, with soap! The shower was by the pier in front of larger restrooms where I could change back into my clothes taking Mutt and my wagon with me. My bikini got washed every time I showered. After Mutt's shower, I stood back just in time for his massive shake! I stored my soap and my toothbrush in my brand new Ziploc. "Thanks Mutt, my Ziploc is great!" Sometimes I felt the need to use soap to brush my teeth, "Yuck! They should flavorize soap!" So I carefully conserved the Christmas toothpaste as I still had some left.

Just before we started along the beach path, the sandwich lady walked along the beach dragging her beach cart. I gave her a small wave, hoping she'd know it was my version of a thank you.

The path along the strip of Beach Park divided by the bike lane felt more like a freeway. With all the teens skating, skateboarding, biking and jogging along with me, it was like a pinball game with me as the target.

As I neared the church there were other homeless lined up from the front to the back of the church. I noticed Jonathan up way ahead in line. He motioned me to join him but my sense of fair play kept me back.

As the smell wafted out, I couldn't believe I soon would be eating something that wonderful. "Mmm." Roast beef, mashed potatoes, gravy, carrots and salad. I stuck the apple in my pocket. It tasted so good. It reminded me of a home cooked meal, like a family might sit around a table in the kitchen.

Mutt enjoyed his share too.

Afterward I helped the cooks clean up. I took a moment to cut my soap in half and gave Jonathan the other half. "For the shower by the pier!"

Full as I'd ever been—at least since the turkey dinner—Mutt and I sauntered back to our alley abode, humming softly in the wind.

That night a lovely vision filled my dreams. A boy and a girl walked hand-in-hand along a path winding through an old- growth forest and singing a haunting song. The girl held a gray and white kitten with dots on her nose. She cuddled the kitten next to her cheek and listened to her gentle purr.

When the girl turned around, the boy kissed her. She smiled as the purr faded away.

I awoke smiling with Mutt nuzzled against my cheek, softly snoring like a purr. *Let that one be a real memory not just a dream. For a moment I felt real happiness.*

Chapter 72
A Daily Routine

Everyday, the nice lady brought sandwiches until spring vacation ended. I guessed her occupation as a teacher, or maybe she had returned to school as a student.

All the while, people smiled as we strolled along on the walking path. People welcomed Mutt and me to Huntington Beach. He just loved the attention and they loved him. I thank God for Mutt as I never talked to anyone, except for "thank you" and "please" that finally rolled out when appropriate. Not conversing kept me from getting close to anyone, whether the person tried to be threatening or kind. It didn't keep Mutt from making friends though. He brought them to us in bands. Sometimes having them around felt like a family with all of them talking to Mutt. He loved the attention and I loved the feeling of belonging.

Several people guessed I might be mute. I didn't change their mind.

Sometimes I found a church would allow a shower. Finger combing my wet hair didn't seem to work and my hair transformed itself to a matted topknot that I captured in a rubber band.

When summer came, days were very similar, sunny warm with sparkling water hosting a parade of birds.

Most days the lady came back with her sandwiches. It was lovely just knowing you would have food every day. She always had kibbles and dog treats too.

Mutt and I swam all afternoon in and out of the waves. I waited until the beach cleared off before we could play catch. I almost believed that I could always live this way. I say almost. I still hoped for a job, but now my grungy appearance made me too self-conscious to even try.

The sandwich lady, told me her name, Karen. I stuck to the name Girl, like Jonathan called me. Karen invited me to her home and after a while we had a few conversations. When she invited me in, I didn't go. I was too old to be adopted though I honestly didn't know how old I was. My hair knot disappeared when Karen left me shampoo, cream rinse and a hairbrush by her outdoor shower. Her big fluffy towels were the best. Sometimes I weeded her yard for her before I took a shower. She offered me a small garden job of changing out a few old plants for some new summer flowers. I didn't want to take money as she gave me so much, but she insisted. *When summer is over, it will be sad when she leaves again.*

Karen let me ride her Boogie Board. Sometimes I put Mutt on there too. You should have seen him riding on Karen's board all by himself. People gathered around just to watch—especially children. People recorded it on their phones.

Karen was a teacher and a writer. We'd often sit on the beach together. I loved when she'd let me read her stories.

She encouraged me to sing. If I had a new song in my head, she praised me. After she brought me an old guitar with new strings for it, she helped me clean it up, fix it and tune it.

Somehow I knew music was in my soul when I began to play with songs flowing out as they danced in my head. Sometimes I'd sing on the beach path and people would leave me some money. I think they liked Mutt's version as much as mine. Jonathan surprised me one day when he joined me in a song or two. His voice really blended nicely with mine.

When we had enough change in his floppy hat, we would

splurge by eating at Taco Bell across the street from the beach.

Sometimes Jonathan would ask a question. I might answer, or not. He didn't press me. He just made me feel safe every night or even on the beach he would notice if anyone bothered me. Once he seemed to appear out of nowhere.

At the beach, one Saturday during summer, I hadn't located myself near a lifeguard station because of the crowd. By the late afternoon, I sat alone on the beach with a few scattered people walking on the path. Fishermen on the pier would be too far away to help.

While I snoozed on the beach, a man sat down, subdued me by sitting on my stomach. He dragged my blanket, over his back, tenting us out of sight. I strained to sit. He muffled my scream. Mutt stood in attack mode barking and growling. Without a sound, there stood Jonathan standing over us, yanking the blanket back from my assailant. Jonathan propped both hands on his hips, tall and intimidating, he roared, "Leave, now!" If my adversary had been wearing boots they would have been shaken off. In his haste, he probably ground off a few toes nails on his bare feet during in his rapid retreat through the sand ending with a belly flop into the waves. While I hugged Mutt, Jonathan disappeared as quickly as my adversary.

After the summer vacation ended, the beach crowd thinned out. Without Karen's daily sharing, I set about to find food. I found a place to play my guitar with more traffic than the beach path. Jonathan joined me and we made enough to feed ourselves.

One day a lady came up to me. "Excusez-moi."

"Bonjour." I quieted Mutt.

"Vous parlez français?"

"Mais oui."

"Où est-il un endroit pour manger?"

"Avec dans un bloc ou deux sur l'autoroute ou à la jetée." I pointed up the stairs and toward the pier.

"Et ausssi, où est la salle de repos?

"C'est alson à côté de la jetée. I pointed.

"Merci beaucoup!"

"Pas de problème. Au revoir."

My head spun. *How did I know how to speak French?* Her questions were simple, just where she could find a restaurant and a restroom. But I understood her perfectly and then answered her. I closed my eyes for a moment. I envisioned a man in a uniform standing with his arm around a girl. "Mutt, I know that uniform! The Marine uniform is familiar to me!" *Am I? Am I regaining my memory?*

"I am wide-awake! I am not dreaming! This just has to be a memory!" Poor Mutt. He sensed my excitement and pranced around my towel.

"Settle, Mutt." I wrestled with him on the towel for a minute, until sand stuck to everything. "A swim! Let's go."

I had learned to make a sundial in the sand. Somewhere around noon, I'd ask someone with a watch what time it was. When I found just the right stick, I'd make a dial with the stick in the middle. Pretty close, the shadow would tell me the time.

By the time we dripped out of the ocean, my sundial told me I might be late. "Quick, Mutt, time to shower for the Lutheran church for dinner."

After a quick rinse off, I scurried up to Coast Highway with Mutt leashed and practically dragging me. Breathing hard, I saw Jonathan waiting for me on the other side of the street. I waved.

Mutt resisted but I sped ahead, running across the highway . . .

"Screeeeech!

Chapter 73
A Rude Awakening?

The sweetest dream floated through my mind. *I could feel the breeze in my face, riding my horse near Poppy's ranch. At my side, a handsome boy wearing a cowboy hat looked over at me. As he tipped his hat back, I recognized Jimmy. Before he dismounted Warrior, he picked a couple of apples, shined them on his jeans and threw one to me. We tied our chestnut colored horses to a branch. Jimmy picked two more apples for our horses. I patted down Candy's soft nose. She loved her apples. Jimmy and I sat with our backs against the trunk. When I turned to face Jimmy, our eyes met as we munched on the apples. What a delicious stare! The kiss! No! No, I don't want to wake up.*

When I opened my eyes, I didn't know where I was. "Jimmy?"

I stared up into a semi-familiar face. "Jonathan?"

"I'm here, Girl, I'm right here." He clasped a hand over mine.

I touched my aching head as I inspected my surroundings. White walls were thick with blinking machines. Pinched on my second finger a white monitor sent information to one of the machines. It was great to see that my heart still bounded a bouncing green line on the monitor. It seamed to be racing. "Why am I in the hospital? What Happened? Where's Mutt?"

"You remember planning to go to the Lutheran Church for

dinner?"

"Sorta."

"Well, my dear, you came barreling across the highway to join me—at rush hour with lots of traffic. A Toyota hit you. Fortunately it knocked you over out of the way of the wheels. Thank our Dear Savior. The car did not trundle right over you."

"My Toyota?"

"I don't think so."

"What about Mutt?"

"Maybe they took him to a shelter. He carried on so and he wouldn't leave your side. He got in the way of the EMT's treating you."

"What hospital is this?"

"Huntington Beach Hospital."

"That's not too far from my home."

"So you know where home is?"

"Yes, finally I know I have one now and my amnesia seems to be going away. I remember lots of things." I reached up and touched my head. Hey, my head's bandaged. Maybe too many memories came rushing back too fast."

"You are absolutely correct about that fact. They kept you sedated so the concussion could heal properly. Karma is with you, child."

"How long have I been here?"

"Three long days. I've been here every day. It is so delightful to see your beautiful green eyes open!"

"A **pink** cast?" I raised my arm. "Well at least it's kind of pretty, only it's pink. Is my arm broken?"

"Just the wrist."

I tried to raise myself. "Ouch!"

"Ah! No!" Jonathan pressed my good shoulder gently back down. "You also have a broken collar bone. So please refrain from executing any gymnastic moves or even rising until the doctor or the nurse comes back."

"Are my parents here?"

"You've cried out for your mom several times. Are you recalling your identity or your family?"

"Uh, yes, I think I am! My name is Natty. Natty Wilson."

"Nice to meet you, my dear Natty. There's a woman from children's services out there. They didn't know how old you were. They thought between 17 and 23. In your belongings, I found a slip of paper with the name Rose Grey. So that is the name I offered."

"Oh? Not Girl?"

He grinned.

A rush of memories of me using Rose for a name filled my head.

"When they brought you in, I told them you were 17. I assumed that they would take better care of you if you were a child. What is you true age? "

"Well, tell the children's services woman she can go right home, I'm 22 and a college graduate, I'll have you know."

"So if you give me your parents' names, maybe the nurses can locate them."

"Robert and Rosalie Wilson." I touched my chin. "They call her Rose. Isn't that odd that I chose Rose for a name when I didn't remember my own?" I remembered the vase of roses at Auntie May's. I grinned when I thought of her.

"Indeed."

"Hey, Jonathan, I'm sorry. I didn't notice how handsome you look. You look like you went through the car wash."

"Well, that my dear, is highly unlikely, though it does sound like a very merry amusement."

He touched his forehead. "Even though I told them you belonged to me, I don't think they believed me. Anyway, they wouldn't allow me stay on the premises the way I presented myself. Imagine, they actually thought me a homeless person."

"Home is where the heart is, they say. I think you are why I didn't mind being—" I cupped my hand around my mouth. "Homeless." My vision blurred. "I love you."

Jonathan wiped the corner of his eye, bent and kissed my forehead. "You have expressed my sentiments precisely, Natty. I guess I shan't call you Girl any more."

"Bet I'll miss that." I looked out the window and wondered exactly what would happen to Jonathan next.

"So, I am grateful one of the EMT's took me home where I showered. He gave me some clothes, gave me a brand new razor and voila, mademoiselle." He reached his hands out to the side and gave a slight bow.

"Well, you are a very good-looking man, and much younger than I thought you were. Your beard looks better trimmed."

"Just to let you know—I shall not reveal the number of my advanced years."

I grinned at him when he threw his shoulders back and straightened up.

"Will you at least tell me what you were in your other life?"

"You mean before I became the H word?" He looked down at his new tennis shoes. "When I lost my wife and my little girl, I started drinking and I lost my job as an English professor."

I started to speak . . .

He raised a flat hand. "When the nurses questioned me about you, I fabricated information. I suppose when I go out to the desk, I better tell them the truth. I'll see what I can find out about not only your parents but also Mutt. When the hospital finds out I lied, I suppose they'll rescind their job offer as a janitor." He strode out of the room with his nose in the air.

"Hey, wait."

He turned.

"Find me a piece of paper and a pencil. I know my parents phone number and address. "Imagine! I have been wandering around the neighborhood where I grew up."

After I wrote down the information, I looked up into Jonathan's brown eyes. "Jonathan? Don't forget to come back to me."

He patted my hand before he left.

My cranium ached from my injury plus being crammed so full of questions, ideas, things, people, places, realizations and happenings, that I thought my skull would burst.

French! I knew the language because with my dad being a Marine, we spent a bit of time in France. I studied French while we were there. He did secret work with the U.S. Marine Corps Special Operations Command, MARSOC.

That memory made me very excited to see my parents.

When the doctor arrived, he stopped me from firing all my brain cells at once. I smiled.

Chapter 76
Neither Here Nor There But Not Gone

I welcomed the doctor. "Thanks for interrupting me from over thinking everything rattling around in my brain."

"Well, hello, I'm Dr. Whittaker. I am so glad to see you sitting up. How are you feeling?"

"A little achy."

"As well you should be, after being hit by a car. Everything looks good, so none of those things rattling around inside fell out. There's a slight break, your clavicle. It should heal quickly."

"My collarbone?"

He nodded. "It's going to be pretty sore for a while, but it's just a seam, a slight break. There shouldn't be a problem if you wear the sling until it is better."

"I think God has been watching over me."

"Quite so. Your friend, Mr. Rousseau told me that you've had amnesia. Do you think your memory has returned?"

"I'm not sure but there's a lot more there than before my accident." I looked at the kind, gray haired doctor adjusting his glasses.

"Maybe we should thank the gentleman who hit you for restoring your memory. He's been asking about you."

"He shouldn't be charged with anything. I remember darting across Coast Highway, not at a corner or a signal. Perhaps I should get a ticket. Please let him know that I accept the responsibility. Please, if he comes around you can tell him I'm okay."

"Well, young lady, you must have quite a story to relate."

"You think so?"

"Do you recall how you became homeless?"

"Too much to tell unless you have a couple of hours."

"So why don't you start telling me your story while I examine you?"

He started with checking my concussion—could my eyes follow his fingers, etc. "I'm going to have the nurse change the bandage around your head as the bleeding stopped fairly rapidly. You are no longer exhibiting any symptoms."

"Sounds good. Did you need to cut my hair short?"

"Just shaved around the cuts. You may have a small scar on your upper forehead. Your hair will hide the scar in back. I also noted another scar back there. Do you know how you got that one?"

"I think I've been using my head as a battering ram in the last year."

While he finished my exam, I gave him a short synopsis of my toils and traumatic adventures.

"Well, you should call the police."

"I'll think about it."

"I think you can go home tomorrow. Your parents have been contacted. Take it easy on yourself. I'll have a nurse fill out the necessary information. The discharge papers will have your instructions for your recovery. You shouldn't drive until you have another check up in a week or so. Are you in pain?"

"No and please don't give me any opioids or other addictive medicine. If I need to, could I take Ibuprofen?"

"Good girl, however you heal faster if you are not in pain, so, I'll give you a prescription, just in case."

The nurse came by to take my order for the meals I would

receive that day. Actually for a homeless person being in the hospital compared favorably to being a guest at the Ritz.

At most any time, I could request pudding, Jell-O, juice, or ice cream. Imagine being able to choose meals from a menu! I know some people that I met actually tried to get hurt so they could go to the hospital. I can see why. The sense of being cared for is a wonderful feeling.

Jonathan came back at lunchtime. I had him in mind when I made my order with extras and two kinds of drinks. He sat next to my tray where he could share. It struck me that I might not see Jonathan once I left the hospital. *What would happen to him?*

Later while I ate my dinner, my special order meatloaf, mashed potatoes, roll with lots of butter, salad, juice and ice cream my parents arrived. I heard people scurrying in the hall, quick footsteps pounded. A bit breathless, Mom and Dad poked their heads in the doorway. When our eyes connected Mom rushed over. We practically shoved the food tray on the floor with all the huggy-kissy stuff. "I can't believe you're here!"

"Me too." Mom touched my cheek.

Then Daddy picked up the milk carton off the floor. He repeated more hugs and kisses. All three of us wrapped together for a long moment rocking just treasuring each other.

I don't think I realized how good hugs felt since maybe the ones Jimmy gave me that summer just before I left Poppy's ranch. That sudden remembrance made me ask, "Poppy? Is Poppy okay?"

"Better than okay. When we called him, he arranged a flight to come down this weekend to see you."

"All right! That also reminds me of Dotty." I looked up at Mom, my face sagging.

"Don't look so worried. She's waiting for you at home."

"I guess I imagined that, that they were . . ." I swallowed a lump almost gagging me, "gone."

Dad took my hand. "I think the only thing we have to worry about now is getting you home. The doctor said that you'll need to stay one more day to be sure you're okay."

"I am still worried, though." I looked away, eyes filling as I thought about the possibility that Matt might have been hit. *What if I never see him again?*

"What's wrong, honey." Mom's brow furrowed.

"I have so much to tell you, but it'll wait until we get home. The important thing is . . . I have a dog." My eyes opened wide with the recalling of where Matt came from and how I renamed him. "Matt, his name is Sir Matthew, Matt or Mutt for short, and I don't know where he is, maybe the animal shelter? Will you find out, please? He's just got to be okay." The room became blurry.

Mom handed me a Kleenex. "I'm sure we can find out."

Chapter 77
Putting Humpty Dumpty Back Together

The next day my parents took me home. What an experience! Had it been only about a year since the last time I rode on 18th Street, two blocks from the beach and only eight or ten blocks from where I'd been wandering for months? Our refurbished Victorian house sat between a couple of lovely old houses, next to the three-story new ones. Mom hung colorful flower boxes on the rail of the upstairs veranda, which shaded the large porch underneath. Mom's roses on the arbor and picket fence were thicker and more beautiful than I recalled. The palm trees that lined the sidewalk seemed to have doubled in size.

As we drove around to the alley and down to our garage, Mom grinned at me. "I made your favorite barbequed ribs, stuffed baked potatoes and an artichoke!"

"Wow! Give me a napkin. I'm salivating!"

Mom scurried out of the car almost before it stopped. Dad pushed the button to close the garage door, while Mom unlatched the side door into the backyard. As I opened my car door, just gazing at the stuff in the garage like my bike still hanging from the ceiling. Instantly, I fell backwards into the car with a wet tongue lashing my face. "Matt! Is it you, Matt?" I hugged him so hard he yipped. "How? Where have you been?"

Dad put his arm around my shoulders. "Your friend Jonathan. He found him in an alley and brought him to us."

"That's Jonathan. He really took care of me when I . . ."

Matt jumped up with a paw on my wrist. "Down, boy."

Kneeling, I cuddled him. "I love you." I nuzzled my face in his fur.

Matt sniffed. I sniffed. Even from outside, I could smell those ribs. "Mmm. Everything really smells way more than good."

As I stood, Matt seemed electrified. He rolled, he leapt, everywhere around me. "Down boy! Hey, Mom? Dad, how do Matt and Dotty get along?"

When Dad opened the back door into the house, Matt charged inside.

Mom couldn't seem to let go of my hand as she led me inside. I checked out the spotless, white kitchen. "Wow! I love the remodel!" I ran my hand across the smooth white marble topping the center island.

"We had to keep busy while you were away." Mom pointed to the living room.

A couple of steps into the room, there were my two furry friends lolling on the green over-stuffed couch, Dotty spread out on Matt's back, kneading him with her paws and licking his head.

When I stared at Dotty, she stared right back.

I wished I had my phone to snap the bewildered, wide-eyed look on her polka-dotted face. As she leaped off, paw on Matt's snout, down to the wood planked floor, she raced to me waving her tail behind. Matt followed suit. They knocked me into the rocker, laughing and giggling at their attention.

"So," Dad rubbed his hands together. "When are you going to catch us up on the last few months? You can imagine how we reacted when we got up to Oregon and the police said you had completely disappeared. Your poor mother, I very nearly dropped her when she collapsed."

"So sorry, Mom. Let me tell you all about that stuff after dinner? I'm starving."

"Well, let's eat then. Rose? Is it ready."

"Come and get it." Mom set the salad on the dining room table.

Needless to say, I ate so many ribs I had to feel my own rib cage to know I hadn't grown some new ones.

Once the double chocolate ice cream with fudge sauce had been devoured, we gathered in the living room for my recitation of the last few months. I grabbed a few Kleenex because I knew one of my base reactions were tears.

"Wait. Let's have a fire. I'll get some newspaper." Dad followed me out.

"I carry the wood." He wrapped an arm around my shoulder.

Things like starting the fire with Daddy and the cozy firelight bathing my parents' pleasant faces were little things I missed the most. The warmth and tranquility of my home almost overwhelmed me.

Back in my seat I watched the flame leap around the logs and catch the paper wads on fire. Even the smoky smell reminded me of what I had missed.

Silence captured us all as we settled in the comfort of our living room. The grandfather clock's ticking and chiming sounded as though someone had turned the volume on full blast. Mom and Dad sat on the edge of their seats, squirming in the uncomfortable silence.

I wadded the Kleenex in my lap.

Dad prompted me. "Okay, why don't we start with the U of O?"

I thought that once I began my tale of woe, I would motor through it like a machine gun. And I did. I didn't even pause for questions.

There were a few tears while I told them about Bud. Especially my few triumphant moments when I talked about my escape, my revenge with Bud's bank account, I laughed so hard I almost couldn't get through the rest of the story.

Dad lifted an envelope. "I opened your bank statement. "I couldn't imagine where all that money came from. At least that let us know you must be still alive."

"Don't think you can talk me into turning it in to the police."

"A 22 year old can do what she wants. In this case, I think you deserve it."

"You bet I do."

Before I knew it, I launched into my escape followed by my second kidnapping. I proceeded right on into my second pile of money, a bit embarrassed at how fast it disappeared.

Grinning when I got to the Mercedes, how it disappeared along with the money, and how I became homeless. That had to include my dear friend, Jonathan, my rescuer. "I hope he hasn't disappeared from my life."

Dad put his hands behind his head and stretched back. "Not long ago, I remember reading a story in the Register about a big arrest in L.A. of a drug and kidnapping ring. Maybe you can call and find out if that Alejandro guy belonged to that gang of thugs."

"I'm fairly optimistic about that one."

Dislodging Matt's nose from my feet and Dottie who sprang from my lap to the back of my chair, Mom lifted me up by my hands catching me into her arms. "You have always made me so proud of you. But my special daughter is not only talented but an amazing hero!"

"That reminds me of Sylvia. I hope she's doing okay."

Mom smiled at Matt. "You know, Jonathan is the one who brought us Mutt."

`"Let's call him Matt, now. He's not a mutt, he is my hero, my Sir Matthew, my dark knight." Dad removed his glasses and smoothed a finger down the side of his nose. He took a note from his pocket and handed it to me. "Here,"

While I remained standing, Matt pawed my leg.

I read the note. The tears rolled as the note blurred.

Dearest Natty, my Girl,

It has been the joy of my latter years to have had you as my friend. I wish you the best. When I have finished putting my life back on track, I will find you.

Go to the top of the mountain and sing your your heart out! You deserve every good thing that will come your way.

With fondness,

Jonathan

PS. I am working at the hospital!

After I laid the letter on the coffee table, I stood quietly reviewing my time with Jonathan.

Dad slipped his glasses back on. "I think you better sit down while I tell you about this Bud fellow."

Chapter 78
Is the End, Really the End?

"Okay Dad, what is it I need to know?"

Dad put his forearms on his knees and leaned forward. "You are indeed lucky."

"At least having amnesia let me forget about that episode of my life until now. That time is not something I want to remember. Do I have to find out anything more? "

"Yes, I think you do."

"That sheriff, Sheriff Tilden, has kept in contact with us, letting us know that he was still looking for you. I called him this morning. He said to tell you how delighted he is that you are home. He wants you to call him when you feel up to it."

I flopped down in my chair. "So why do I have to sit down to hear about creepy Bud?"

Dad cleared his throat. "After you left the Sheriff's office, he got a search warrant to do a little recon of Bud's house and property." Dad pulled on his ear lobe.

"Okay, shoot."

"Anyway, it was just as you said with the basement and all. Even though Bud burned the cabin to the ground, they still found evidence of you in the rubble in the basement. Some finger prints and what all. Bud had already high-tailed it out of there. Good for him because I was about to go up there, drag him out of his cabin and give him a Marine Corps martial arts demonstration."

Dad wiped his brow. "God had you in his hands, my dear one."

"Don't I know that? But you helped me too, Daddy, with those martial arts demos! I put those lessons to good use—with both the villains in my life. You would have loved to see the way your methods translated into triumph. Then there was Matt and Jonathan. I believe God gave me what I needed to survive. Even Poppy, you know how he recites verses? Well, he whispered in my ear. Some of those verses flashed into my psyche just when I needed them most."

"Poppy's a pretty inspirational guy."

I nodded. "Then there's Auntie May. What luck to find her!"

"Anyway, when Tilden checked the local hospitals because you had told him that you shot Bud, they found nothing. He hadn't checked into any of them. A couple of days later they got a call from a nurse. When she went to work on Monday morning, she found the doctor badly beaten and bound in zip-ties. The doctor tried to call the police but Bud caught him."

"The doctor didn't die, did he?"

"Fortunately his nurse found him and began first aid until the ambulance arrived. Luckily, his attack yielded some good samples of Bud's DNA from the doctor. Apparently, he really fought back!"

I let out a huge breath I'd been holding. "I couldn't live with myself if the wound I gave to that SOB made him seek out treatment and then kill the doctor that helped him. Bud's crazy."

"You are right about that fact! The police did more searching. They borrowed a cadaver dog from Roseburg to take him back to Bud's crime scene. That dog's nose turned on his high-gear sniff."

"Did they find that empty grave, the one I told them about?"

"That's not the only one they found."

"Really? I worried when I found that envelope of credit cards."

"There were at least six others. Six others! And the graves weren't empty. You can't believe what the police found." Dad leaned forward. "After hearing your story, this just sickens me. You know what else?"

Somehow I knew. I knew what they found.

"Wedding gowns! The girls all had been beaten, cleaned up and dressed in wedding gowns! They were posed with a bouquet in their hands. Cotton pickin' insane!" Daddy stood up pounding one fist into the other.

With my own fate in Bud's hands, I knew exactly where I'd be right now if I hadn't escaped. I shuddered.

Tears dripped down both of our faces when Daddy drew me into his arms. I'd never seen him cry before, let alone sob, but there we were, the two of us clinging with Mom joining in.

In the back of my mind, I can still hear the last words Bud spoke to me.

"I'll get you no matter how long it takes."

That's something I decided my parents didn't need to hear.

Chapter 79
Putting My Life in Order

After my story telling, I climbed the stairs like a ragdoll. The room had a musty smell, so I opened the window I supposed the door hadn't been open for a while. Totally drained, I flopped on my bed.

Since my room hadn't changed much since I attended high school, I truly felt home. The blue paint reminded me of the time my poor dad wanted to surprise me. He painted my room pink. My anti-pink reaction slipped out the minute I saw it. "Oh! No!" I felt so bad, but when he offered to repaint it blue, I helped him. It turned out to be a really fun time with my dad. The sky blue color, a few trophies for swimming, and play posters from a couple musicals I'd acted in, brought forth a bunch of high school memories. I relaxed and thought of my dear friend Marilyn who I hadn't seen in a couple of years.

As I sat on the edge of my bed, my brain went to work on what I needed to do to and what I should do first. I found a pad with a pen and listed:

1. Call my friends
2. Withdraw some money
3. Phone - credit cards
4. Driver's license
5. Insurance
6. Car
7. Clothes

8. Make up (I only had one lipstick and a mascara.)

9. Look for a job

10. Look for an apartment

As I approached my closet, I wondered if Mom had done like I asked her to do before I came home—clean out my clothes and give them to the church to distribute to the needy. When I slid the doors open, "Yup," nothing left but my robe and nightie hanging on a hook, two of my favorite dressy dresses, three jackets, two sweaters, and an expensive Coco Chanel bag. An old boyfriend of Mom's gave it to her a long time ago. (Daddy wouldn't let her carry it!)

In one of the drawers there were several sets of undies, a sweat suit, a T-shirt and a pair of shorts. So I'd survive if I didn't go shopping for a few days. Knowing that I had money made me happy that nothing had to be done today—nothing except call my friends.

Marilyn's number came first to mind, my friend since kindergarten. No wonder I memorized her number, the one from way back then. We had landlines for the first 12 years of our lives. We didn't get cell phones until we were teens. All my friends now had cell numbers, which I hadn't memorized—one of the downsides of iPhones. I hoped Mom still had their numbers as she used to call my friends and update them during my absence.

On the bedside table sat my cute little silver phone. I lifted it out of its cradle, half suspecting that it wouldn't be working, but I should have known my old fashioned parents would never give up a landline. I punched in Marilyn's number. While it rang several times, I wondered if they still had the same number. Her mom answered giving me the news that Marilyn had moved to Newport Beach. She also gave me a taste of what would happen when I talked to anyone who knew about my disappearance. A million questions came at me like pins and needles dredging up things I wanted to forget.

Since I didn't want to tell her right now, I promised her if she gave me Marilyn's number, she'd get the whole story later. I wrote Marilyn's number on a scrap of paper.

So! I would need to get a new phone soon. I had nothing in which to store my numbers. Phone books or operators are useless for cell numbers.

I needed to find out: if you lose your phone and your laptop could you get your same number, address book back? How many programs, apps, and numbers would be retrievable? What about photos? I thought I knew how to do some, because I have storage on the cloud.

The realization hit me like a sledgehammer on a fingernail. Everything I lost would need an explanation to recover or get a new one— everything I had to replace. Would I need to worry about my credit score? *One thing at a time . . .*

When I called my friend Marilyn, she forced me to tell my story before she told me her life's updates. After I'd finished telling her my adventures, she responded with, "You should write a book!"

"Okay. What's up with you?'

"Boring!"

"Come on."

"All right. I have a job with an Aetna insurance company, an apartment in Newport and a new boyfriend, Alex Segal who is a successful lawyer. See, not much to tell. With you now! That's a story! You need to write a book!"

"Remember, we had English together. Did you see how excited I got whenever we had to write anything? It always came out a blank page or a song. Can you imagine how long, and boring that song would be?"

That's when I got the idea what to do with all the notes I made on a million scraps of paper.

Marilyn suggested we go shopping after she got off work. "I'll come to your house at 3:00 next Friday. I have an appointment near you so I'll be off early. "

"Great. I can't drive for a while."

"You know—thinking about never seeing you again left a pretty big empty spot in my life."

"I know. Me, too. Glad we can fill those up soon! See you Friday."

Recalling the last day in Oregon reminded me about calling the two other Tiers of our Oregon trio, Vicki and Mindy. Mom had their numbers as they called often to get an update.

Vicki plays violin with the Eugene Symphony Orchestra. She is getting married in a couple of months to Don who is also a symphony member. "Would you be a bridesmaid?" she asked.

"As soon as I get a calendar, I'll pencil you in! Are you kidding? Of course I will!"

When I caught Mindy, she was staying in a hotel while she toured with a string quartet. She plays the cello and the harp. The group is also practicing for Vicki's wedding.

Both of them made me feel quite loved when they gushed about how worried they were, relieved that I'm back and excited that I was okay. They both wondered when we would all get together.

"Just because there's the wedding, we shouldn't wait a couple of months."

"You have to see the bride's maid dress and get fitted."

"As soon as I get a car I'll drive up!"

Taking a deep breath, I had to decide if I should even call my 'boyfriend'. Mom said Sean only called once to ask about me while I was missing. Last semester, his letters had been few, just like his calls. When I left Oregon, I thought I'd wait and surprise him. Now he's the last person I thought to call, but the only friend whose cell number I had committed to memory.

After staring at the phone for a few minutes, I punched in the number, really hoping he wouldn't answer.

Chapter 80
While I Was Gone

"Sean?" My throat closed.

"What the hell! Is this Natty?"

"It is. I'm home."

Dead silence lay between us.

"It is so good to hear you're back. What happened to you, anyway?"

Without giving a detailed summary of my last months away, I mentioned my two adversaries, my memory loss and my homeless months.

"Wow! Are you writing your memoirs yet?"

"Well, I wrote plenty of scribbled notes. We'll see what I do with them. What's happening with you?"

"I . . .uh . . .have a new job in mergers and acquisitions."

"Do you like what you're doing?"

"Not sure yet. I am leaving for Denver in two weeks."

"Oh?"

"Look. I have to be honest with you."

"I want you to be."

"Do you remember Jennifer Slayton?"

"The one a year behind us at Edison?"

Even knowing what I knew he would tell me, I needed to hear it.

"One day I went fishing on the pier. Jen came over to ask me about what happened to you. When she began to console me, we just hit it off. It's not something I should explain over the phone. Do you want to meet for dinner some time before we go?"

"She'll be going with you?"

"Well . . .Yes."

"I think this is a better way to discuss this with you. It was good talking with you, Sean. I hope we will always be friends but long distance relationships often result in couples growing away from each other. That's just the way it goes. Thanks for a couple of fun years. So long, Sean. Be happy."

"You too."

With the receiver in my hand, I just stared forward, trying to assess my feelings—a little sad—a little free. Growing up and out is hard sometimes.

Sean's temper used to upset me. I thought about the last time I tried to do something nice like wash his car. You'd have thought I planned to use a Brillo pad.

Matt whined. It almost sounded like I love you.

"I love you too!"

Poppy arrived just before I opened the game closet. There was still 'Chutes and Ladders' along with other games from my toddler days. Poppy said he'd be back with some boxes from behind the liquor store to help me.

After I fixed us some iced tea, we began filling the boxes with things to give away and things to save. I separated ones to take to the children's ward, ones I wanted to keep and ones that were in bad shape. A large green bin filled up quickly with worn out toys. With a plop here and a plop there, I left my childhood behind. When I missed a throw into a box or a bin, Matt would retrieve it for me. Dotty just watched and didn't even move when Matt leaped over her.

Lifting my ice tea, I toasted him, "Thanks Poppy. I never could have done all this with my arm in a sling."

With the game cleanup done, we spent the afternoon playing cribbage. Afterward, he and I cooked a spaghetti dinner. That's where I learned all my great pasta recipes. Poppy and I loved bread and butter, so our garlic bread really added to the salad and spaghetti.

Besides cooking, Poppy loved playing games. No wonder I always had fun when I visited his ranch. Following dinner and a bowl of ice cream, I suggested Monopoly. Poppy's face lit with his wrinkles curled into a picture perfect smile. His eyes twinkled as he answered. "You bet!"

Dad sat back in his chair, patting his tummy. "Do we have to?"

Mom pinched his cheek. "You bet!"

When Dad won, then he said, "Well, that was kind of fun!"

We rolled our eyes.

Before I went to bed that night, I found Mom sitting in the dining room with a box of folders and a trash can. "What's up, Mom?"

"Well, I didn't want you to feel bad, but after you disappeared, I quit my job. I spent a part of everyday looking for you. Believe it or not I think I did find some people who had seen you. I kept all the information and a list of people I either contacted or might contact. Much of it is not necessary now since you're . . . "

"Oh Mom, if I hadn't been so stupid."

"No! Don't you dare regret what can't be changed! I think God has a way of sending us on journeys we might not like but that brings us to the time and place where we are supposed to be."

"I can sort of see that. Meeting Jonathan enriched both of us. Then there's Matt! I wouldn't wish I bypassed having either of them in my life. Besides, facing adversity, meeting it head on and achieving victory has made me a stronger person. Not to mention, I have a nice little bank account to send me out into the rest of my life." I grinned.

"When your dad and I started home from Grant's pass, we decided to go back up to your college dorm just to see if anyone had any helpful information. We also talked to Vicki, Mindy and couple of your teachers. We got the name of the musical group you were planning to join.

When we gave Sheriff Tilden your credit card numbers, we found places you stopped, gas stations and the Wolf Creek Inn. We talked to a lovely woman who remembered you quite well. She gave us your tale of a visitation by their spirits. She let us search the room, even though the police had done so. We also found where you purchased gas. When you transferred money into your German account then to your regular account, that's where we hit the wall. But we also found hope in those findings. Sheriff Tilden thought he would find a way to reveal whose account sent the money.

"Anyway, I am cleaning this out and throwing away most of it."

"That's a good idea! I am going to try and put this behind me." I kissed Mom's forehead. "Behind you too."

"Oh I almost forgot. The musical group in Huntington Beach—they were thoroughly investigated but all had strong alibis, like being in Newport Beach."

"I'm glad. If I wanted to contact them again, I hope they won't be too mad about being considered suspects."

Mom stood, held my hand for a moment then hugged me. When her eyes filled with tears, so did mine. "Night, Honey."

"Would it bother you if I played the piano for a little while?"

"That's one of things I really missed when you left home for school. Please . . . I'd love it."

When I looked in the piano seat, my old notebooks were there. As I played, I jotted down some note sequences with words for a new song I'd been thinking about. I sang softly."

I didn't notice Mom behind me until she touched my shoulder. "I think your voice is even more beautiful than I remember. I love you."

"Me, too, you!"

We squeezed our hands together.

"Oh Mom? Could I borrow some clothes for tomorrow until I buy some more?"

"You look better in them than I do!"

"See you in the morning."

"You bet, but not too early, please. You forget we're retired now! What's early for us is a whole lot later than it used to be."

"Okay, so I won't wake you!"

"I'll lay out an outfit for you to wear. Do you need to get some things done tomorrow? I can drive you."

"What would I do without you, Mom?"

"You see what happened the last time your did that?"

"Okay, would you have time to drive me to get a few things?"

"Sure. It'll be like the old days before you could drive."

"Not really. I promise not to be sassy like my old teen-age self!"

Chapter 81
Knitting an Unraveled Life Back Together

Sitting in a place dark and dank, I heard the rusty hinges screech open. Almost silent footsteps moved toward me. I shook. Squinting my eyes, I really didn't want see it, no matter what, but he was there. The blurry figure of Bud stood at the end of my bed staring with his ghastly red eyes. I gasped. He whispered, "Do not make another sound."

I sucked in my breath.

Clutched in one hand, a huge knife flashed in a spear of light. In the other was a garish, lacy, satin wedding gown dripping blood. He started around the bed toward me. I cringed away from him, gasping for air.

"I told you I would find you. You can't ever escape from me—ever!"

"No!"

The knife came slashing down.

"Ahhhhhhhhhh!"

My blood-boiling scream brought my parents scrambling in. They hugged me while I trembled in their arms.

"Bud came. Right here at the end of my bed. It seemed so real!"

My dad pushed my hair out of my face. "I'm going to sit right here until you fall asleep. He's not going to find you."

I didn't think I could fall asleep after that, but sleeping in my own bed wrapped me in a cocoon. With my father next to me, holding my hand, I fell asleep.

Before I woke, I managed to dream about Marilyn and I shopping for new clothes, twirling around in front of a mirror like we were models. Setting a more positive thought for taking on the day, my eyes popped wide open at seven. Beside my lingering thoughts about my nightmare, my mind zoomed through the myriad of things I had to do before I start living.

It gave me something to contemplate other than fear. I made a decision about what to do with some of my newfound wealth. Once you become homeless, it is almost impossible to come back without help. I didn't want to be an enabler, but I do want to help some deserving people.

After showering, I added a new item to my list of things to buy today—a hair dryer. I dressed in Mom's outfit, dark blue leggings and a tunic with tan and navy stripes. I twisted my hair up in a knot then applied a little almost dried up mascara. When I donned my old tennis shoes, ripped and grungy, I set my first priority on shoes. I borrowed a pair of flip-flops from Mom. "Sorry I woke you, Mom."

The sun streamed through the window lighting up the white kitchen with a spark that revived me. Mom poured me a cup of coffee. "Bob, do you want some granola and a cup of coffee with us?"

"I'll just read the paper while you girls talk shop!"

"Daddy, will you keep Matt company while we're gone?"

"You better watch it or he'll be my dog. I fed him this morning."

"Thank you."

After finishing breakfast Mom grabbed the car keys to her little Smart car. She used this car for errands that she and Dad didn't do together or if he had an appointment.

"It's pretty comfortable with my long legs in this little car. Thanks, Mom. I really need to do these things, if it's okay with you." I listed them.

At the bank I reinstated my credit card by paying the fines and the $300 that I had owed when I missed payments the last twelve months. On the way to the Apple Store, I bought a wallet. Mom's empty Chanel purse now had a wallet ready to fill up with several hundred dollars I took out for shopping.

A great shoe store in Huntington Beach sold wholesale shoes. I bought new Vans tennis shoes, a pair of Cole Hahn loafers and black pumps. Next thing was a must have. We headed for the Apple Store.

Even though I imagined some possibilities, using the Cloud, I could retrieve lots of what had been on my original phone and laptop. Verizon hadn't given my number to anyone else. When I got my new iPhone and laptop lots of things came back. *Let's have the whole day go this well.*

The rest of the week became a whirling target. I hit a few local boutiques for job-hunting clothes and shoes.

I spent a couple of days on my laptop and my cell, answering ads and making appointments for job interviews.

Chapter 82
Unforgettable

Friday morning I woke with a most lovely sensation of being kissed, a vision of Jimmy flashed for a moment. "See you soon!" When I opened my eyes, a strong sunbeam flashed through the window. A verse ran through my head. "Delight yourself in the Lord and he will give you the desires of your heart." Romans 8:22

Friday came a lot quicker than I thought. Time to have fun. I dressed in an easy dress to pull on and off for trying on clothes during my shopping date with Marilyn this afternoon.

Excitement to see my friend made me antsy for the afternoon. At 3:15 the doorbell rang. Marilyn's always prompt so no surprise when I opened the door. We flew into a huge hug.

When I drew back I noticed she had put some blonde highlights in her gorgeous red hair. With her top down on a perfect afternoon, we flew along Coast Highway to Fashion Island. Our hair caught in the breeze with our laughter rising. Each time we see each other it seems no time has passed at all. First, we hit Bloomingdales laughing and giggling. We both selected a couple of sets of fancy underwear. I needed a more outfits for work and some casual clothes. Instead of Mom's Chanel bag, I bought a more practical conservative, black leather purse. While we changed, we laughed at our antics trying on things. "But it wasn't *that* funny to pinch my muffin top when I tried on those tights. They just weren't the right size!"

"Yeah, right!" She pinched me again. "Though you have lost weight."

Laden with multiple paper bags, we stood behind her car. "Is that trunk big enough to hold all of our fabulous buys?"

We managed.

"We still have one more place to go. It's all denim and you're going to love this store." Marilyn revved up her engine. Off we sped, before we finally pulled up in front of a little boutique that sold specialty jeans.

Inside the store, Marilyn held up a mini skirt. "Hey, this skirt'd be great on you. See these signatures?" She pointed to the pockets. "The cowboys sign the rear pocket and sell their used Levis. The boutique makes them into skirts, cutoffs, purses, jackets or just decorates and resizes them for resale."

Marilyn picked Levis with Tex scrawled across the rear end, embroidered with pink flowers around the signature. She looked great in them. She slipped on the perfect pink T-shirt.

"That's Gucci. You have to get that outfit." After trying on several, I bought the pair of Levi's signed, 'Mustang' on the derriere. "Best fitting jeans I ever owned!" I spun around looking at my rear view. "My appearance definitely improved after having lost some weight in the last year—bad time, good diet." I paired the jeans with a light green T-shirt that matched the leaves and stems. Fuchsia flowers wound down one leg of the Levis, from the right front hip to the hem. "Let's wear them tonight."

"Yeah, let's. That green top is sensational with your gorgeous green eyes."

"You're just saying that because it's true. I'm so glad your eyes don't match your pink shirt!"

Marilyn gathered up her package containing the outfit she had worn. "I have reservations at Muldoon's for dinner. Promise me, after a glass of stout, you're not going to get all teary over breaking up with that loser boyfriend of yours."

"Sean could be okay when he wanted to be. With more downs than ups, I think I'm glad we ended it. Is it possible to find someone that sets your heart a flutter, just looking at each other?"

"Yeah, sure. You're not going to remind about some teen guy you met years ago."

"I know it's childish, but honestly, I've never been as happy as that last summer we spent together. However, I'm not looking for anyone right now even with my 'gorgeous green eyes.' Not until I get my life back together."

"Muldoon's should be fun. The Irish Stones are playing. They've not only got great voices, they also are quite comedic. I heard them several weeks ago."

"Well, that's what I need after my last year!"

We stepped inside. The wood paneled interior resembled an old Irish Pub. A little crowded, but not nearly as crowded as it would be after dinner. Our table wasn't ready yet, so we sidled up to the bar to wait.

The Irish Stones began setting up for their show.

"Two stouts, please." It wasn't more than a few minutes later the stouts landed on the bar as the bartender splashed them down using a one-handed grip. Marilyn scrunched up her nose, "Ew!"

"All that because I sprinkled salt on my stout? Mmm, taste it." I licked the foam from my lips.

"No thanks."

When I felt the tap on my shoulder, I turned. I've always been a sucker for blue eyes, so I smiled up at him.

He shook his head back clearing a mane of blond hair

away from his forehead. "Can I buy you a drink?"

"I'm sticking to this stout for right now." I held up my glass. "Are you with the band?"

"I'm the Stone."

"Oh." I sipped from my mug of stout."

"Excuse me. My partners are eyeing me. Better go join them." He scratched his phone number on my napkin before he hopped up on the tiny platform with two other guys.

His guitar, the banjo and the violin tuned up. When they played the intro to a song I once knew, *"Will you Go Lassie?"* I smiled as I remember my grammy singing it.

The audience gave them a healthy ovation. Amid their applause, we were called for dinner. Absentmindly, I slipped his phone number in my pocket.

The dining room was elegant in a quaint way, lace tablecloths and crystal vases with fresh flowers. A waitress led us to our dinner seats and we sat across from each other. "After we eat, I hope we can get a seat in the bar. The Irish Stones are better than you said they were—especially one."

"Pretty handsome dude!"

My cheeks burned.

At dinner we both ordered their Shepherds' Pie, as good as my Irish grammy used to make. All through the meal we laughed. We reviewed old times like when she grabbed my bikini top that I had undone for a tan on my back. She ran down the beach with it, while a bunch of guys on the beach guys poured ice on my back.

When she asked if I ever sang anymore, I discussed the possibility of getting back into music.

"Well, you never know if a bit of magic will come your way. God knows you deserve it."

I checked my phone. "I can't believe we spent three hours laughing and talking. I told my parents I'd be home early this evening."

"So they give you a curfew? Why don't we stay for a few more songs if we can find a seat?"

"Sure. They didn't give me a curfew. I just have to call and tell them I'm okay and staying for a few more songs. You remember how they are worriers, especially when I disappeared, gone all those months."

"Yeah, Yeah, yeah."

I called.

Just as we reentered the bar, two seats emptied and we dashed in ahead of a couple vying for the same spot at the bar.

By now the tone of the music had livened up. Making everyone stomp their feet, clap or sing along twice as loud as the band played. I sang so much and so loud, my voice got hoarse. *If I want to stay in music, I have to sing more and train my vocal chords.*

The *'Stone'* kept looking at me. When he winked. I grinned back.

Marilyn leaned over. "He's a hunk and he's flirting with you."

"Remember when I asked you if there really could be someone who could stir your heart with just a look? Maybe I found him. At least I might like to know him better."

Just after I told Marilyn I might like to know him, my phone rang. "You're not going to believe this!"

Chapter 83
Another Chance

I put my hand over the phone. "Sean is at my house saying he's not leaving until he talks to me."

"Do you want to go home?"

"Not really. However, he'd probably make some kind of scene if she tells him where I am."

"Okay, Let's go."

I smiled at the 'Stone' waving at me. *I'd like to see him again.* I left with that thought on my mind.

In the parking lot, I turned to Marilyn. "It's been a long time since I truly had fun. Thanks."

"Let's go again next Friday. The Irish Stones will be there all month."

"For sure!"

"Same time, same game."

We drove out of the parking lot smiling.

At home, I unloaded my packages from her trunk. With packages practically smothering me, I walked to my front door. Juggling them around, I couldn't be sure I could open it with the key.

Sean opened the door before I could ring. "Your parents went to bed when they heard you out there."

"Look Sean, why are you here?"

He closed the door.

"I talked to Jennifer and . . ."

"Don't say it. She's not going with you."

"I just told her that I would never be sure, if didn't talk to you first.'

"What did she say to that?"

"Didn't make her very happy."

"No kidding."

He reached for me.

I backed away.

"Come on, Natty." He pulled me close. "Just kiss me."

"So you think that's going to fix everything?" I pushed him away. "I'm so over you. Chill. We're done."

"You don't mean that."

His puppy-dog look assured me of my decision. I outgrew him.

When I opened the door, he paused.

"Goodbye, Sean. Good luck in your new job."

After he was outside, he turned and glanced back over his shoulder.

Resisting slamming the door, I just closed it gently.

I never thought I'd be glad about breaking up with Sean. Leaping up and clicking my heels, I thrust my arm in the air.

While I climbed the stairs, I reached into my back pocket. Across a cocktail napkin, I read the phone number with the message, "Come next Friday."

Out with the old and in with the new.

Chapter 84
Moving Right Along

The following week brought me back into a life of normalcy, if you want to call having your mother take you to job interviews, normalcy.

Following several more interviews, as well as two-second interviews, I decided to accept Wells Fargo's offer as a systems analyst. The best part was I won't start for a month, making plenty of time to hunt for an apartment and go to Oregon to see my college friends.

Poppy was excited for me to stay at his ranch in Oregon and I was too! I just didn't know how exciting it would all turn out to be.

When I saw the doctor, he released me to drive. "Just remember, I still don't want you to lift anything heavier than a book. Use your left arm and continue to use the sling to give a little relief. See the nurse and set up some therapy sessions."

"Thank you, Doctor."

"Good luck!"

I grinned.

Driver's License came next. With a phone, I could now make an appointment to get it taken care of without spending hours in line. I read through the book reviewing the material on the test. My dad accompanied me and drilled me on the laws, all the way to the DMV. I just hoped my picture came out better than the last one I had taken.

At the Mazda dealer, Dad helped me get a really good deal on a MX 5 Miata. I always wished for a Miata, so I sat in a deep burgundy convertible with a lighter burgundy top. When the top rolled back, I loved the sporty look.

After a test run, Daddy worked a deal for me with all cash. I knew I could have negotiated a good deal by myself, but this might be the last time I got to play Daddy's little girl. He seemed to revel in that role!

The paper work is so time consuming. I just wanted to pile in my new car and ride with the top down. Finally!

After he showed me how to put the top down, I shook hands with the dealer.

"Ride with the wind!" He saluted.

"I shall!"

As I sank into the leather seats, my thoughts turned back to the Mercedes I confiscated. I shut the door, waved goodbye to Dad and I drove out to face the world. It would be fun to have my good friends back again.

"Siri."

"What can I help you with, Natty?"

I smiled. "Did you miss me?

"I don't have an answer for that."

"Siri, Where is the nearest gas station."

"Thanks, Siri. I'm glad you're back."

I know Dad always wanted a Corvette, so did Mom. If they hadn't been paying my college expenses, they'd have one. Once I got myself straightened out, maybe I could help make that happen.

On the way home, I hit the drugstore and market near our house. Half my car filled quickly with hair products, a dryer, and make up. Next I bought filet mignon and shrimp to cook a special dinner for my parents to celebrate and also to break the news. I need to live on my own. I was going to look for an apartment.

After we we finished our shrimp cocktail, I broke the news about an apartment.

"But you just got home."

"I know Mom, but I'd like to live closer to work."

"You always used to say you never wanted to live away from the Beach."

"Newport has a beach."

Dad smiled. "Not that I want you to go, but you might consider buying instead of renting."

"I have some ideas of what I want to do with my recent 'bonus' and it wasn't to spend it all on myself."

"If you should find a fixer, I'd help you."

"Well, if you have to go, we have some of Grandma's furniture and you could take anything in your room."

Their reaction surprised me a little. "That's a couple of good ideas. Sets the tone for a chocolate sundae." I cleared the table and brought the sundaes. It was sweet to be home.

After dinner, I snuggled on the couch with Matt and Dottie. *I am so very thankful.*

That week I checked with a couple of banks. If I could buy a house with a $250,000 mortgage, my loan payments would be just over $1,300 depending on the interest rates. That's less than the rent of some of the places I priced. With my new job, that would be doable, not for a single family home but for a condo—especially a fixer. I relished doing fun jobs together with Dad again, like we did around this house.

As I dressed for Friday night, I found myself trying on one new dress after another. In the end I decided on my new green shirt. I pulled on my jeans with Mustang on the rear. I fluffed my hair and finished my make-up. Twirling in front of the full-length mirror I confirmed that the jeans were quite flattering.

With a vision of one Irish Stone drifting though my mind, I hadn't been this excited to see someone for a very long time.

Since Marilyn had to work later than last week, I picked her up in my new Miata. On Coast Highway, our hair billowing out in the wind, nothing could wipe the smile off my face.

Chapter 85
I'm Back

Marilyn and I stopped at a couple of furniture stores just to see the approximate costs of getting a sofa and chair for my new place. Cost Plus World Market's furniture would certainly update Grammy's furniture, besides they're a lot cheaper than the bigger stores.

We landed at Muldoon's a little later than the week before. That meant we couldn't get a seat in the bar, SRO. It took a minute staring at Mr. Blue Eyes and he finally connected with my green ones. He dipped his guitar in recognition that he had seen me. *Was that hunger? Or did my stomach just flip?*

We stood for a moment before they called our table. I ordered the shepherd's pie again. It was so good last week.

Since we were laughing so hard, I appreciated that any romantic couples sat elsewhere. We got a little serious when I told her about my plans to buy a place.

Marilyn asked me a few questions about Bud. When I told her that he still hadn't been arrested or even found, her brow furrowed. "You're not going to buy a single fam home, are you?"

"Why not?"

"You need to have plenty of people around you, just in case he does find you."

"He's not going to find me. He didn't have enough info.

Don't worry about me. I'm fine."

When the waiter brought our check, I grabbed Marilyn's hand. "My treat. Come on. Let's go listen to the band." I laid the money on the table.

As the audience sat again for a slow number a couple gathered up their coats. Marilyn and I dashed to beat the rest of the people aiming for those seats. We sat directly in front of the band.

When the band started up with a lively set of music, the audience joined right in singing and clapping.

"Blue Eyes" raised a flat hand and the audience quieted. "Ladies and gentlemen, I wrote a song this week. Would you like to hear it?"

Applauding and "yeahs" filled the room.

Here it is. *"Just When I Saw her."*

Once his beautiful tenor voice hummed, and he began a melodic ballad, mesmerized aptly described the look on my face.

"Hey, Natty."

I turned to face at Marilyn.

She cupped her hand over mouth. "Don't look at me. He's singing this to you."

"Come on."

"Just listen to the words."

As he sang, he stared through the crowd, gazing right at me. Standing near me, even the audience noticed and turned around staring back at me.

Blushing, I began to admit or believe that maybe he did write it for me.

The after-dinner music picked up the beat. It had the crowd on their feet. Smiling, singing and clapping until our hands stung, the final set ended. We stood to leave.

Blue Eyes and another one of the band guys hurried

over.

"Hey, what's your hurry?" They dragged a couple of empty chairs over and sat. My "Stone" held my hand and gave a gentle tug, so I sat next to him.

"Mus, yours truly and this is Fergus."

"Glowing at Fergus, Marilyn sat down. "I'm Marilyn guys, this is Natty."

Marilyn was immediately ensconced in a conversation with Fergus leaving me staring at those very blue eyes.

"Good evening, Maddy."

"You could call me that, but it's Natty."

"Welcome back, Natty."

"Your music is wonderful. It reminds me of songs my grammy and Poppy used to sing with me."

"How about my new song?"

My face reddened, I'm sure. "Lovely."

"It matches the woman I wrote it for, a woman with green eyes, just like yours."

"Does that line usually work for you?"

"I don't know."

"Because?"

"This is the first time I've used it."

Fergus stood. "How would you beautiful lassies feel about a walk on the beach?"

Marilyn looked at me. "Depends."

"Aren't those granny diapers?" Fergus turned red, tilted his head to the side and pinched his ear while we all laughed.

I looked at Mus. "I guess the green-eye thing worked. Can we follow you? I'm not leaving my brand new car here in the parking lot."

Chapter 86
Starry, Starry Night

Wondering about my judgment, I felt safer with Marilyn and Fergus joining us. Just to feel even safer, while they were in listening distance, I let my parents know where I went and with whom.

The guys had a tarp in the back of their van that worked as a beach blanket. Surprisingly there were a few people still on the beach sitting around fire pits roasting marshmallows.

Mus told silly Irish jokes with Fergus. The more we laughed, the funnier they got. When the guys started singing, I joined in, with Marilyn as our audience.

"Doesn't she have a beautiful voice, now?" Mus slugged Fergus in the shoulder.

"That she does."

As the time drew late, I called my parents to tell them not to worry or wait up.

Mus asked me about my singing and I told him about the Three Tiers group and how I had once planned to be a singer.

In the cool evening, it seemed natural when we cuddled up with the guys and watched the stars dazzle in the clear, black velvet sky. Though the Oregon sky had more stars, this beautiful sight made my heart light.

I started humming a song I wrote with my friend Jimmy when we went on a midnight hike.

"That's a beautiful melody." Mus leaned back and caught

me in one of his magnetic stares. "I think I've heard it before. What's it called?"

"Doesn't have a name—my friend and I wrote it a long time ago."

It must have been early the next morning when we finally headed back to our cars.

"Hey, good time, huh?" Fergus put his arm around Marilyn. "Let's do it again some time."

"Here! Here!" Mus opened the driver's side of my car. "This car kills it."

"I love it."

He leaned his forehead against mine. "How about lunch tomorrow? I was going to say breakfast but it's nearly breakfast time right now and I think I am going to sleep until lunch. Give me your number." He drew back and reached for his phone.

"I have yours. You left it for me last week. Remember?"

"Yeah, but how will I know you will call? You didn't call this week."

"I guess you'll just have to wait."

His smiley expression collapsed. "Okay." He brushed his lips against my cheek with a peck of a kiss. "Good bye."

The goose bumps rose and I thought I'd topple over for sure.

The next morning about 11:30 my phone rang. My lids snapped open wondering if I had slept all day? "Hello?" I rubbed my eyes.

"Are you ready for lunch? It's after eleven."

"What? Who is this? Mus?"

"Yep."

"How did you get my number?"

"What are friends for? Fergus got Marilyn's number. When he called her, I got your number."

"You didn't think I'd call you?"

"Just wanted to be sure."

"I suppose you know my address too?"

"Yep. How about I pick you up say at 11:45?"

"It's a go if you make it at twelve."

"You're on! Oh, wear a bathing suit and bring a towel and maybe a windbreaker."

On the dot, Mus showed up. I peeked out the window. Two surf boards stuck out of the back of his pick-up truck.

It had been a long time since I surfed. Could I still?

He just knocked when I surprised him by opening it. Dad sat in his chair reading the newspaper. "Dad, this is Mus, my dad, Mr. Wilson." He stood.

"Nice to meet you, sir."

They shook hands.

"You too. Take care of my girl."

"Yes, Sir."

"I was a Marine you know." He winked at Mus.

"Yes, sir."

Once out to the pickup, I looked at the gear. "How did you know I could surf?"

"Can you?"

"I'm not sure. I used to be able to."

"Well, you don't really have to know how. We're going windsurfing! But 'breakfast slash lunch' first. What are you in the mood for?"

"You're going to laugh. How about MacDonald's? I'm excited to try wind surfing and a restaurant will take too much time!" Since I hadn't told him of my travails, he couldn't have realized how many times I dreamed of a Big Mac!

"Okay," He opened the car door. "A Big Mac coming up!"

Out on the bay, he showed me the essentials of the sport. I was really surprised at how easy the sail lifted out of the water. I caught on immediately. I took a thrilling ride as my board scooted off across the water. "Hey! I'm pretty good at this!"

Then . . . when I had to turn around, I couldn't go back. "I guess I bragged a little too soon!"

After a session on how to catch the wind in my sail, I did okay. "Wow! This is fun!"

A couple of hours later we laid out on the toasty sand to warm up and dry off.

On our way home, I felt a little sad as I didn't know when I'd see him again. I hummed to myself, I thought.

"There' that song again."

I rolled my eyes at him and smiled..

"How about dinner tonight?"

"Uh . . . Not tonight. I have to pack."

"Oh? Where are you going?"

"My grandpa lives in Oregon. I'm going to spend a few days with him so I can see my roommates from college. One of them is getting married next month and I have to get a bride's maid's dress."

"Then you won't be here tomorrow or the next day or Friday night?"

"Don't look so glum. I am coming back."

"Like when?"

"I'll be back late Friday night. I have a late flight to L.A. and that's a long way back to the beach. I'll crash in my own bed on Friday night."

"Well then, rest up!"

"Of course I will, but why?"

"Because you have to be at the birthday bash that Fergus and I have planned for Liam on Saturday night. We split the cost of a ticket to bring his girlfriend, Arianna, all the way from Belfast. You'll be recouped by then."

"Wow, that is a gift!"

"We built a cake she can pop out of. You could help her get ready."

"Sure." I looked at my toes. My cheeks turned warm in the cool breeze. "Thanks. I had a great day."

"Thanks for being a good sport. It was kinda cold out there, but if you don't have a wet suit it'll be way too cold in a couple of weeks."

When I started to get out of the car, Mus raced around the car and opened the door. He took my hand. When I stood next to him, he opened my fingers to expose my palm. When he gently kissed the center of my hand, my knees felt so weak he put his arm around to catch me.

"So sorry. I must have tripped."

"No problem."

As he released me, there were those blue eyes holding me steady.

"What do you say I drive you to the airport in the morning?"

"No . . . I have it all planned."

"Ok, I'll see you next Saturday night." He turned quickly and raced off before I realized there were tears in my eyes. And I did kick myself for not accepting his ride offer.

Chapter 87
Home Again

My week away proved exhausting but enjoyable. We tried to cram every fun thing we could think of into four days. Mindy was between tours. Vicki took the week to do some planning for the wedding, which is why this week worked for all of us.

The navy blue dresses Vicki picked for the bridesmaids made us all looked elegantly slender. I could envision wearing my dress again unlike so many other bride's party dresses one would never use again. Vicki's gorgeous dress fit perfectly, just enough lace to be chic. The veil trailed with a lace train.

"That's a wow!" I hugged her.

We tasted wedding cakes, sampled dinner menus, picked out flowers then had a shower for Vicki. My face hurt from laughing so hard. I had a couple of texts from Mus saying he missed me. Being so busy, I never got around to texting back except one, "Me, too."

Out at Poppy's ranch, Candy still had a lot of oomph. She really got excited seeing me again. I even slept in the barn one night just to be with her. I didn't even know if Mus liked to ride horses. I hoped so. In between the wedding preparations, and helping address the invitations, Poppy and I took rides and played some music. I told him about Mus. I knew they'd like each other. No matter how much fun and how great it was to spend time with my friends I could hardly wait for Saturday night to arrive.

Thinking of him, I wondered if Mus might be able to come to the wedding. *I guess I'll have to wait and see how it all goes.*

Thursday night, I bid a semi-sad farewell knowing this would be the last time my friends and I would be young, single, and carefree girls. Time to grow up.

Poppy rose early to say goodbye to me on Friday morning, but then he usually woke early—always something to do for the ranch. When I said goodbye to Candy I worried. Poppy and Candy weren't that old, but I knew they wouldn't be there for me forever.

I slept on the plane. I had arranged for a Limo—not the fancy kind—an airport limo. The lonely ride back home from the airport made me wish I'd have let Mus drive me.

Book 3
Here, Now, Forever

Chapter 88
Endings Are Beginnings

No sleeping in Saturday. Matt hadn't left my side since last night. With Matt licking my face, plus the smell of coffee and bacon frying, I was awake. As the aroma wafted from Mom's kitchen, I stretched, and smiled in expectation of seeing Mus that night.

Mus called me to make sure I would be there for the party. He warned me to be a little early as it might be a tad crowded. Besides, he wanted me to help with the birthday cake surprise.

Somehow I knew it would be a special evening, I just didn't know how special.

That night, I decided to wear my jean outfit I wore when Marilyn and I first saw The Irish Stones. I took extra care with my makeup and hair. There might be a lot of cute girls there. Hero worship is hard to resist.

I picked Marilyn up on the way. She told me she had been seeing Fergus all week.

"Don't let that lawyer sue you. What was his name?"

She rolled her eyes. "I can't be tied down with just one man!"

The four of us doubling some time would be great. We all had such fun together.

After arriving. Mus met us at the bar. He brought us all stouts. Fergus and Marilyn disappeared to a corner table.

"Come over here, I have a little something for you." Mus

followed me to a private table. "Very cool jeans!"

I sat, sipping my Stout.

Mus leaned close and swiped the foam from my upper lip.

A chill swirled down my back.

"How was your trip?"

"Really great."

"He took a gentle hold on my chin and turned my face toward him. Our eyes connected. "Those are the most beautiful green eyes. I mention them again because I've only met one other person with eyes as green and beautiful as yours."

"You're trying that green-eyed line again?"

"It worked, remember?" He laid a wrapped, cylinder-shaped gift on the table.

"Okay, I'm falling for it. What green-eyed girl?"

"This is a very special green-eyed girl I met at my pa's ranch. He stared off as if his mind had gone searching. "It was a very sad day for me, because my pa said we had to get rid of all our wild barn kittens. Then this delicate girl came with her grandpa. I gave her my favorite gray one with a sprinkle of gray dots on her face. The twinkle in the girl's green eyes made me feel a lot better knowing the kitten now belonged to a good home. I've never met anyone else like that girl."

My cheeks felt hot. "What's your name?"

"Mus."

"I know that, I meant to ask you about it, before. That's a strange name." I pushed my hair behind my ears.

"You missed a strand." He gently tucked it in.

My stomach fluttered as I stared directly into those sapphire blue eyes. I felt like my grin touched my ears as he handed me the gift roll.

Mus couldn't sit still.

Unwrapping the cylinder carefully, I hung the curled ribbon on my ponytail. Even though I could feel the blood pulsing through my veins in anticipation, I took my time. I slipped a rolled up piece of notebook paper from the cylinder, which was a paper towel cardboard roll.

"Is Mus short for something?"

"James is my real name. When I got sick of being called Jimmy, my pa started calling me Mustang for the way I handled the orneriest of the horses we used to train. Mus is short for Mustang." He touched my cheek and looked over at my backside. "And I think you're wearing my jeans."

I remembered that my back pocket said, "Mustang."

"I first knew how special you are, when I recognized the your green eyes but it was the song! The song you've been humming—GO ahead. Unroll it!" His voice climbed several notes higher.

My hands shook when I stretched the roll of paper out to reveal my own handwriting penning the very music and words to the song I'd been humming for the last week.

"Nice to see you again, Natasha."

"No one calls me Natasha any more."

"Why not?"

"That name belongs with the boy I left in Oregon 10 summers ago."

"And my heart belongs to the green-eyed girl who left me 10 summers ago in Oregon."

One handed, he reached behind my neck, drew me close and kissed my lips so softly that I almost melted in my seat. We sat there holding hands lost in each other's eyes. I think my heart beat right out of my chest. Like we were the only two people in the world, the audience burst into applause and shattered that idea. I'm sure I turned red as a tomato.

When the rest of the band came back, Jimmy took my

hand and led me to the stage. "I'd like to introduce Natasha, a member of the Irish Stones for this evening's performance. She wrote the song I am about to sing."

Actually, I wanted to join him singing but my damp face burned and my throat swelled closed. His eyes never left mine as the song filled the air and my heart. A standing ovation erupted through the crowd.

On one of the breaks, I stole out to assist Arianna into her costume, her blonde wig and makeup. When she had carefully made herself beautiful and unrecognizable, Marilyn and I helped her climb into the cake. As we wheeled her in, the audience's applause exploded with everyone singing 'Happy Birthday'. The noise practically blew the windows out! Liam went wide-eyed as the audience spread and we pushed the cake near the front of the room.

Mus gave her a seductive intro and a drumroll imitation on his guitar. Out of the cake, Arianna exploded and stepped out.

Everyone expected a girl. They just didn't know who the girl would be. Liam didn't recognize her until she came right up to him, put her arms around his neck and showed him her shoulder with the tiny tat, a heart with his name inside. As soon as he realized it was Arianna, she flipped off the blonde wig with her own red hair bouncing down around her shoulders. Liam picked her up and spun her around and round. When he took her face in his hands and kissed her, another whole round applause rose from the crowd. Fergus raised a sign informing the crowd that this was Arianna, Liam's Irish fiancée here from Ireland.

The rest of the evening, everyone danced and sang. I learned the Irish jig. Best birthday bash ever.

Chapter 89
Beginnings

Now one would wonder if that ending could be any better. However, it was just the beginning of my life as one of the Stones, not only a band member, but as Mrs. James Stone. He's still Jimmy to me, though he says it doesn't irritate him when I say it with an Irish lilt. Sometimes Matt comes along to join the band. (He still wears his service jacket.) He sits or lays quietly until his cue to join us with his Irish whine. I think he was the group's most popular member—Sir Matthew Stone, Laird of the Stones. He actually manages to hit many of the notes in the chords we sing. Though his most popular gig is on YouTube.

A final surprise came when Jonathan came to listen to the Irish Stones, I asked him up to lend his beautiful baritone voice. He had applied to a school in France to teach English. "I'll be going at the beginning of next year."

I gave him a congrats with a hug.

To wrap up my greatest fear, I found Bud. Besides taking money from another of his accounts, I sent him a warning. "If you ever try to find me, you'll have nothing left." Then I gave the police my findings. I wait for the time when they notify me he is in custody.

Alejandro is in prison. His charges included; drug dealing, possession, human trafficking, and murder. He'll be in there for a long time. It also did my heart good to know that many of the girls he kept went home upon being released. I hope they are recovering. Sophia is also incarcerated. I am so glad to find out that she has no children, just the picture she carried around and used for her ruse.

Silvia is in her first year of college. She earned a scholarship with the good grades she got plus a Courage Award she received from her local church for seeing that Alejandro now takes up residence where he belongs.

With Bud's money and the Lutheran Church, I set up a charity to help the homeless giving them a place to live, childcare and also a chance at education and/or job training. The only caveat is no drugs or booze and to be actively seeking a job, training or education. With our concerts and our website we are raising enough money to keep it going.

Guess what my Dad is driving these days? Mom wraps up her hair, Daddy puts down the top and you might see them riding around their red Corvette.

After the wedding, the Irish Stones played at my old spot in Eugene, 'Sam Bond's Garage.' My friends and their husbands met Jimmy and they all got along so well. (They'd heard about him for years.) That trip also made it possible to stop by Auntie May's. Not only did she love Jimmy, Pookie and Matt couldn't stop playing together until they fell asleep curled up next to one another.

And I just stepped into the rest of my life.

Through all my ordeals, the realization that I never felt alone brought me out of the dark and into the light. Just as Mom said, "God has a way of sending us on journeys we might not like, but that bring us to the time and place where we are supposed to be."

I will instruct you and teach you in the way you should go; I will counsel you and watch over you."—Psalm 32:8

Visual mysteries abound in the workings of an author's mind, especially when the author is also an artist.

After taking a class, "Drawing on the Right Side of the Brain" she emerged with a novel swirling through her mind.

All her books are set on the Oregon coast, and special dogs nose their way into all her stories. You will also find mystery, suspense, and romance.

Karen Nichols relocated to Oregon from Southern California where she was a teacher. She wrote and illustrated a number of children's books. Her artwork appears in books, logos, ads, and on book covers. Her fine art, sculptures, novels and poetry books are currently displayed in Backstreet Gallery in Florence, OR.

Her articles have appeared in the *Siuslaw News*, and she was the managing editor for Carapace Scrawlers Writer's Journal.

Karen enjoys teaching creative writing and has been on a number of panel discussions and seminars. She has been instrumental in developing the Florence Festival of Books and also the Florence Regional Arts Alliance.

She lives with her husband, Ralph, in Florence, Oregon.

Made in the USA
Lexington, KY
24 November 2019